Readers love
KATE MCMURRAY

The Long Slide Home

"…I am still greatly enjoying this surprisingly emotional and character driven series. It still amazes me that while this appears to be a fluffy baseball series, it is so much more than that."

—Prism Book Alliance

"Watching these two navigate through their friendship to something more was really beautiful."

—Scattered Thoughts and Rogue Words

Devin December

"*Devin December* is an achingly sweet romance novella about finding love where you least expect it. This novel was immensely delightful, and Andy is so fierce and brave that I couldn't help but fall in love with him!"

—Just Love: Romance Novel Reviews

"Great job, Kate, I always loved your stories and will continue to read."

—Inked Rainbow Reads

The Silence of Stars

"I loved this book… The story just leaps out at you in the best way possible…"

—Bike Book Reviews

By KATE MCMURRAY

Blind Items
Devin December
Four Corners
Kindling Fire with Snow
Out in the Field
Playing Ball (Multiple Author Anthology)
The Stars That Tremble • The Silence of the Stars
A Walk in the Dark
What There Is
When the Planets Align

THE RAINBOW LEAGUE
The Windup
Thrown a Curve
The Long Slide Home

Published by DREAMSPINNER PRESS
www.dreamspinnerpress.com

OUT
IN THE
FIELD

KATE McMURRAY

REAMSPINNER
PRESS

Published by
DREAMSPINNER PRESS

5032 Capital Circle SW, Suite 2, PMB# 279, Tallahassee, FL 32305-7886 USA
www.dreamspinnerpress.com

This is a work of fiction. Names, characters, places, and incidents either are the product of author imagination or are used fictitiously, and any resemblance to actual persons, living or dead, business establishments, events, or locales is entirely coincidental.

ISBN: 978-1-63477-175-7
Digital ISBN: 978-1-63477-176-4
Library of Congress Control Number: 2016900162
Published May 2016
v. 2.0
First Edition published by Loose Id LLC, 2012.

Printed in the United States of America
∞
This paper meets the requirements of
ANSI/NISO Z39.48-1992 (Permanence of Paper).

For all the baseball fans out there—especially my dad, for bringing me to my first Yankees game when I was twelve, creating a rabid fan in the process, and Avi, for all his support and the occasional pair of tickets.

First

EAGLES COURT RODRIGUEZ
AS TRADING DEADLINE APPROACHES

by Cary Galvin, Sports Net

After last season's disastrous performance in the Division Series and the slow start they got this year, the Eagles are eager for young blood. The rumor out of Brooklyn this week is that the Eagles are offering Ignacio Rodriguez a pretty lucrative deal before the end of the upcoming trade deadline. We're not yet halfway through the season and Rodriguez already has Rookie of the Year written all over him—and I'm not just saying that because we played college ball together!

Manager Bill Haverman and GM Teddy Rothschild are pushing for a younger team and investing in the farm system, a strategy they think will bring wins back to Brooklyn in the long-term. But a short-term investment in younger players like Rodriguez could affect the team's play-off chances as early as this year. What that means for older players like Steve Mistry, Roger May, and Matt Blanco is anyone's guess, but I suspect they may be a part of history soon.

That would be a real shame, of course, because if any player ever represented Eagles baseball, it's Matt Blanco....

Chapter One

ALL BASEBALL players have OCD. That was the only explanation, Matt Blanco thought, for all the pregame ritual. He carefully went through his home-game routine: he closed his locker and tapped the door twice; he fiddled with the collar of the T-shirt he had on under his uniform; he touched the wall in the hallway leading out of the locker room. As he walked toward the dugout, he caught sight of June Redstone, the elderly widow of a former star of the team, and leaned toward her as he passed; she dutifully kissed his cheek.

He heard the din of the crowd roaring as he got closer to the field. The rise in volume was probably due to Matt's teammate Jefferson Jones jogging over to the bull pen to warm up. Normally Matt would have trotted out to the field and waved, but today he had other things on his mind. Namely his new teammate.

Matt was trying really hard not to think about his new teammate.

He sneaked into the dugout and pulled on his cap. The new guy was nowhere in sight, luckily. Shortstop Manuel Cruz sauntered over and plopped down on the bench, where he kissed the thin gold bracelet on his wrist, part of his own pregame ritual. That completed, he grinned at Matt. "You're out here a little early," he said.

"Eh. Warm-up was done sooner than usual. I figured I'd come and look at my adoring fans."

"Sure," said Cruz. "Did you hear about Miller?"

"No. What about Miller?"

Cruz leaned back, his smile smug. "As of Monday, he'll be wearing a Red Sox uniform."

"Oh fuck, no." Matt didn't especially like Evan Miller, but he was a terrific third baseman with a pretty high batting average.

"They took him and a handful of Triple-A guys in exchange for Rodriguez."

"Oh."

And speak of the devil, who should appear in the dugout just then but Ignacio Rodriguez, apparently the Brooklyn Eagles' new starting third baseman. It was his first time in the Eagles' blue-and-white home-game uniform, but he wore it like he'd been born in it.

Matt had attended the big press conference the day before. He'd learned two important pieces of information: first, Rodriquez had been batting above .400 when he'd been in the minors, playing for the Pawtucket Red Sox, which was probably why he'd been such a hot commodity when it came time to trade players; and second, he was about the best-looking man Matt had ever set eyes on, if you liked your men Latin and young—which Matt did. Although, man, this guy was *young*. He also had close-cropped black hair, dark skin about the same color as Matt took his coffee, a long nose, a wide mouth, and a tight body. When Rodriguez grinned, light seemed to bounce off his teeth.

The stats were good. The other thing was a huge problem.

Cruz leaned in and whispered, "What do you think of the new kid?"

The new kid was talking to Bill Haverman, so Matt felt safe offering an opinion. "Good numbers, if you buy the sabermetrics." It wasn't always enough to have good numbers, though. Maybe that was an old-school opinion, but Matt's experience bore it out. Players with good numbers didn't work well with some teams. If Rodriguez bombed, it wouldn't be the first time the Eagles had traded for an ace who ultimately had an abysmal season.

"That's something," said Cruz. "I talked to him yesterday. He seems like a nice kid. Also, Mistry's finally off the DL."

"Oh, I hadn't heard that either."

"Dude. Where have you been all day?"

"PT."

"Everything okay?"

"Dandy. Ain't nothing wrong with me except that I'm an old man." That and his knee had been sore all week, but he wasn't eager to volunteer that information.

"Good to hear, I guess." Cruz patted Matt's thigh.

Terry Wistler, the batting coach, walked over and glared at Cruz. "Focus" was all he said before he moved on to something else.

Matt looked at Cruz, who shrugged. "I was sloppy yesterday," he said. "So what did you end up doing last night?"

"Friends of mine had a party," Matt said. Cruz didn't need to know that at said party Matt had met a hot guy who knew absolutely nothing about baseball. Matt had then taken the man to a hotel room in Brooklyn he'd reserved just in case. It pained him a little that he couldn't say this to Cruz, who was probably his closest friend on the team after pitcher Roger May.

Roger wandered into the dugout then. Matt nodded at him. Cruz said, "Sounds fun. You get laid?"

"I got laid," Matt said. He grinned.

Cruz thought sex threw him off his game, so he stayed celibate most of the season. He made exceptions for special occasions—during the All-Star break, the night he'd hit his two hundredth home run—but he stuck to that for the most part. His abstinence, however, did not keep him from getting the scoop from everyone else. For a straight man, Cruz was a terrible gossip.

"And you, sir?" Cruz said to Roger. "You and your lady friend have a good night?"

"Lauren and I are married now," Roger said. "She's not my lady friend. She's my wife."

"You pitching tonight?" Matt asked.

"Nope. I'm starting tomorrow."

While Cruz and Roger shot the shit, Matt looked around. Rodriguez pulled his batting helmet out of its slot and weighed it in his hands. He put it back. He seemed nervous. As unofficial team captain, Matt knew it was his duty to go try to calm down the new guy, to be friendly and welcoming. But that would involve actually talking to Rodriguez.

Besides, just then Haverman started barking orders. For all intents and purposes, the game had begun.

FROM A practical standpoint, this game was no different from the thousands of others Iggy had played. He stood at third, gazing out at the landscape before him, noting where each of his teammates stood, noting how this batter tended to hit the ball. It was easy and familiar.

And yet it wasn't. For years he'd dreamed of just getting into the stands of FSB Stadium. Now he was on the field.

Not only that, but Matt Blanco—legendary Eagles first baseman Matt Blanco, the greatest player who had ever played the game as far as Iggy was concerned—was standing just on the other side of the infield. And he kept shooting Iggy looks.

Iggy couldn't figure out what any of those looks meant. Had he done something to offend Blanco? Was he this surly with all new players? Iggy worried briefly that Blanco might know something about him that he didn't want anyone to know yet, but he couldn't figure out how that could be the case. Iggy maybe hadn't been as discreet as he could have been, but he didn't think anyone knew his secret.

The inning ended, and Iggy jogged back toward the dugout. Given the way the top of the order had been batting, he thought it unlikely he'd be up that inning, so he took a deep breath and tried to relax.

But then Matt Blanco walked up to him and wrecked any hope of that. Because the thing was, not only was Blanco Iggy's idol, he was incredibly handsome, even more so close up than Iggy had imagined. He had olive skin and dark hair—classically Italian good looks—as well as a square jaw lined with stubble. He looked relaxed and casual, like he was perfectly in control of the game.

"Hey, Rodriguez. Nice play against Jackson," Blanco said.

"Uh, thanks." God. Blanco's dark eyes were incredible, much more intense than they seemed in photographs. And Iggy had looked at a lot of photos of Matt Blanco over the years.

"I, um. I mean…." Blanco took off his cap and ran a hand through his flattened hair. He seemed… tongue-tied. Nervous. But how was that possible? This man was one of the greatest ballplayers there had ever been. Iggy was just a rookie. "It's always weird adjusting to a new team."

"It is, yeah. Although you haven't had to in a long time, eh?"

Blanco shrugged. "I guess not. Anyway. Nice work. Welcome to the team." Then he turned and walked toward the shelves where the batting helmets were stored. Iggy might have felt insulted for the abrupt end in the conversation, but he realized Blanco was up second that inning.

Everyone who knew Iggy had assured him that playing for a big-market team in a city with a voracious tabloid industry would be okay if he just kept his head down and didn't draw attention to himself. What was it his friend Cary had said? "Gay men have been playing baseball for a hundred years, and no one's ever been the wiser."

So there was no way Matt Blanco knew Iggy's big secret. Unless he'd cottoned on to the fact that Iggy was seriously in lust. Iggy had a hard time keeping his gaze away from the man, who was now in the on-deck circle taking practice swings with a weighted bat. Iggy ducked behind Manuel Cruz so he could better covertly watch Blanco's arm muscles strain and stretch as he swung.

He turned away. Lusting wouldn't do him any good. Matt Blanco was so far out of his league, it wasn't worth wasting his thoughts on him. It was better to focus on the game. No matter how horny he was or how much he missed sex, there was too much at stake to risk it.

He chastised himself for thinking about sex in the middle of a game. Instead he found a spot on the bench and watched Blanco bat, which effectively put his attention back on the field.

Chapter Two

EVERYTHING HURT.

Andy Su, Matt's physical therapist, stood frowning at the edge of the bench where Matt lay on his back, unwilling to move lest some other part of him he hadn't known he had decided to start hurting.

"You're going to have to take it easier on your left knee," said Andy.

In frustration, Matt lifted his head, and then dropped it quickly back on the bench, which caused pain to blossom at the back of his skull. He groaned. "I think my knee is the least of my problems."

Andy sighed. "You're just sore. You've been overexerting yourself instead of taking it easy like I told you. But everything that hurts now will feel better in a couple of days. Except for that knee. It needs time to heal, or you're going to tear something. If you don't back off, I'm talking to Bill about putting you on the disabled list."

Matt groaned. "Fine, I'll go easier on it."

"That means no running unless you have to. That means you tell Bill to put in a pinch runner if it hurts during a game. That means you stop the insane workout routine you've had going for the last two weeks. I mean, what the hell, Matt? You know better. What's gotten into you?"

"Nothing has gotten into me," said Matt. Nothing he'd admit to, anyway. He'd developed a crush on the rookie third baseman, but that was really small potatoes. It wasn't the first time he'd developed a crush on another player, and it probably wouldn't be the last, and these things never lasted long. By way of explanation, he said, "You said working out more would build up my endurance so I wouldn't get so tired after a game."

Andy frowned again. "I did say that, but there's a difference between an extra fifteen minutes of circuit training and the two-hour workouts you've been putting yourself through."

"Fine, fine. Point taken."

"Good."

Andy helped Matt back to his feet. Matt imagined he could hear his body creaking as he stood. He groaned again as his muscles cried out.

"You're not as young as you used to be," Andy said.

"Yes, I get that."

"Your body is your livelihood. I understand that completely. You want to stay in shape so you can keep on playing baseball until you've reached a ripe old age. But that also means you have to take care of it."

Feeling tired of the lecture, Matt started walking toward the locker room.

Andy called after him, "Same time next week!"

Matt pushed through the door to the locker room and fantasized about taking a long, hot shower and then going home to sleep for a very long time. But, of course, sitting on a bench right in the middle of the goddamned room was Ignacio Rodriguez.

Matt loped over to his locker and pulled it open with so much force that it banged into the locker next to it.

"Uh. Everything all right?" Rodriguez asked.

"Fine."

"Okay."

Matt was about to strip and head for the shower, but he felt self-conscious suddenly, aware that even if Rodriguez had zero interest in looking at him, he was still right there. Matt glanced behind him and saw that Rodriguez sat with a towel wrapped around his waist, and he was fishing through a duffel bag for something. Then he stood and went over to his locker and started pulling clothes out of it.

Curiosity piqued, Matt said, "You lose something?"

"Um." Rodriguez turned to face him. His face and chest had gone crimson. Matt had to put some extra effort into not letting his gaze settle too long on that chest. "Well, I…." Rodriguez put his hands on his waist and shook his head. "I think I've been hazed."

Matt really tried to hold back the chuckle. "Someone stole your underwear."

"It sure looks that way." Rodriguez sighed. "What are we, thirteen? I thought shit like this stopped happening after you graduated from college."

Matt chuckled. "Come on. You know baseball players are basically just overgrown teenage boys. Normal men grow up and get jobs in accounting or whatever, but we spend our adult lives playing the same game we've been playing since we were kids. Some of us never grow up."

"I guess."

Rodriguez pulled a pair of jeans and a T-shirt from his locker. Matt really wanted—and at the same time, really didn't want—to see what was beneath that towel, so he turned back to his locker and considered his options. He spent way more time than he should have hedging about whether he felt comfortable stripping in front of Rodriguez. He pulled his T-shirt off and glanced back at Rodriguez, who was still standing there, holding his clothes. When Matt turned to find out what was wrong, he heard the hiss of Rodriguez taking in a sharp breath.

Matt's thought process worked quickly. Rodriguez had gone red again as Matt turned around. He couldn't possibly be embarrassed, could he? The man had been playing major-league baseball for more than half a season, and he played in the minors and college before that. There was no reason for this situation—two professional players in a locker room—to be unusual. And yet Rodriguez seemed to be waiting for Matt, just like Matt was waiting for Rodriguez. Which didn't make any sense, unless….

"Everything all right?" asked Matt.

Rodriguez nodded. Then he shook his head. "It's not a big… I mean, you wouldn't understand, and I…." He frowned.

"I was a rookie once too."

"I know, but…." Rodriguez looked up. Matt met his gaze. There was so much anguish there. "I…. Please. Just go shower. It's nothing."

"Are you sure?" Their gazes were still locked. Some of Rodriguez's pain looked familiar. He wondered if some of what he saw there was in his head or if it was true. "Wait, are you…?" he started to ask.

But Rodriguez started to answer. "I…."

Their eyes met again, and suddenly Matt understood. He took a step back. His back collided with the row of lockers. "Jesus Christ," he said.

Rodriguez sat back down on the bench. "Oh God, oh God, oh God."

Matt closed his eyes and tried to gather his thoughts enough to say something rational. "Okay," he said. "Here's what's gonna happen. I'm going to go take a shower. You do whatever you need to. When I come back, we're gonna talk about this." Not that there was much to talk about. If Matt's hunch was correct—something he would bet on given Rodriguez's reaction—then it wasn't like Rodriguez was going to go off blabbing. Nothing like a secret that would bring both of them trouble to keep them both quiet.

Matt closed his locker and went off to get a towel. He showered quickly, thinking about Rodriguez the entire time, his mind bouncing between erotic fantasies and whether it was a great or a terrible thing that Rodriguez had turned out to be gay also. He grabbed his workout clothes and put a towel around his waist, realizing on the way back that he'd have to be naked in front of Rodriguez sooner or later, so he might as well get that over with.

When he got back to the locker room, Rodriguez was gone.

IGGY DRESSED in record time—sans underwear, but it couldn't be helped—before running out of the stadium. The subway seemed safer, more anonymous than bumming a ride or calling a cab, so he hopped on a train and then spent the whole ride trying to calm himself down. He had plenty of time to do that, since he had to transfer trains three times to get to his apartment. He'd just signed a contract worth $25 million, but somehow he couldn't figure out how to get an apartment in New York City that was convenient to his job.

On the way he considered the old school-yard taunts he'd put up with his whole life. In Iggy's neighborhood, the worst thing a boy could do was fail to be completely masculine. The kids Iggy knew growing up were always waiting for boys to slip up, to do something that didn't fit with their precise definition of masculinity. Iggy routinely failed to pass those tests, mostly because it had taken his voice longer to drop than it had for the other boys. Cary had told him later that it was also because he had such a pretty face. On top of that, his ability to hit almost any ball pitched to him from the Little League mound had intimidated a lot of the other boys. Iggy had repeatedly been called "gay" or "fag" starting from a young age. He knew now kids on the playground couldn't have known how close they were to the truth. At the time his standard retort had been "It takes one to know one!" The one thing the arbiters of masculinity could never suffer being called was gay.

And that was where that look in Matt Blanco's eyes had come from, Iggy realized as the train finally pulled into his station. Iggy had almost confessed the very secret he held closest, all because Matt had almost asked while looking at him with that sad expression. Perhaps it really did take one to know one.

That didn't help Iggy's panic subside. Once safely inside his apartment, Iggy pulled out his phone and dialed Cary, who had been his best friend since they'd played ball together in college. Cary answered on the third ring. Then a jumble of confused words tumbled out of Iggy's mouth. "He knows, he goddamned knows, and I think he is too, and what the hell am I going to do?"

After a long pause, Cary said, "Wait, what?"

Iggy began pacing. He took a deep breath. "Matt Blanco—*the* Matt Blanco—knows that I'm gay. And I think he is too."

"Holy shit! Give me a sec to go somewhere private." Something rustled in the background, and then Cary came back on the line and said, "Back up. Tell me everything."

Iggy related what had happened in the locker room that evening, but after some discussion, he agreed with Cary that it wasn't absolute proof. It sure seemed like something, though. Tension had filled that room before Iggy had given himself away, but at the time, Iggy hadn't been able to put his finger on the source of it. To Cary he said, "So now the question is if he was acting all weird because we're both gay, or if he's actually attracted to me. Oh God, what if he's attracted to me? What if he isn't?"

"Calm down, Ig. One crisis at a time. So Matt Blanco, one of the most beloved players in baseball right now? That guy. He could be gay."

"Yeah. More than could be."

Iggy realized late in the game that this was a dangerous conversation to have with Cary, who had gone into sports media instead of playing after college. Cary often said that he owed his career as a reporter for Sports Net, a fairly prominent sports-news website, to the fact that he'd played college ball with three guys who were now in the majors. Either way, he worked in an office that was a hotbed of gossip. On the other hand, Iggy trusted Cary with his life and knew nothing he told Cary would make it to the site without his permission.

"It's never even been implied, though," Cary said. "You know how the New York media is. Those players are all under microscopes. Blanco stays out of the gossip pages by some miracle, sure. There's never even been a hint of anything in any place I've ever worked."

"I don't know what to tell you, just what I saw with my own eyes." He felt a little more rational as he dropped onto his sofa.

"What are you going to do?" Cary asked.

"Nothing."

There was a long pause. "But you… like him, don't you?"

"Sure. He's a nice guy."

"Is he as hot in person as he is in photos?"

"Hotter."

Cary sighed. "Man. That team has an attractive lineup. Too bad Evan Miller got traded. Now that's a man I can…." He paused. "Well, that's a man I could get behind. In more ways than one."

Iggy groaned. "Not to be selfish, but can we focus on me for a second?"

"Just so we're clear, you *like* him, like him. You want him."

"I…." It was impossible to deny. Cary had known Iggy too long. He knew about the framed baseball card, he'd seen the poster in Iggy's dorm room, he'd known for years that if there was one player Iggy would have killed to get his hands on, it was Matt Blanco. "I barely know him," Iggy said, which was true. "I mean, I've known *of* him for years, and you know that I worshipped him when I was in college, but I don't really know the real him at all. We've barely even had a conversation. He could be a giant asshole. And he's kind of a lot older than me. More than ten years."

"Those are valid points," Cary said. "But also, I feel like you have an opportunity here. How many people get to meet their idols? You've not only met yours, but you're playing on the same baseball team. In more ways than one even! I think you should go after him."

Go after him? "Are you crazy?" Iggy's voice screeched as he spoke.

"I'm not saying you should fuck him, although you should if you get the opportunity, because when does that ever happen? I just mean you should get to know him. And if he *is* gay, then you have an unexpected ally on your team, don't you?"

"I guess."

"I know it's risky."

Iggy sighed. It wasn't even the risk that bothered him. He lived in a glass closet where most of his friends and family knew he was gay, but hardly anyone he knew professionally did. Sometimes a tiny part of him hoped that the general public would find out. Having to keep the secret brought so much stress, not to mention loneliness, to his life. He was terrified of dating now that the New York media had decided he was worth paying attention to, and he knew that his sexuality making headlines would effectively derail his career. The gay athlete was always persona non grata in the locker room. It stood to reason that either the fans or his teammates, more likely both, would turn on him, and that would create a lot of tension that would distract from the game.

Iggy knew all this, and still that didn't seem like the biggest problem here. "It's also, you know, I've worshipped this guy for years. And he thinks I'm just some rookie kid. That's just to begin with. But what if… what if he *is* a giant asshole?"

"Ah," Cary said. "What if he doesn't live up to your expectations of him?"

"Yeah."

"Well, I can't help you there. Although maybe you seeing that he's a real person instead of a god will help with your hero-worship complex there. Then you can fuck him."

Iggy laughed despite himself. "Thanks," he said.

"No problem."

When Iggy got off the phone, he flipped on the TV. ESPN was doing some kind of special on the shape of the top teams now that the trade deadline had passed. Iggy was featured quite prominently, but he found he couldn't watch himself on TV. He flipped around until he found a dumb-looking action movie and settled in to watch, hoping it would take his mind off Matt Blanco.

THE DREAM always started the same way. Matt stepped out of the dugout. He picked up his bat and walked to the on-deck circle, where he took a few practice swings. Then it was his turn at bat. He paused to acknowledge the crowd, which gave an uproarious cheer. He walked up to the plate and swung the bat again. Finally, just like Babe fucking Ruth, he pointed. Where he pointed varied, but it was usually toward the left-field bleachers.

Anytime he had the dream, he was confident that his bat would connect and he'd drive that ball out of the stadium. Everything from the wind to the velocity of the pitch was under his control. He choked the bat, he lifted it, he saw the pitch, and he swung.

What happened next was a crapshoot. Sometimes he got the home run he expected. He'd run triumphantly around the bases. Best case, the bases were loaded before he got up to bat and he became the hero of the game. That version of the dream usually ended when he was hoisted up on the shoulders of his teammates. Sometimes the bat whooshed right over the ball, and he'd wake up just after he heard the slap of the ball hitting the catcher's glove. Sometimes the bat connected, but the ball soared into an outfielder's glove. Sometimes the ball hit him in the head.

He had the dream a few nights after his encounter with Ignacio Rodriguez in the locker room. Instead of Cruz or Roger, the person who slapped his back before he got up to stand on deck was the Rodriguez kid. But Matt knew even in his dream that Rodriguez was clearly not a kid—he was a man, and a sinfully attractive man at that. His touch was affectionate, supposed to be encouraging, maybe even a promise for something to happen later. It felt a little like a kiss before being sent off to war, only Rodriguez was right there in the trenches with him. More than that, Rodriguez was probably the better player, now that Matt's knees ached, now that his batting average had plummeted. In the dream he was aware of these things, but they didn't matter, because then he was at bat, then he saw the pitch, then he was swinging.

Slap! Strike one.

"No," Matt said. "That's not how that was supposed to go."

He choked the bat and held it up. He could see everything as if it were in slow motion. He saw the pitcher spit, his right leg draw up, and his glove rise, saw the way his fingers fit around the ball before he threw it, saw that ball flying right for him. He had this one. He could control it. He moved the bat forward slowly, knowing it would connect. Then *whoosh!* *Slap!* Strike two.

Matt cursed. He glanced toward the dugout, where Rodriguez waited expectantly. He could not disappoint this man. He would not. He went through the routine. Practice swing, point to the left-field bleachers, Babe fucking Ruth. He had this.

And again, there was the windup. The pitch. The ball hurtling toward him. The bat slicing through the air. And *slap!* Strike three.

Matt fell onto his knees. He cried out in anguish. The crowd booed.

He woke up with a start.

After a long breath, Matt sat up and assessed the situation. He was in bed alone, his room was pitch-dark, and his knee throbbed. He lay back down and knew no more sleep would be coming that night.

Chapter Three

BOTTOM OF the eighth, Eagles up 2–1, one man on second, one out. Iggy watched from the dugout as Manuel Cruz went up to bat. Cruz was known mostly for his adept fielding and his elegant swing but wasn't really a power hitter, and still Iggy heard Bill mumble, "Hit it out of the park, Cruz. Come on."

He didn't quite accomplish that. Instead, Cruz swung the bat and sent a grounder right between first and second. The Mariners' center fielder picked it up and tossed it to first before the first basemen tossed it to third. Double play. Iggy picked up his glove. Top of the ninth.

He kept rehearsing the mechanics of the game in his head, like an announcer might. It helped to keep his mind off Matt Blanco. He hadn't been able to bring himself to so much as say hello to Blanco since the other day in the locker room. He knew there was a limit to how long he could avoid the situation, but he wasn't ready to face it yet, wasn't ready to find out what the consequences of the situation might be.

Coming up with his own play-by-play also kept his mind on the game. It was a litany, but it helped him focus. *First pitch, ball. Second pitch, strike. Third pitch, foul. Fourth pitch, pop fly, caught by Cruz. First out.* And so on. It was an easy inning, the rookie relief pitcher mostly just throwing heat for the hell of it, ninety-five-mile-per-hour fastball after ninety-five-mile-per-hour fastball, and none of the batters able to do much except hit the occasional ball into a fielder's glove. Then Don Richards, the Eagles' stadium announcer for the past several decades, declared the Eagles the victors, and the game was over. Iggy kept up the litany. *Slap Cruz's hand. Now Jones. Now Blanco. Don't make eye contact with Blanco. Now go back to the dugout, bump fists with Bill. Now inside.*

This was a Sunday afternoon game, the last in a series against the Mariners that the Eagles swept easily and predictably, and it was broadcast only on the New York Sports Network, which the Eagles owned, so in sum: nobody except the diehards cared. They had a night game the next day against the Red Sox, the sort of game everyone did care about, so most of the team was planning to shower and then go home to rest up. Iggy was most of the way through that process—was in fact in his street clothes and about to leave—when Matt Blanco sidled up to him and said, "So there's a decent pizza place a few blocks from here."

Iggy broke out in a cold sweat. He swallowed and said, "Okay. Good to know."

Blanco took a deep breath and glanced around the locker room. Jefferson Jones was icing his shoulder, and most of the coaching staff was around, critiquing various players. Blanco said, "Haverman suggested that I play nice and invite you to do something social. I know everyone's beat, but you have to eat, so I thought I'd take you to this pizza place. Okay?"

There was a tiny bit of hostility in Blanco's voice—or it might have been just plain frustration—but either way he seemed about as excited about that slice of pizza as about getting a root canal. "Oh," Iggy said. Remembering what Cary told him about taking the opportunity to get to know Blanco better, he added, "Yeah, okay. I like pizza."

Blanco nodded. "Meet me by the staff exit in ten. I gotta go talk to somebody first."

Iggy dutifully met Blanco at the staff exit a few minutes later. Blanco pulled a New York Giants cap over his head and brandished a pair of sunglasses. Iggy put on his own sunglasses and trailed Blanco down the block.

After they'd been walking for about five minutes, Blanco said, "Look, I lied."

"About what?"

"About Haverman. He didn't make any suggestion. But I didn't want it to look like I was asking you out on a date. Which I'm not. It's just pizza."

Iggy wished he could see Blanco's eyes, but they were doubly shaded by the sunglasses and the brim of his hat. "Okay," he said.

"You ran out on me last week."

So here they were. The moment Iggy could no longer postpone. "I know, and I'm sorry. I just—"

"I was worried you were spooked or something."

"Or something," Iggy muttered.

"I didn't mean to spook you, for what it's worth." Blanco turned sharply and then looked back at the sidewalk and kept walking. "Well, Ignacio—"

"Please call me Iggy."

Blanco turned to look at him again.

"Everyone calls me Iggy. My family and friends, I mean. I'm sort of hoping it catches on with the press, because even though it's a little weird, it's a hell of a lot better than I-Rod, which is what the *Post* has been calling me. That sounds like a sex toy."

Blanco laughed. "It does, yeah. Well, in that case, call me Matt."

"Of course." Iggy reminded himself that Matt Blanco was, at the end of the day, just a man, a man in the same profession he was. It wasn't that big a deal that he was on a first-name basis with *the* Matt Blanco. He was just on a first-name basis with Matt, his teammate.

"Here's the place," Matt said suddenly. It was a nondescript storefront with a red awning. Under his breath he added, "It's not the best pizza you've ever tasted, but it's pretty standard New York style, and they use a lot of cheese."

"Sounds great," said Iggy.

"You were just living near Boston, right? This is better than the pizza there, I'm sure. This is Brooklyn, after all."

"I believe you."

It surprised Iggy that Matt seemed so nervous that he was talking to fill the silence. Iggy took a deep breath in an effort to calm his own nerves, which felt frayed and exposed.

Matt led them to a table in the corner. "What do you want?" he asked.

"Uh, pepperoni?"

Matt nodded. He took off the shades and the hat and then walked up to the counter. A man with dark hair and a beard manned the register. Matt said, "Hey, Tony, how's it going?"

"Ah, Matteo. Nice to see you. I saw that home run you hit on Thursday."

"Thanks. Can I have a large pie? Half pepperoni, half mushroom."

"For you, anything."

Matt bought a couple of bottles of water and brought them back to the table. He handed one to Iggy and sat down. "Tony'll bring it out when it's ready."

"Thank you."

They sat in awkward silence for a moment, but that awkwardness did a lot to humanize Matt in Iggy's mind. Matt might have been a god among athletes, but he was also a man with a brain and a heart and an inability to deal with some social situations. Iggy found himself chuckling.

"What are you laughing at?"

"You."

That pulled a smile from Matt. "Why am I funny?"

"You just… are. I think I only just noticed that you're just this guy in a pizza place and not a Hall-of-Fame-bound baseball player. I mean, you are that, just, you know."

Matt smiled. "Yeah, I know."

"You must get that a lot."

Matt shook his head. "Actually, no. Most new people I meet either have no idea who I am or never get past the starstruck phase. I'm glad you found the middle ground."

Iggy wasn't sure he had. There were so many things about fame that he hadn't considered. Would he achieve the kind of fame Matt enjoyed? Did he want to? "Does that bother you?" he asked. "The ignorant and the starstruck, I mean."

"Sometimes." Matt took a sip of his water. "Yeah, I guess it does. The last person I dated knew absolutely nothing about baseball, which was refreshing at first. Except it turns out I don't know shit about anything except the game, so we ran out of things to talk about." He sighed. "I didn't sign on for a life in the spotlight, you know. I just want to play baseball."

"I know."

"Yeah, I guess you do."

Iggy did not feel particularly encouraged by Matt's words. Was that how Matt met potential hookups? Only going out with guys who didn't know who he was? Was that what Iggy's life had in store? That didn't sound so hopeful.

Tony brought over the pizza. It sat inauspiciously on a steel platter, but it smelled delicious. Iggy hadn't known he was hungry until he got a whiff of the food. Tony pulled a pizza cutter from his pocket and ran it over the pie four times.

"How's your mother?" Tony asked.

"She's good. She and Dad finally finished the renovations in their basement, so she's already planning the next project."

Tony chuckled. "Always has a plan, that woman."

"I'm just trying not to get roped into this scheme."

Tony said something in Italian to Matt, which Matt answered by saying, "Yeah, yeah. *Capisco*. Go back to tossing dough around."

"Are you bilingual?" Iggy asked.

"Mostly. My *nonna* was off-the-boat Italian. She lived with us most of the time while I was growing up and didn't speak much English. What about you? How's your Spanish?"

"Pretty good. My parents are Dominican, but I was born in Arizona. My dad thought it was important for us to know English, so he made sure mine was good, but my mother's English is only so-so."

"If your dad wanted you to be assimilated, I'm surprised they didn't give you a more Anglo name."

"Eh." Iggy shrugged. "I'm named after my father's brother. He died six months before I was born." Iggy waved his hand. He didn't want to talk about his family, and all this conversation was doing was distracting him from the matter at hand. He took a deep breath and then said, "So about last week. I'm really sorry. I shouldn't have run out like that."

"It's all right," said Matt. "I understand why you did."

"Is this a safe place to talk?"

"Yeah." Matt hooked his thumb back to point toward Tony. "Tony is my mother's cousin."

That didn't really seem like an answer, but Iggy said, "Well, anyway. I'm sorry for ditching you. I guess I panicked."

Matt nodded. "Yeah. I was surprised, but I understand. I panicked a little too, frankly." Matt's eyes were wide.

Iggy thought about what Cary had said. If nothing else, he'd have an ally on the team, someone who had been through all this shit before and could help Iggy figure out how to deal with it. Not just being gay, but the media attention, the pressure to play well. Of course, Iggy really did *want* Matt, precisely the way Cary had said. Was there even a prayer of something happening between them?

Out of uniform and close up, Matt was even hotter than Iggy would have guessed. He kept his dark hair cut short, his olive skin betraying his Italian heritage, and he had those incredible dark eyes. He was, of course, in peak physical condition. Iggy noticed subtle signs of Matt's age—he had crow's feet and frown lines—but if anything, Iggy thought that just made him sexier. He was healthy and vibrant and aging well, and the signs of age implied knowledge and experience.

Iggy said, "Well, I guess it's all out in the open now. I mean, between us, at least."

Matt pushed his plate aside. He shook his head. "This is nuts."

"I am surely not the first gay baseball player you've ever met."

Matt shook his head. "Nope. You're not. Just… this is not how I would have expected this to play out."

"Oh." Iggy wasn't sure what to think of that. What had Matt expected? Still, he didn't feel he could ask. Instead he asked, "So that guy is your mother's cousin?"

Matt turned and looked back at the counter. "Yeah."

"Are you from New York?"

Matt nodded. "Grew up in Bensonhurst."

"Where's that?"

"South Brooklyn. Kinda near Coney Island."

And with that, they were on to safer topics of conversation.

IGGY WAS saying, "Then Faber nailed the ball, and everyone thought it was a home run. I mean, Faber was waving to the crowd, and the kids in the stands had their gloves out. We were all just standing there waiting for the ball to go out. Everyone thought that was a home run except Hernandez, who was playing center field. He jogged backward until he hit the mat, and then he held his glove up, just totally relaxed. I think he even yawned. And that ball fell right into his glove. That was the greatest catch I ever saw."

Matt chuckled. They were walking back to the stadium, swapping stories of great plays they'd witnessed, and Matt was enjoying himself to the extent that he was reluctant to just let Iggy go when they got back to the ballpark. Once they'd both loosened up and let go of some of the panic and tension, Matt found Iggy friendly and easy to talk to.

When they reached the fork where Iggy would have to make a subway/parking lot decision, it looked like he was headed toward the subway. Matt said, "I've got my car here. I'll give you a ride."

"Oh," said Iggy. He looked at the parking lot entrance and scratched his chin. "All right. I live on the East Side."

Matt motioned for Iggy to follow him. "You're gonna have to narrow it down."

Matt's car looked a little lonely in the staff parking area. Everyone else seemed to be gone for the night.

Iggy said, "Um, Upper East Side. Seventy-Eighth between Park and Lexington."

Matt wrinkled his nose. "Wow. Really?"

"Yeah." Iggy sighed. "I've been getting that reaction a lot. I should have stayed in the hotel until I understood the lay of the city better, but my signing bonus was burning a hole in my pocket, and I let the realtor talk me into this place. It's a great apartment, don't get me wrong, but leave it to me to invest in an apartment in the one neighborhood in the city where property values are going down. And that's not to mention how hard it is to get between there and the stadium."

"It can't be that bad."

"No, I guess it isn't. But my neighbor, Edith—"

"Edith?"

"None of my neighbors are younger than eighty, okay? Anyway, Edith says the neighborhood's gone to hell since the construction on the Second Avenue subway started."

Matt laughed again. "Yeah, it's definitely not that bad. Anyone describing the Upper East Side as having gone to hell has no perspective at all and has probably not left the Upper East Side in thirty years."

"But it's not even that." Iggy followed Matt over to the car. "The place is just so… big. And it's just me rattling around in there. Until a month ago, I was sharing the first floor of a house in the Boston suburbs with one of my teammates from the Paw Sox. I don't know what to do with all the space."

"Welcome to the big leagues, kid."

"Yeah, yeah." Matt watched Iggy survey the car. "Somehow I expected you to drive something a little ritzier. A Camry? Really?"

"It's a hybrid."

"Uh-huh."

Matt hit the Unlock button on his key chain, and they both got in the car. Matt mentally worked out the route he'd have to take to get to Iggy's place. Not too bad; once he dropped Iggy off, it would be a quick drive through Central Park to get to his own apartment.

Once they were in the confined space of the car, Matt was suddenly much more conscious of Iggy. He put the car in gear and pulled out of the parking lot. He'd driven this way so many times he could do it without thinking, which was good, because most of his thoughts circled around Iggy. Primary among those was that Iggy was so young. Matt had been hoping that getting to know Iggy would demystify him enough for Matt to get over his crush, but the opposite proved true; the more Matt got to know Iggy, the more he liked him. The attraction seemed mutual, which didn't help. Still, he reminded himself, the difference in their ages was an issue. Matt was nearing the end of his career while Iggy was just starting. Not to mention their profession didn't take too kindly to gay players. They should not get involved. It would make everything too complicated.

And yet….

Iggy reached down to scratch his knee as Matt rolled to a stop at an intersection. Matt tried really hard not to look.

"Where do you live?" Iggy asked when he righted himself.

"Upper West Side. So I'm not that much more convenient. A lot of the guys have apartments in Lower Manhattan or in Brooklyn closer to the stadium. I kind of like being far away, though. The drive takes only about a half hour if traffic's not bad. That's the best you can say about any distance between two points in this city."

"Yeah, I've noticed that."

Matt pulled onto Franklin Avenue. He drove in silence for a few blocks.

Then Iggy said, "I guess I understand why you'd want to be isolated."

It was nice to have someone who understood. "When I bought the apartment, there was a little bit of an uproar, like I was betraying Brooklyn somehow. But a lot of the Mets and Yankees have apartments in Manhattan or even the suburbs. Hell, Overbey moved to Westchester after he got married. Now, of course, nobody gives a shit, but you know, there was a lot of attention being paid to me after I started playing well."

"Is there still? I mean, I've seen photos of you in the tabloids."

"Eh, sometimes." Matt tended to get his photo taken when he went out with his teammates, but he otherwise worked very hard to stay under the radar. He only picked up men at private parties, for one thing. "I don't know how much people really care about my personal life. If I don't draw attention to myself, the public mostly just seems to care about my batting average."

"Okay. I guess that's good. I wanted to know what I'm in for."

Matt laughed. "Yeah? So what you're saying is, you think you'll be as good as I am so that you attract the media's attention." Although Matt knew he already had. Iggy Rodriguez was the rookie everyone was talking about that season.

Iggy grinned. "I know I will be. I'll be better."

Matt stopped at a red light and kept laughing. "A little cocky of you, don't you think?"

"I have ambitions," Iggy said. Matt glanced at him as the light turned green and saw the shit-eating grin on Iggy's face, which made him understand that Iggy wasn't being completely serious. "Doesn't every player dream of being a legend?"

"I don't know about you. I just want to play baseball."

"Aw, come on. Don't you have an idol? One of those Hall of Famers that you imitated when you were a kid?"

Matt had a ready answer but didn't want Iggy to know that, so he hedged and then said, "I know it is cliché, but I loved Babe Ruth when I was a kid. He was the first player who blew all those old records apart, you know?"

"Yeah. I always liked DiMaggio. I watched archival footage in college and studied his swing."

"Sure. I was a kid in the seventies. My dad was a big Yankees fan, so we went to a lot of games. I watched those hitters in the late seventies, like

Thurman Munson and Reggie Jackson. Man, I loved Reggie Jackson when I was a kid. I remember watching that World Series on TV, the one where Reggie hit three home runs? That totally blew me away."

"It must have been something to see."

Matt winced, Iggy's comment reminding him how young Iggy was, but he put it out of his mind. "It was amazing. Of course, I'm obligated to tell you that, both as the Brooklyn Eagles' first baseman and also as a born-and-bred Brooklynite, I was obviously an Eagles fan as a kid."

Iggy chuckled. "I won't tell anyone you were a Yankees fan." He shook his head. "I still don't believe all this."

"Believe what?"

"You may be a closet Yankees fan, but I loved the Eagles as a kid. Jack Nesbit, Carlos Lopez, those were my heroes."

"Yeah? Nesbit retired the year after I was signed to the Eagles. He's a really great guy. Usually comes to Old-Timers' Day."

"Would it be completely silly if I asked him to sign a ball?"

Matt smiled. "Nah, I think he'd be tickled."

They were still laughing and swapping stories of games remembered when Matt pulled up to Iggy's building. Matt said, "Well, I guess this is the part where I tell you I had a great time, and I'd like to see you again." He hoped it sounded like a joke, but he mostly meant it the way it sounded. God, he was in trouble.

Iggy raised an eyebrow. "I'll see you at batting practice tomorrow, Matt." Then he got out of the car.

Matt sat in the car for a moment and tried to adjust his expectations. Iggy had still been eating school lunches when Matt had been signed to the Eagles. And if that weren't enough of a reminder of how old Matt was, his knee was starting to throb. He sighed and put his car in gear.

Chapter Four

MATT WAS feeling good and limber after physical therapy. He shook out his arms as he walked into the locker room. His only real goal was to find a clean towel and wash off all the sweat.

He was surprised when Iggy strolled into the room. Matt had thought he was the last athlete in the stadium. "Is anyone else here?"

Iggy walked to his locker but didn't open it. "No. I was working with Terry, but he just left with Su. So it's just us and security."

Matt turned back to his locker and dug through it until he found a towel. Giving it due consideration, he decided he would not be changing in front of Iggy if they were the only ones in the locker room. He was too self-conscious about being naked in front of someone he was that attracted to. Plus, now that he was in the same room as Iggy, as often happened when he was near Iggy, he was half-hard.

When he moved to walk to the showers, he noticed Iggy was staring at him. "You want something, kid?"

Iggy smirked. "You."

All rational thought fled Matt's head. Or maybe that was all the blood rushing south that made him light-headed, because Iggy always looked so amazingly sexy, maybe especially while he was fresh from a workout in a T-shirt and an old pair of uniform pants, his hair damp and sticking out every which way, beads of sweat on his exposed skin, a pink flush everywhere. Matt could smell him, could actually smell sweat and desire and the promise of sex.

The smart thing would have been to make a joke, or to tell Iggy to fuck off, or to push past him and go to the showers. Matt moved his hand, intending to do just that, but instead it landed on Iggy's shoulder. He lightly caressed the damp T-shirt. Iggy opened his mouth and moved in.

Their lips came together in a crash. Iggy even tasted amazing, all metallic masculinity with something sweet mixed in. Once their mouths opened to each other, Matt couldn't hold himself back. He tore Iggy's T-shirt over his head, then got his hands on all that sepia-toned skin. It was smooth, if a little clammy, and Matt could feel his muscles rippling underneath the surface. Iggy's fingers dug into his hips. Then, before Matt was really aware of what was going on, Iggy slammed Matt's body into his locker. The slap of metal on his back stung, but he didn't care. He wanted to touch Iggy everywhere, and he couldn't get over how good it felt to get his hands on the flesh that had been tempting him, taunting him, for weeks. He groaned, and Iggy pushed him harder. The vents digging into his back finally pulled him out of the haze.

"You sure we're alone?" Matt managed to say through short breaths.

"Positive." Iggy pulled at Matt's shirt and managed to get it off. Iggy ran his hands down Matt's chest, then bent his head and licked across Matt's collarbone.

Matt thought he heard a sound coming from the hallway outside the locker room. Iggy's lips and tongue slid across his skin, leaving behind tingles and goose bumps, but his fear of being discovered won out. "Iggy, wait."

Against Matt's shoulder, Iggy said, "Don't you fucking tell me to stop. I've been wanting to do this for too long."

That was a sentiment Matt felt down through his toes. He couldn't imagine separating himself from Iggy, tearing away from this thing he wanted so badly. But if anyone walked into the locker room, he and Iggy would be right there in plain view. Thinking fast, he said, "Showers." At least there, they would have a reason to be naked together.

Iggy grunted his consent. Without losing their grip on each other, they each managed to wriggle out of their pants. Through a combination of pushing and pulling, they stumbled into the showers. For show, Matt turned the knobs on two of the showers and stood there naked, letting warm water run over him as he took in the sight of Iggy. Yeah, Matt thought, no room for misunderstanding here. Iggy was naked, his skin glistening, his cock hard.

"C'mere," Matt said.

Iggy closed the space between them.

Everything was slick and wet and hot. Matt kissed Iggy, tasting him, feeling the heat of his mouth. They moved their lips together, slid their hands over each other's skin. Water cascaded over their bodies.

Matt glided his fingers into Iggy's wet hair and pulled him close, deepening the kiss. He slipped his tongue into Iggy's mouth, tasting him, savoring him.

Iggy dug his fingers into Matt's back. Matt thrust his hips forward, and their cocks rubbed together. God. *God.* Goose bumps broke out everywhere, and Matt groaned, his heart rate and anticipation mounting. He knew sweet release would come disastrously fast, but he didn't care. This was so damn good, and Iggy seemed to be right there with him, grunting and biting now.

Matt figured there'd be time to draw it out later. Because he certainly was not letting Iggy get away without a later. He wrapped his hand around both of their cocks and rubbed them together. His skin seemed like it was all exposed nerves, and everything was hot and fresh and intense. Iggy made little mewling sounds and dug his nails deeper into Matt's skin. That small bite of pain made his dick throb. He leaned forward and pressed his lips to Iggy's jaw, darting his tongue out to taste skin, rubbing his face against the rough stubble. He trailed bites and kisses along Iggy's neck and nibbled at his collarbone, all while continuing to pump their cocks. Matt uttered curses and moans as everything seemed to rise higher. Everything, every pore in his body, every cell was tuned toward Iggy, and he pushed and tasted and pulled and pressed. His knees wobbled, but he willed himself to keep standing, to see this through.

When he was about to hit the point of no return, he pulled away a little. Iggy threw his head back and moaned, and Matt could not think of anything sexier or more beautiful than Iggy wrapped up in ecstasy. Iggy's cock vibrated in Matt's hand, and he came, spurting against Matt's abdomen. Just the sight of that sent Matt hurtling over the edge. He slid his hand up and down his cock a few times, and then he was right there with Iggy, just as lost, as his orgasm exploded over him and everything was pleasure and relief and wonder.

Matt threw his arms around Iggy and held him close. "Jesus, that was—"

"We should clean up just in case security comes through or something."

"Oh, right."

That was a little disappointing, but Iggy was right. He stepped under one of the sprays and grabbed a bar of soap. He watched Iggy soap up and liked the sight. Iggy kept shooting him looks, little smiles, and Matt wondered what was going on in his head.

While Matt was still cleaning up, Iggy turned off his shower and said, "I'm gonna go get dressed. Probably it's better if we don't do everything at the same time."

"Sure. Wait for me; I'll give you a ride home." Or back to my place, Matt thought. His old body liked the sound of that, and a jolt of arousal passed through him again.

"That's not necessary," Iggy said.

"It's no trouble at all."

Iggy ducked out of the shower room before Matt could put forth his best arguments. He thought of some pretty compelling things to say while he washed his hair: *This was hot. We should do it again. We could keep doing it all season. The bed in my apartment is pretty comfortable. No one has to know.*

He grabbed a towel and supposed he had no reason not to be naked in front of Iggy anymore. He felt naked in more ways than one as it was, but he didn't mind having someone on the team know his secret. It was kind of refreshing to just be honest for a change. He whistled and hummed to himself as he walked back toward his locker.

When he got there, Iggy was nowhere in sight.

Chapter Five

IGGY'S PREGAME ritual included a thirty-minute run on the treadmill to loosen up. He listened to a playlist of Queen songs to get himself psyched, and jogged between the gym and the locker room mentally singing along with "We Are the Champions."

He took a deep breath before pushing through the door, worried Matt would be there—he was *so* not ready to face Matt yet—but he was spared.

"Pick up the pace, Rodriguez," said Jefferson Jones.

Iggy glanced at the locker room clock, and—*fuck*—he was running late. He changed into his uniform quickly, sliding the gold cross he'd gotten as a gift from his grandmother at his first communion under his undershirt. He'd given up on his faith as a teenager, but he whispered a prayer to St. Sebastian, as he always did before a game, and pressed his hand to his locker for fifteen seconds and headed out to the field.

Matt was at the bench already, stretching out his hamstrings and chatting with Roger May. Matt's dark hair was a little tousled and his muscles rippled through his uniform as he stretched. Iggy tried to make himself invisible, walking softly over to the shelves that held the batting helmets.

It wasn't regret he had, per se. How could he regret such an amazing sexual encounter? Being naked with Matt in the showers had been one of the hottest experiences of his life. But it had been so... brazen of him. Iggy didn't do things like that. That was, he'd initiated sex plenty of times, but not with sexy famous men he didn't really know well. He still wasn't really sure what had come over him. But the encounter had left him feeling embarrassed and confused, and then he'd made it worse by straight-up panicking and bolting from the locker room without so much as a "see ya later" to Matt.

Iggy picked up his batting helmet and cradled it in his hands as he looked at the batting order. He'd be batting fifth today, which he supposed bought him enough time to get his head in the game.

"Hey, Rodriguez," said Roger May casually. "How's it going?"

"Fine," Iggy said, trying not to look at Matt.

"Santiago is pitching for Texas today. He's got a wicked curveball, but you can still hit it if you know it's coming. He tends to hook the ball high and to the left, so watch for that."

"Thanks," said Iggy. "I appreciate the tip."

Iggy chanced a glance at Matt, who stood at the end of the bench, staring at the ground with a frown on his face.

Roger slapped Matt on the back. "'Course, Blanco still can't hit a curveball."

"Fuck you. I could hit a curveball clear to the Empire State Building."

Cruz emerged from the stadium and kissed his gold bracelet before giving everyone within slapping distance a pat on the ass. "How goes it, boys?"

"Discussing the finer points of Santiago's curveball," said May.

"That man could not throw a straight fastball if his life depended on it. He's got a goddamn crooked arm, and everyone's like, 'Oooh, his curveball is amazing.' We all know Blanco could hit that shit out of the park."

"That's what I said!" Matt sounded exasperated.

Cruz laughed. "Santiago's ERA is in the double digits. I'm not worried about Santiago. He's gonna walk half the order. But I heard they got Lucky Chase on reserve to clean up his mess. I am worried about Chase. No one can hit anything he throws."

"So we earn enough runs when Santiago is pitching that it doesn't matter if we don't score in the ninth," said Iggy.

Everyone turned and stared at him. He'd just said something patently obvious and felt like an idiot for it. Why hadn't he kept his mouth shut? Why had he propositioned Matt? Why was Matt so goddamn beautiful? Why was Matt staring at him now like he had three heads?

"I like this kid," Cruz said, slapping Iggy on the back hard enough to propel him forward a step.

After Iggy got his balance back, he slid his helmet back into its slot. Bill started shouting at everyone to get their shit together. The voice of Don Richards boomed through the loudspeakers as he welcomed everyone to a night of Eagles baseball. Iggy glanced at Matt, which was a mistake, because Matt was staring at him.

Everyone stopped what they were doing as the national anthem rang out through the speakers. Iggy's gaze kept sliding toward Matt, who stood stiff, facing the American flag that hung over the Jumbotron. Beard growth shadowed Matt's face, making Iggy think about shaving, which made him think about showers again. Aware that the stadium cameras liked to catch the players singing along, Iggy schooled his features and focused on the flag. When the anthem was over, the players poured out of the dugout. Iggy took a deep breath, trying to shake visions of naked baseball players in the locker room showers.

Matt passed by Iggy as they both walked to their respective bases. He turned and looked at him, a pained expression briefly passing over his face, before he asked, "All right?"

"All right."

Matt nodded and jogged to first base.

But things were not all right. Iggy managed to focus on the game for the length of the first inning. Cruz had clearly underestimated Santiago, who struck out two of the four batters who went up to the plate—including Blanco, who totally whiffed all five pitches. That two of them had been called as balls was remarkable and probably said something about the umpire's biases.

By the fifth inning, Iggy was telling himself that he should probably talk to Matt, give him an explanation. Surely Matt understood how impossible this situation was. There was no relationship potential here, and Iggy knew his feelings were too tangled up in a decade's worth of hero worship for him to separate out the incredible sex from Matt the man and Matt Blanco the baseball player. It was too fraught, too messy, too easy to get caught.

Too tempting.

But, no, it was over. Matt wouldn't meet his gaze when they were both in the dugout.

The Eagles squeaked out a 2–1 victory, but more because Texas lost than the Eagles won. Well, May had been having an excellent game up on the mound, on his way to a no-hitter until he started to show signs of fatigue in the sixth and gave up a run. Bill had pulled him then. The Texas fielders had played messy ball, though, fumbling what should have been easy catches and mishandling the ball when it was hit to the infield.

Team spirits seemed low when Iggy returned to the locker room. Eager to get home, Iggy stripped and headed for the showers.

That was a mistake, perhaps. Most of the team had beat him there, including Blanco, as naked as he had been the evening before when Iggy had rubbed against him under that very showerhead. His body was long and lean. Water sluiced down his pecs, his abs, his groin, everything well defined and perfectly made. Matt's cock was flaccid, but Iggy couldn't help but think about how it had looked hard. Iggy closed his eyes, trying to remember the batting averages of every member of the team. He'd managed to talk down his cock, more embarrassed than aroused now, not that anyone was even looking at him. He opened his eyes. Matt glared at him, finished rinsing his hair, and ducked out of the shower room.

Iggy couldn't help but think that he'd irretrievably fucked up.

As he changed into his street clothes, Cruz asked, "What did you do to piss off Blanco?"

"What? Nothing."

"Did you comment on his swing? Because he hates that."

"No. I've barely said three words to him all day."

Cruz appeared to consider that as he stacked his cleats on their little shelf in his locker. "It's probably not you, then. Blanco's had a stick up his ass all season. Sorry you had to bear the brunt of it today."

"Oh. No big deal."

But it was a big deal. Iggy knew he had to fix this, if only for the sake of team harmony. He just had no idea how.

MATT KNEW he was being a child. He drove home from the game, annoyed with himself for not handling his feelings for Iggy like a rational adult. And he drove to the stadium the next morning vowing to do better.

Iggy stood at his locker when Matt walked in. Matt's locker was close to Iggy's, so there was no way to avoid seeing him.

"Hello," Matt said.

"Hi. Listen. I'm sorry for—"

"Forget it."

"No, I really think I should apologize for...." Iggy glanced around the locker room, which was hardly empty. There were a half dozen guys changing into clothes for their pregame workouts. "For what happened two days ago."

"No apology necessary. Nothing bad happened. Did it?"

"Well, besides me—"

"*Did* it?" Matt asked, his gaze darting around the room before settling on Iggy.

"Nothing happened," Iggy said, catching on.

"That's what I thought."

"We can't avoid each other forever," Iggy whispered.

The whisper drew Matt's attention to Iggy's mouth, which was not a great place to look if he was trying to talk himself out of his attraction. Iggy pursed his lips. Matt knew Iggy was right. If they couldn't resolve whatever was going on between them, it had the potential to affect the whole team. Of course, that was a good reason to not get involved with each other to begin with, but that cow was already out of the barn.

Or else nothing happened, and they would both act as though they weren't still hot for each other. Unless, of course, Iggy had been disappointed by Matt. Iggy was young and beautiful and Matt was… not.

Iggy left the locker room without another word, and Matt stood at his own locker, a T-shirt in his hand, wondering what the hell he was supposed to do now. He still wanted Iggy with every fiber in his body, but there was no way to satisfy that need without creating a bigger mess. And Matt did not create these kinds of messes. He avoided drama, kept out of trouble; he played the game.

So that was what he'd do. Iggy would have to remain a brief flight of fancy.

In the dugout later, he walked up to Iggy and said, "Dallas is playing one of the rookies at right field today. According to the scouting reports, he tends to hit toward third, so be ready for that."

Iggy stared out at the field. Matt worried for a moment that Iggy hadn't heard him, but then Iggy said, "Thanks."

"No problem. And Romano is on the mound today. I know you're still struggling to hit the curve, and Romano's got a mean one too, but it goes wild about a third of the time. So only swing if you really think it's in the strike zone."

Iggy turned to him. "Why are you—"

"Being a good teammate."

"Okay." Iggy let out a breath, and then his Adam's apple bobbed as he swallowed. "Thank you. Um. I used to play in the minors with Estevez. He's the DH today. Fast as lightning, but his swing doesn't have a lot of oomph. He tends to hit pop flies to the infield."

"Got it. I'll watch for that."

Iggy nodded. "I gotta…." He pointed vaguely toward the equipment at the other end of the dugout.

So Matt told him to go. He watched Iggy fiddle with his batting helmet and pick up a couple of bats and wondered if things were really over between them.

Chapter Six

AFTER HE dropped his stuff in his hotel room, Matt got a drink at the bar. He was feeling restless and hoped one of his teammates would materialize to do something entertaining, but everyone seemed to have gone to bed. He was loitering in the lobby when he heard Bill Haverman curse. He redirected his attention toward the check-in desk.

"What do you mean you're short a room? My assistant called to confirm this yesterday. We had a block of thirty rooms. The same thirty rooms we always have when we play in this goddamned city."

Bill was nearly red. Matt was hesitant to get involved, but he found himself moving toward the front desk. He heard the clerk say, "I'm sorry, sir, but there's also a convention here this weekend, and we're booked solid."

"We're the goddamned Brooklyn Eagles," said Bill.

Matt spoke up, keeping his tone friendly. "What seems to be the problem?"

Bill threw his hands in the air. He shot Matt a grateful look. They'd pulled this routine before; Bill would fume and fuss about some service he wasn't getting, and he was easy enough to turn down, but once you got Matt Blanco on the scene, customer service people tended to get starstruck and give in. It was kind of their version of Good Cop/Bad Cop.

"I'm sorry," said the clerk. "There are just not enough rooms. Maybe if a couple of your players doubled up, just for tonight? I can get another room tomorrow. I wish I could make a room materialize out of thin air, but I can't." The clerk's eyes were wide, and there was a little bit of a plea there, like he actually did want a room to appear so this nightmare would end.

"I want to speak to a manager," said Bill.

The guy behind the desk paled. "Uh, I am the manager."

Bill slammed his fist on the desk. To Matt, he said, "I didn't realize they were booked solid. I've already handed out room keys to most of the team. They're probably all settled in, so it's too late to change. And it doesn't make sense to have one man stay at another hotel."

Matt's own room key sat securely in his pocket. He asked, "Who's out a room?"

"Rodriguez."

"Always the rookie who draws the short straw, eh?" Matt's mind worked quickly, and he said, "If you can't work this out, he can bunk with me." He immediately wanted to take it back.

"All right. I'll go find him." Bill turned back to the guy behind the desk. "If this ever happens again, we're staying somewhere else in the future. You got that?"

"Yes, sir," said the manager, duly chastened.

Bill turned around and surveyed the room. "I think I left Iggy in the restaurant. I'll let him know what happened. If you're spending time with him anyway, would you talk to him about that thing he does with his elbow when he gets pitched a curveball?"

"Of course."

"Great. Thanks, Matt. I owe you one."

Bill produced Iggy a few minutes later. He had a black duffel bag slung over his shoulder and was looking at the floor. Bill slapped them both on the back before heading out of the lobby. A long, awkward silence followed.

Matt couldn't help but notice the small things. Iggy's eyelashes were long and lush, strangely pretty for a guy. His T-shirt pulled against his shoulders in a way that Matt found really sexy. The cuffs of his jeans were shredded where they dragged at his heels. And he just stood there, looking a little sad.

"So, ah," Matt said, "I'm on the fifth floor. We should take the elevator."

Iggy looked up. "You volunteered to room with me?"

"My room has two beds."

"But—" Iggy's jaw snapped shut, and he shook his head. "All right. Well." Their eyes met, and the air around them seemed to still as an electrical current zipped between them.

That was something, Matt thought. Attraction still pulled them together, even though Iggy had continued to avoid him. Matt hadn't forced the issue either, hoping everything would blow over. He felt little hope for that now, however. Arousal uncoiled in Matt every goddamned time he looked at Iggy.

Then Iggy smirked. And Lord have mercy. Matt wondered if they should maybe clear the air, but Iggy shifted his weight and adjusted the duffel bag on his shoulder, and Matt promptly forgot what there even was to talk about.

"The fifth floor, huh?" said Iggy.

"Yes, right. Come on." Matt led him to the room. He thought to himself that, for better or for worse, his night had just gotten a lot more interesting.

IGGY CRANKED the heat up in the shower, hot enough to scald his skin. When he stepped under the water, he got a shock to his system, and still that wasn't enough to push the arousal from his body.

But did he even want to? Getting involved with another player was a terrible idea, and yet Matt Blanco was just on the other side of the bathroom door, and they were alone together for at least the rest of the night. And Matt wanted him. He knew from the way Matt's eyes widened when he looked at Iggy, knew from the way he leaned in when he was speaking, as if his whole body was drawn to Iggy. Iggy knew exactly what that was like, because he felt it too, was drawn to Matt like lightning to a rod.

Tonight Iggy could have Matt. And why shouldn't he have him?

There were a lot of reasons, actually, but most of them fled Iggy's mind as he thought about those looks Matt had been giving him since the lobby. This was a messy, complicated situation, and still Iggy wanted Matt more than he wanted to play baseball.

He told himself to forget the awkwardness between them. He pushed aside the fact that they were teammates, that Matt was Matt Blanco, that they were anything but two men who liked each other. Then he took a chance.

When Iggy stepped out of the bathroom—wearing only the towel he had loosely draped around his waist because any other clothing seemed superfluous—the first thing he saw was a stern-looking Matt, lying on the bed and flipping through the channels on the TV. Without looking at Iggy, he said, "Red Sox won today. So did Tampa. That kid Robertson hit two home runs against Hardy."

"Uh-huh. Matt?"

"Yeah?" Matt looked over.

"I'm done in the bathroom. Squeaky clean. Inside and out. Thought you should know."

Matt's eyes seemed to focus in the general area of Iggy's crotch. "Oh," he said.

Iggy adjusted the towel to make sure it stayed put. He wasn't quite sure what to do. Part of him still couldn't get over that he'd made the first move. He felt self-conscious suddenly under Matt's gaze. For a long moment, he merely stood at the door to the bathroom and Matt remained on the bed.

But he knew Matt was into it. He didn't think it was cocky of him to assume that Matt found him attractive; Matt had demonstrated as much already.

Matt flipped off the TV and tossed the remote to the side. It hit the wall with a loud snap, but Matt didn't seem to notice. Instead, he cocked an eyebrow. "Come here."

"Yeah?" asked Iggy.

"Either you come here or I go there, which would be a shame, since I'm already lying on this nice soft bed."

It was sex, Iggy told himself. It was sex with an attractive man who would never in a million years tell anyone. Really it was ideal. Iggy's reservations faded away.

He walked over to the bed. His towel started to come loose again, but he stopped caring. He grabbed it and tossed it aside, and he stood naked in front of Matt.

Matt rose up on his knees on the bed. He shuffled over to Iggy, took Iggy's face in his hands, and kissed him.

Matt's mouth was hot, his lips soft, his taste vaguely minty. A day or two of beard growth scraped against Iggy's face, but he liked that, liked the reminder that he was kissing a man, a real man, not just his fantasy.

Iggy put his hands on Matt's sides and pressed into the muscle there, felt the heat of Matt's skin. Matt's body was hard and strong and substantial.

This was different from the quickie in the showers. The lights were glaring in the room, meaning Iggy could see every inch of exposed skin, every hair, every wrinkle, every ripple of muscle. This wouldn't be rubbing one out with the hope they didn't get caught. They had all night. Sure, they had to play the next day, but fuck it. Iggy had played on no sleep plenty of times before.

He broke the kiss and leaned back a little. He ran his fingers over Matt's hair. Matt closed his eyes and leaned into Iggy's touch, so Iggy kept stroking his scalp. He kissed the edge of Matt's hairline, kissed his cheek, trailed kisses along his jaw. Then Matt captured his lips. Iggy opened up, dipped his tongue into Matt's mouth, slid it along his teeth. He wanted to get closer to Matt's lovely light skin, so he moved his hands up to the buttons of Matt's shirt and started to undo them. The shirt was clearly old, well-worn from too many washings. Iggy really liked that about Matt, liked that a man who made enough money in a year to buy a small country still lived rather modestly. Matt continued to surprise him, but all of those surprises were good.

He buried his guilt about leaving Matt alone in the locker room that afternoon. It got lost somewhere as Iggy touched and tasted and experienced Matt's body, his texture, his scent. He pushed Matt's shirt off his shoulders and finally touched all that skin. It was surprisingly soft and smooth, yet still firm and hot.

Matt groaned. He curled his hands around Iggy's asscheeks, digging his fingers into Iggy's flesh, pressing and pulling. Matt's touch was rough, but the kneading motion went right to Iggy's dick, made his skin tingle.

"Christ, but your ass is a thing of beauty," Matt murmured into Iggy's shoulder. "I want to fuck you so bad. Have since I first set eyes on you."

How could Iggy say no to that? "Yes, yes, fuck yes," he said. "But do you—"

"Condoms and lube in my shaving kit in the bathroom."

Bingo. Iggy laughed.

Matt laughed too, but then he bit Iggy's shoulder and said, "Not that funny." But he kept laughing.

This was how sex should be. Joyous. Full of laughter and heat and excitement. Matt was so hot up close, beautiful in his way too. Perhaps he was no longer a young man, but he was still vital and alive and strong. He used that strength to push Iggy away.

"On your stomach," he said. "Be right back."

Iggy did as he was told, lying facedown on the bed. He pressed his face into the pillow, unable to contain his excitement, adrenaline rushing through his body. He was really going to do this. He was going to spend the night with a man he'd fantasized about for years, a man he'd been wanting and thinking about almost constantly for weeks. It was impossible. It was too much, but it felt completely right.

He couldn't see what was happening, but he sensed that the lighting had changed. He heard the squeak of the hinge on the bathroom door. His pulse quickened as he sensed Matt coming closer. Little flutters grew in his belly as he waited, wanting this so badly that he twisted his hands in the quilt to calm down. Like he could be calm when he was lying naked on a bed in Matt Blanco's hotel room. Like he'd ever be calm again.

Iggy nearly jumped out of his skin when Matt caressed his back. Matt's breath feathered against the base of Iggy's spine, and Iggy started to shake with anticipation. He tried to tell himself to relax, but it was useless. Matt straddled one of Iggy's calves. Iggy couldn't deny that Matt Blanco was *right there*, and he was *naked.*

Iggy's breath hitched, and he had trouble getting it going again as Matt lowered himself on top of Iggy and started planting the sweetest, most tender kisses along the knots of Iggy's spine, from the base of it toward his neck. The kisses were wet and hot and sizzled against Iggy's skin. By the time Matt got to Iggy's nape, he used his teeth, nipping and pulling. Iggy groaned and bucked his hips, loving this but tortured by it too, needing just a little more to really get off.

Matt shifted Iggy's hips up and put a towel under him. He rubbed a lubed-up finger against Iggy's entrance, and that felt amazing. Iggy's heart beat so fast he thought it might burst waiting for this, needing it. He rocked back and raised his butt to give Matt a better angle. Matt answered by shoving two fingers inside, and Iggy could not stop the groan that escaped him. It hurt but in the best way, and the mild pain started to give way as Matt gently stretched him.

Iggy turned his head on the pillow and looked back at Matt. "We're really," he said as he panted, "going to do this?"

"Do you want me to stop?"

"Not if both our lives depended on it."

Matt smirked. "You've got a hot little ass, you know that?"

"Thank you. You've got a very nice cock. Do you plan to do something with it?"

"Fuck you into this mattress."

The words made Iggy shiver. "Get to it, then."

Matt shifted on the bed. Iggy couldn't quite see what he was doing, but he guessed based on the way his arms moved that he was rolling on a condom. Then he was out of Iggy's field of vision, and for a moment Iggy wondered if he really was imagining all of this. But then Matt was back, caressing Iggy's arms, pressing his palms into Iggy's skin, the head of his cock pushing against Iggy's entrance.

"Yes," Iggy moaned.

Matt mumbled something that sounded like "Such a hot ass," and he started to press inside.

Iggy and Matt groaned together as Matt pushed forward. Matt really did have a beautiful cock, but it felt much bigger than Iggy had thought it would. Granted it had been quite a while since Iggy had bottomed—or had sex at all—but it hurt more than he expected. Matt gave him a moment to adjust and wrapped his arms around Iggy's chest. He shifted his hips out and then back in, and the head of his cock hit Iggy *right there*, and he saw stars. His whole body felt it and jerked in response.

"That's the spot, isn't it?" Matt said.

"Less talking, more fucking."

Matt drove in and out of Iggy, slow and gentle at first, but as Iggy started to push back, and as he cried out, "Harder," Matt picked up speed. Iggy shouted, "Don't tickle me. Really fuck me." Matt laughed, and then he let loose.

And it was awesome. It hurt, but it made Iggy's body sing, made his blood rush, and it was so goddamned good that he never wanted it to stop. He felt like he was all bruised skin and sweat as he curled his fingers into the quilt, as Matt grabbed at his skin hard enough to leave marks, as Matt unleashed a fury of thrusting and pounding and grunts and moans.

"Holy shit, you're tight," Matt said. "I'm not gonna last long."

Iggy was so lost in his own pleasure that he couldn't respond. Matt kept rubbing the sweet spot and pushing Iggy right up to the edge of the cliff. Iggy needed more friction on his cock to make him fly to pieces, but then all this would come to a crashing end. As Matt's pace became more frantic, as he started muttering curses in between the grunts and groans, Iggy slid a hand under himself and grabbed his cock.

That was everything he needed. He needed Matt fucking him fast and hard, crying out about how good it was, unleashing everything he had. He needed Matt's cock inside him, lighting up all those nerve endings, sending pulses of pleasure and light and sweat and goose bumps and blindness through his whole body. He needed just enough friction on his cock to pull out that orgasm. He rode the edge for a while, until he felt Matt tense up behind him. He kept stroking his cock, squeezing hard enough to get the pressure he wanted.

Light and pleasure and everything exploded as the orgasm ripped through Iggy's body. He groaned and arched his back and shot on the towel. If sounds came out of his mouth, he didn't know what they were. He flew through the air, flew there with Matt, felt Matt's hands clutching at him. They were flying apart together. Then everything was mellow and delightful and sparkling, and Iggy fell forward onto the mattress. Matt collapsed on top of him.

They stayed that way for a minute or more, until Matt said, "Santa Maria."

Iggy laughed. "Your Italian is showing."

"Shush. The English-speaking part of my brain may have fallen out of my head. I'd better go find it."

It was only when Matt lifted himself away that Iggy realized how much he liked Matt's weight on top of him. How much he liked everything about Matt. How deep the pool of trouble he'd waded into was.

AFTER MATT took care of the condom and the towel and turned off the remaining lights in the room, he paused to look at Iggy splayed out on the bed. The sight called to him. He slid under the covers with Iggy.

"You're not going to pull another disappearing act, are you?" Matt asked. The idea of Iggy bolting again made Matt tired. They'd just had really explosive sex, and Matt wanted to do it again, and there was no reason they couldn't come to a mutually beneficial arrangement. Or so he hoped.

"Where would I go?" Iggy settled into the bed and tugged the quilt over his body.

"Well, let's review." Matt sat up. "We made eyes at each other one evening and almost confessed some things, and you bolted. We had sex in the locker room last week, and again you bolted. That looks like a trend to me."

Iggy was silent for a long moment. Matt was fairly convinced he wouldn't answer, until he said, "Look, this is all very strange for me."

"How so?"

Iggy sighed. "It's crazy enough that I got pulled up to the majors. That's been my dream since I could hold a baseball bat. Then, on top of that, I was traded to the Eagles. It's like, if I could have designed my life, this is how things would have turned out. And then on top of *that*, I am currently in bed with Matt Blanco. I had a poster of you on the wall of my dorm room in college."

Something about that hit Matt the wrong way. He jerked away from Iggy a little but didn't get out of bed. "Really?" he said.

"Yeah. I mean, come on, the best player on my favorite team. That's a no-brainer. It doesn't hurt that you're hot. So you'll excuse me if I'm a little freaked out that I am now… you know, having relations… with the guy whose picture once looked down on me from the wall as I fell asleep each night."

That freaked Matt right the fuck out. He did get out of bed. Realizing he was still naked, he grabbed the sheet and pulled it in front of his crotch. "Jesus. So is that why you wanted to have sex with me? To realize some teenage fantasy. Because I've got news for you, buddy—"

"No. No, of course not. Matt, get back in bed."

"No."

Iggy sat up, letting the quilt fall to expose his naked—and beautiful—chest. "Look, I have never done anything like this before. It's not like I go around pursuing my idols. That day in the locker room? When we, I don't know, had that moment or whatever? I knew we understood each other, first of all, and that kind of blew my mind. I thought it was going to be hard enough to be on a team with you, considering how much I idolized and, yes, fantasized about you when I was in college. And then I saw in your eyes that you were…." He shook his head. "I was going to tell you that afternoon, tell you all of it, but I freaked out. I still can't believe that you're gay. And the times we've been together, they've been like a dream. And that's why I bailed. Because I'm still trying to reconcile this thing I worshipped with you as a real man. And you *are* a real man. I'm learning that now. You are a complicated, interesting, sexy man, and you're not the perfect man of my fantasies, but I still think you're really great, and for whatever reason you're attracted to me, but we play on the same team and…. Can you see why I might have some trouble wrapping my head around all this?" He frowned. "And now you're completely spooked. Great."

Matt had avoided sleeping with fans—for the most part—because he didn't want to be worshipped. And it wasn't even as though he thought that he and Iggy really had something. They still barely knew each other. But he thought it would be different this time. After everything, all he really wanted was someone who saw him as he really was, who loved Matt and not Brooklyn Eagles First Baseman Matt Blanco. *Because let's face it; there won't be a Brooklyn Eagles First Baseman Matt Blanco much longer.*

He let out a breath and sat on the edge of the bed. "I'm sorry for freaking out."

"You have a right to. This is a very strange situation."

Matt looked back at where Iggy lay propped up on his elbows, naked chest still exposed. Matt said what was foremost on his mind. "I like you, Iggy. A lot."

"Thanks. I like you too. And not just in the man-of-my-fantasies way."

Matt laughed. "So what now?"

Iggy put a hand near Matt's back, not quite touching but present all the same. Matt leaned a little to indicate it was okay for Iggy to touch him. "Well," Iggy said, pressing his palm into Matt's skin, "I don't see as we have a lot of options."

Matt figured this was coming. That this little interlude between them couldn't last long. He just hadn't expected it to be over quite so soon. That was disappointing. But he said, "Yeah."

"I mean, clearly we're going to have a torrid affair, during which time we might get to know each other better. You're going to dispense with all the myths about you that I'm still holding on to. Really, it's all a terrible tragedy that we're going to have to have really great sex for the rest of the season. Can you imagine a worse fate?"

Matt laughed. He turned around and lay back down on the bed next to Iggy. He slid his legs under the quilt. "I bet you were a little terror as a kid."

Iggy moved closer and snuggled in next to Matt, pressing the whole length of his body against Matt's side. "It kept me from getting beaten up," Iggy said. "As did baseball. The kids stopped calling me a faggot when I started leading our team to state championships."

"Yeah, I get that," Matt said. Baseball had saved his life too.

That shared understanding eased Matt's mind enough that he was able to drift off to sleep with Iggy in his arms.

Chapter Seven

MATT WONDERED if there was anything worse than playing in the rain. It was Sunday afternoon. The game against Dallas—which looked like the team most likely to be facing the Eagles in the Championship Series, assuming both teams got that far—had gotten enough fans in the stadium for the seats to look packed, despite the threat of rain. The sky was an ominous shade of gray, and the clouds cast strange shadows over the outfield. But no actual raindrops had fallen yet, and as Bill was fond of saying, the game must go on.

Except that by the third inning, it was drizzling. Matt dutifully trotted out to first base for the top of the inning and was thankful that at least the brim of his hat kept the rain out of his eyes. He glanced across the field and made eye contact with Iggy, who looked just as miserable. Because not only was it raining, but it was cold, only about sixty degrees Fahrenheit even though it was still August, and Iggy, with his Arizona-bred constitution, was shivering. He found the strength to smile at Matt, though, right before Jones threw the first pitch of the inning.

Three outs later, Matt sat on the bench to wait for his turn at bat. Iggy plopped down next to him. "Some weather," Iggy said.

"Yeah. Roger looked at the radar earlier, and it's only supposed to get worse. There's a massive storm heading this way."

Cruz sat down on Matt's other side. "You're always the optimist, Matthew. See that white patch in the clouds over there? Where you can kind of see the sun? I choose to believe that all this is breaking up."

Matt laughed. "Okay, Manuel. Good luck with that. But your delusions can't fight nature."

"Does Eagles management just not believe in rain delays?" Iggy asked.

"No," said Cruz. "Not since they got that quick-drying sand stuff for the infield."

"And they never cancel games due to weather because of those new tarps," said Matt. "If there is a rain delay, well, we'll just cover the field until the monsoon stops."

"You're on deck, Cruz," Bill shouted.

Cruz got up. Everyone was huddling under the overhang of the dugout, so Matt felt a little crowded even with the extra space on the bench. He looked over at Iggy, who was shivering again. Matt's initial instinct was to put an arm around him, but he refrained.

Iggy said, "Man, it's cold. Although not as bad as that game I had to play in Colorado at the beginning of the season. It snowed."

"It snowed during the 2007 World Series. Remember that? I was in the stands for that game."

"Really?"

"Yeah." Matt leaned close to Iggy. "Don't tell anyone, but I've always had kind of a soft spot for the Sox. It was kinda nice to see them win that one."

Iggy nodded.

"You're freezing," said Matt.

"A little. I left my jacket in the locker room."

"Do you want me to try to rustle one up for you?"

"No, you don't have to do that." Iggy sighed.

Matt burst into laughter. "God, listen to me. I'm talking like I'm your father."

Iggy laughed too. "Yeah, don't ever do that again."

Cruz came back. "Well, aren't we peas in a pod?" he said, sitting down next to them.

"Rodriguez!" barked Bill.

Iggy stood and, on the way, gave Matt what he could only interpret as a Meaningful Look, with pursed lips and a raised eyebrow. Iggy was out of the dugout before Matt could fully react, but he made a mental note to warn Iggy against such things later. Not that he hadn't liked the look. Although, truth be told, he was mostly looking forward to *later*.

Roger appeared out of nowhere and took Iggy's spot. He had an apple in his hand. "Where the fuck are we in the rotation?"

"Iggy's batting eighth."

Roger looked toward home plate and narrowed his eyes. "Why is Rodriguez batting eighth?" He bit into the apple.

Matt had lately been wondering the same thing. Iggy's stats, particularly his on-base percentage, should have put him higher up in the lineup. If Matt were in Haverman's shoes, he would have put Iggy third or maybe even have him bat cleanup. Of course, that would shake up the lineup, which would likely make Matt lose his spot; he usually batted first or second.

"Batting order is like the order of succession, isn't it?" Roger said.

Matt chuckled. "You think the kid's rookie status has pushed him further from the crown?"

Roger lightly punched his arm. "Could be. You're batting first, so I guess that makes you the king."

Matt wondered why Roger chose now to have a philosophical discussion about strategy. Roger took another bite and chewed on the apple, smooth as you please, like nothing was bothering him.

"I gotta ask you a question," Roger said eventually.

"Sure."

"Not here."

There was a neat *klok* of the bat at home plate. Iggy hit a line drive right past the third baseman. He took off for first and made it there safely.

Overbey, who was batting ninth, walked up to the plate.

"Blanco!" bellowed Bill.

"I'll find you after the game," Matt said.

"TV room," said Roger, referring to the room in the basement of the stadium equipped with five televisions. Mostly the room was the place Haverman sent players when he wanted them to analyze their techniques.

The Eagles eked out a narrow victory, after which most of the team headed for the locker room, and Matt tracked down Roger in the TV room. He was somewhat surprised to find Roger watching footage of Iggy.

"The rookie's good," Roger said.

"He is, yeah."

"He seems to be a good prospect. Unlike that other new kid, Letum. I heard he was doing great stuff in the minors, but he doesn't run very fast." Roger fiddled with the remote and replayed one of Iggy's at bats. "Rodriguez is good, no doubt. Can't hit a curveball for shit, but we can work on that."

This was an old sport. Before Roger and his wife, Lauren, became a more serious item, he and Matt would sit around and assess all new players on the team, pick their performances apart, and then pull them aside to give them tips. Roger was fond of saying that a team was only as good as its worst player, though Matt thought that was only true to a point. Good fielding could make up for a lousy pitcher and vice versa. Strong defense or a solid group of power batters could bring a team to victory even if something was lacking. Of course, everyone performing at the top level was ideal, but in Matt's experience, these occasions were rare. Sometimes great players stank up the field if they weren't working well with the team dynamics. Two seasons ago, the whole Eagles lineup had been plagued with injuries, and they'd failed to make the play-offs despite having one of the best teams in the league on paper.

Matt said, "I think Iggy's curveball thing is fixable. Terry's been doing extra batting practice with him and claims he's improving."

"Good to know." Roger put the remote down and turned toward Matt. "So you like Rodriguez?"

"Yeah, I just told you I like him. He was a good trade. Losing Miller sucked, but at the end of the day, I'm kind of happy not to have to deal with his ego."

"Sure, I'm with you there. But do you *like* Rodriguez?"

"What?"

Roger took a step closer to Matt and lowered his voice. "Cruz made an off-color remark the other day. Something about how you and Rodriguez seemed to be getting pretty chummy, and if he didn't know better, yada, yada. I laughed, but I thought you should know."

"Oh." Panic exploded in Matt's chest. "Shit."

"I don't think he actually suspects anything. That was just Cruz being Cruz. But if he noticed that you and Rodriguez are getting friendly, he may not be the only one, and—"

"Shit." Matt took a deep breath in an effort to get his racing heart to calm down. He looked at Roger, who looked back expectantly. He sighed. "Yes, I *like* him. Christ, what are we, in ninth grade?"

"Matt."

"Don't bother," said Matt. "Anything you tell me will be something I've already thought, except the thoughts that I'm having are much, much worse."

"Is he even—" Roger started to ask.

Matt could only nod.

Roger took a moment to think about that. "You know because you've already slept with him."

Matt nodded again. He wished he could open up a trapdoor in the floor and fall through it. In all the years they'd been friends, Roger had never judged him, at least not to his face, but he sure had a way of magnifying Matt's mistakes.

"Fuck," said Roger.

"I know," said Matt. "I know how it looks, and I know what the risks are, and I know, Roger, believe me. I fucking know how this could play out."

"But you like him."

"I like him a lot."

Roger frowned. A heavy silence pressed on them. "Is this a regular thing, you and Rodriguez?"

"I don't know. It's… new."

"Christ on a crutch, Matt, this is up there with the stupidest things you've ever done. With a teammate? It's like you're asking to get caught."

"We're being careful."

If looks could kill, Matt surely would have died from the one Roger was shooting him. "I'm not doing this to yell at you. I'm doing this because you're my friend, and I don't want bad things to happen to you."

And that was when Matt's defenses kicked in. "Now, wait a minute. This could be a good thing."

"How is this a good thing?"

"Well, to begin with, he's definitely not going to tell anyone. We can both keep the secret."

"Right. And if someone catches him on the way into your apartment building, your whole fucking career is over like that." Roger snapped his fingers.

"You're overreacting."

"Am I? I don't know how, but by some miracle you've managed to keep this under wraps for your whole career. You don't think those guys in the locker room—Caballo, Cruz, all of them—you don't think they'd turn on you if they knew they had a gay player in their midst and that he had, in fact, fucked a fellow teammate? I don't think it's legal for Eagles management to fire you, but they *can* make your life miserable."

"So we won't get caught. It's not like I'm throwing this in people's faces. I don't *want* to get caught."

"I sure as hell hope he's worth the risk."

Matt's anger kept ratcheting up. Almost testing Roger, he said, "He's really good in bed."

Roger winced. "Don't tell me shit like that. I don't want to know about it." He shook his head. "Do you have an escape plan? What the hell will you do when you *do* get caught? Because that's not an *if.* One of these days, it'll all come out. You know what the media here is like."

"We'll deal with it if it happens." Matt sighed. He had no idea what they would do, which only added to the churning in his stomach. He had no escape plan, no excuse. He wasn't willing to admit to Roger that he feared everything Roger was saying would come true. "It's not like I have a disease, Roger."

"I never said that. You know I don't think that. I don't give a shit who you fuck. I'm worried about your career."

"Right." Good and angry now, Matt stalked out of the room.

IGGY FELT cold down in his bones. He stood in the locker room after the game. Though the hot shower had thawed him somewhat, all he could think was that he wanted to hide under some big warm blankets for a while.

He was pulling on a sweatshirt as Matt came back from his shower wearing only a towel. He glanced at Iggy as he opened his locker. Then he went about getting dressed. Iggy tried not to watch and instead focused on gathering his things. Matt leaned over and said, "I need to talk to you about something, but not here."

"Okay."

Matt backed away. "Sure, I can give you a ride home," he said.

Iggy got it and nodded. "Thanks, Matt."

He waited for Matt to get dressed. They slapped backs and asses and hands on their way out of the locker room, and then Iggy followed Matt out to the employee parking lot.

In the car Matt said, "Apparently Cruz has been joking around with the other guys that the two of us are, well, you know."

That made Iggy nervous. He looked at Matt, trying to ascertain his reaction to that news. His face was completely neutral. So Iggy tried levity. "Doing exactly what we're doing?"

Matt smirked. "Yeah. It's just idle talk. Cruz thinks he's being funny. He doesn't know the truth. I just thought you should know. We should maybe, you know, put a little effort into not attracting Cruz's attention. Or anyone else's."

"I understand."

"Good. Uh. Thanks."

They chatted about the game on the way into Manhattan. Iggy supposed that was all Matt wanted to say. He smiled to himself, liking that Matt had sounded casual and not freaked out.

But then they stopped in front of an apartment building that wasn't Iggy's. "My garage is just down the block," Matt said.

"Am I to understand that I am coming home with you this evening?"

Matt smirked again. "You understand correctly. Get out here so the garage attendant doesn't ask questions. Go inside and mention to the doorman that you're waiting for me. I'll be there in a moment."

"You trust a doorman but not a garage attendant?"

"I've been living in this building for six years. I give generous gifts at the holidays. I trust Raul with my life. You never know who's going to be working at the garage, though."

"Gotcha."

Iggy didn't have to wait long. Matt walked into the building a few minutes later. He winked at the doorman and then led Iggy toward the elevator.

Matt's apartment looked more like a showpiece than a lived-in space. The entrance led to an open kitchen full of shiny stainless steel appliances and dominated by a huge butcher-block island in the middle. To the left was a living room that looked like something out of a furniture showroom: brown leather sofa, brown rug, mahogany coffee table and bookcases. Everything looked very dark and masculine. It was gorgeous. It was impersonal.

"Did you hire a decorator?" Iggy asked as Matt walked over to the refrigerator.

"What? No. You want something to drink?"

"Whatever you're having. Seriously, this place is amazing."

"Thanks. I picked out most of the pieces myself." He handed Iggy a diet soda.

Since it seemed to be a point of pride, Iggy opted not to voice his observation that the whole space was a little too perfect.

Matt walked into the living room and sat on the couch. "I have a cleaning lady who comes through here when I'm out of town. I think she's a little OCD." He grinned.

Something about that cracked the tension Iggy wasn't aware had been developing in his back. He rolled his shoulders and sat next to Matt on the couch.

Iggy wasn't quite sure what to do. He popped the top on his soda and took a swig. Matt picked up the remote control for the TV but didn't turn it on.

"So that was some play in the eighth, huh?" said Matt.

That was when Iggy realized Matt was nervous. It was interesting to see this little flaw in him—that he defaulted to baseball when he was unsure of what else to do or say—and it went a long way toward putting Iggy at ease. "It was a good play. Matt?"

Matt turned to look at Iggy.

"Relax." Then Iggy leaned in and kissed him.

It was a soft, slow kiss, without any particular urgency, intended to make Matt relax by letting him know that Iggy wanted to be there with him.

When Iggy moved away, Matt looked flustered. He ran a hand through his hair. "I'm sorry."

"What are you apologizing for?"

Matt sighed. "It's nothing. Stupid argument I had with Roger is on my mind."

"He's your friend?"

"Yeah. We came up through the minors together, got pulled up at the same time, have been on the Eagles forever, you know? We're like brothers."

Iggy reached over and played with Matt's hair.

"You must have known that," said Matt.

"I guess I did, yeah."

Matt shook his head. "It's strange sometimes, being with you. I like you. I'm worried I'll let you down."

"How can you think that?"

"Well. You were a fan before, right?"

"Of you? Yeah."

"Well, and that's weird. I make it a point not to sleep with fans because I never know if they're into me or my fame. But you…. Things are different with you."

"I'm not interested in your fame."

"I know. But you've been following my career, right? So you may have ideas about me, and there's no way I can…."

"Stop. No. I mean, yeah, I followed you for a long time. So yes, at first it was about that. It was about you being Matt Blanco, baseball hero. But now? I've gotten to know you, the real you, who you are off the baseball field. And I like him—I like *you*—a lot more."

"Oh."

"I know you're not just baseball. You're friendly and charming and a genuinely nice guy. You're clearly interested in art and design too. Right? I mean, this painting, for example. I bet you can tell me a lot about it."

Matt's gaze went from Iggy's hands to the painting hanging on the wall above the TV. "It's by an artist named Eric Mandelbaum. He paints mostly urban landscapes. I found him and liked his stuff. My sister is an art buyer for a gallery in San Francisco." He placed both of his hands in his lap and laced his fingers together. "This one… I like the colors, I guess."

It struck Iggy that Matt had mentioned once before that one of the things he found refreshing about being with Iggy was that he could talk about things he was comfortable with, most of which were probably related to baseball. "Or we could talk about that play. Cruz was great. I didn't know he had it in him."

A faint smile formed on Matt's lips. "Yeah, he's got reflexes like a cat."

Iggy couldn't fight the smile that broke out over his face. Matt really was adorable. "Hey, Matt?"

"Yeah?"

"Take me to bed."

The smile on Matt's face became a smirk. "Demanding little thing, aren't you?"

"You like it."

"I do." He stood up and offered his hand. "Come on. I don't think I gave you the proper tour. The bedroom is right this way."

IT WAS nerve-racking having Iggy in the apartment. Matt's home was his sanctuary; the only people who came over regularly were his parents, because his mother was the sort of busybody who liked to stop by spontaneously. Matt rarely brought men back to his place. If he did, they stayed in the living room. They'd exchange blowjobs or fuck on the couch, and then that guy left. Just getting to that part required the man earning a tremendous amount of Matt's trust. He knew he was playing with fire even picking up a guy. He often gave fake names and tried to ascertain if the guy knew anything about baseball. If the guy said "Is that the one with touchdowns?" or "Those uniforms aren't very flattering," he got a green light. Because any gay man who paid attention to the sport knew that yeah, on an out-of-shape player, the standard baseball uniform could look dumpy. But on a hot guy in peak physical condition, a baseball uniform could show off his muscular chest and make his ass look fantastic.

The bedroom was the giveaway. It was where he hid everything relating to Eagles First Baseman Matt Blanco: over fifteen years of accumulated ephemera, everything from World Series rings—Matt had three—to his Rookie of the Year plaque to merchandise samples from his endorsement deals to old jerseys. He kept his regular rotation of uniforms in his locker at the stadium, but he had a couple of spares in the closet clearly emblazoned with *Blanco*.

Iggy was halfway out of his shirt when he stumbled into the room. Matt was distracted from his distress about Iggy being the first man he'd let in this room by the sight of Iggy's deliciously perfect torso. Those abs looked like they were sculpted from clay. Iggy whipped his shirt off and tossed it aside. He smirked at Matt and then looked around the room.

"Wow," he said.

"Ugh, I knew this was a mistake," Matt said, moving to push Iggy back into the living room.

Iggy put his hands up and kept Matt where he was. "No offense, but your living room is really sterile. But this? This screams *Matt Blanco*."

"I know, it's stupid, but—"

"It's not stupid. It's perfect. That room out there is not you, but *this*. This is you. I like it."

Matt didn't know what to say. He scratched at a nonexistent itch at the back of his head.

So he let Iggy stay. He trusted Iggy, and not only because they found each other in similar circumstances. Something about Iggy really got to him. He was young—*so* young—and naive, but also friendly and charming and so fucking sexy that Matt thought he'd go crazy trying to keep his attraction under wraps in public.

"I heard a rumor once," Iggy said, "that a certain womanizing New York Yankee sends all his conquests home with an autographed ball. Made me wonder if he just kept a bucket of them in his bedroom. I see no such bucket here, though."

"Well."

Iggy took a step closer and put a hand on Matt's chest. "Most of your conquests don't even know what a baseball *is*, do they?"

Matt shrugged.

"So it's different with me."

Iggy ran his hands up to Matt's neck, snaked them around so he was holding Matt by the shoulders. The look in his eyes was smoldering, dark, and heavy-lidded, and Matt found himself falling under Iggy's spell.

"It's different with you."

Iggy leaned forward and nipped at Matt's lower lip. Matt closed his eyes and bent his head a little, wanting to kiss Iggy so badly but not finding those lips waiting for him as he expected.

Instead Iggy said, "You ever been fucked by a ballplayer?"

Oh God. "Can't say that I have." On the rare occasions that Matt fooled around with other players—and those had been exceedingly rare, mostly because the few gay players he'd met in his career were so far in the closet it wasn't worth the effort—he preferred to top, as if that preserved his masculinity somehow. Even he knew that was bullshit, and he liked bottoming. He had a mild submissive streak that liked giving up control, liked not having to worry for the thirty or so minutes he let someone else drive.

And then there'd been that Mets catcher he'd gone on a few dates with, but that had ended the day the catcher decided he wasn't gay anymore and found himself a wife. They got divorced a year later, which didn't surprise Matt but made his whole relationship with that guy seem like a colossal waste of time. Matt couldn't believe he'd risked getting outed for a man that fickle. That should have taught him not to date players.

Matt wasn't sure this situation was much different, but Iggy lit him on fire the way no one had in years. For whatever reason, Iggy felt worth the risk.

Iggy shoved him toward the bed. Matt stumbled and fell on his back. He lost his breath for a moment, panicking at the idea of letting this younger man push him around, but then he realized he was hard as steel. "Yes," he mumbled, scrambling out of his warm-up pants and pulling off his T-shirt. He stroked his cock a couple of times.

Iggy's eyes widened as he stared. "Yes, what?"

"Yes, fuck me."

Iggy pushed his own pants to his ankles and kicked them off. He was hard too, and his cock bobbed as he walked. His skin was so beautiful, all smooth and dark. Matt loved Iggy's looks, loved how the two of them looked with each other. They were hot together. Hot enough to set the sheets on fire.

Matt was willing to provide the match. He scooted back on the bed to make room for Iggy and then spread his legs wide to make his intentions clear. Iggy groaned and crawled onto the bed between Matt's legs.

"You're something else," Iggy said. Then he curled his hand around Matt's achingly hard cock and pulled it into his mouth.

Matt nearly screamed. He bit into his fist instead and stifled a moan as Iggy's warm mouth enveloped him. His cock felt raw, exposed, electric. The texture of Iggy's mouth on his sensitive skin, smooth and rough at the same time, made his balls start tingling.

He grabbed a bottle of lube and a couple of condoms from the nightstand and handed them to Iggy. Iggy let Matt's cock out of his mouth and took everything. He poured a healthy amount of lube on his fingers and then pressed one to Matt's hole. He was gentle at first. Too gentle.

"Shit," Matt muttered. "I'm not breakable."

Iggy lifted his head and smirked. "You want more, big guy?"

"Yeah."

Iggy shoved two fingers inside.

The burn was familiar and yet not. Matt hadn't bottomed in a long time, and he knew he was tight. But man, that felt good. The veins stood out on Iggy's arms, showing that he was really pushing it, not just playing now, and that was what Matt wanted, all that masculine strength unleashed inside him. "Fuck yeah," Matt said. "More."

Iggy poured more lube and then added a third finger.

It was a lot, but the pain reminded Matt that he was alive, he could still do this, he was with a man he trusted not to hurt him. This wasn't like college, when the first man he'd gone home with beat the shit out of him. It wasn't like some anonymous encounter that only existed for both parties to get their needs met. No, this was real, and Matt knew Iggy wouldn't hurt him, and he wanted Iggy to run this show, to make him feel good, to take control away.

His erection had flagged when the pain first started, but now that his body was stretching and relaxing, Matt took hold of his cock and rubbed it back to life.

"Yeah, baby," Iggy said. "Stroke yourself. That is so ridiculously hot." As Iggy's fingers continued to move in Matt, stretching him and searching for secret places, Iggy bowed his head and sucked one of Matt's nipples into his mouth. Every part of Matt's body felt wired to his dick, and that move alone had him hard and throbbing again. He wrapped his free hand over the back of Iggy's head to keep him in place, because Iggy's teeth and tongue on his nipples brought about all manner of tingles and itchy need.

Now he needed to get fucked. He needed something bigger than Iggy's fingers in him, needed to be filled up, to get pounded, to hurt, to come. His body quivered under Iggy's ministrations, undulating and moving and arching off the bed as he tried to move, to get more of Iggy inside him, to get more, more, more, now, now, now.

"If you don't fuck me right this second, I'm gonna go crazy," Matt said.

Iggy chuckled and eased away. Matt had to wait for him to roll on a condom, and he couldn't keep himself from writhing in anticipation. Iggy was a substantial man in all ways, but that was what he wanted. A big fat cock inside him, tearing him up, splitting him in two. Then he wanted Iggy to be there at the end to put him back together.

Iggy poured more lube on his covered cock and moved closer to Matt. Then he lowered his body and took Matt's lips in a hot kiss, mouths open and tongues licking and teeth scraping, so hot and delicious Matt wanted to revel in it. But then he felt the blunt head of Iggy's cock pressing at his entrance, and he wanted that more.

He shifted his hips up, inviting Iggy to move forward, and he was rewarded with the head of Iggy's cock pushing through the ring of muscle. Matt groaned and arched his back, sliding into it, wanting more. He grabbed at Iggy's skin wherever he could, dug his fingers into his arms, his back, finally his ass. He pulled and tugged and pressed their bodies together until Iggy was buried inside him and let out a satisfied sigh.

"Your body, Matt, Jesus—"

"Less talking, more fucking."

Iggy let out a strangled laugh. He kissed Matt again. He rocked back and away. Then he drove back inside.

And then they were in business.

Iggy sat upright to get a better angle. He drove into Matt again and again, digging his nails into Matt's thighs, his hips, pressing hard enough to leave bruises. Matt loved it, loved the acceleration of pleasure, the lightning bolt through his body that came every time Iggy hit *that spot*, the speed and the pain and the excitement. He tried to push back at Iggy to get more friction, but Iggy held him to the bed. Iggy dictated the speed. Iggy was in control. In his entire life, Matt had never been so excited to let someone else control him.

He moved his hand toward his cock, but Iggy slapped it away. "Don't you dare. You don't come until I tell you."

Matt's cock got harder, if that was possible. A dribble of precum spilled from the slit.

Matt didn't know what to do with his hands, so he grabbed Iggy. He groped Iggy's arms, his delicious pectoral muscles, the ridges of those abs. He tweaked Iggy's nipples, which made Iggy throw his head back.

"This is too good," Iggy said. A sheen of sweat broke out over his body, but he kept on pounding at Matt, kept making Matt's body careen toward the end. "I'm not gonna last much longer."

"More," Matt said. He needed more to come. And he needed to come. It was like an ache building in his balls now. Just a little more friction….

Iggy grabbed his cock. As he pounded away at Matt, he started to lose some momentum, and his movements became more erratic, but he stroked Matt at some approximation of the same rhythm. He pressed his thumb into the space at the base of the head, and as if he were looking for the detonation button, Matt thrust his hips up to get him to press there again. The rough texture of Iggy's hands—athlete's hands, calloused from wielding a bat, dry after sweating in a glove—was just what Matt needed. Everything came together at once, mixing pain and pleasure and texture and rhythm to that one spot in Matt's body.

Matt flew apart.

He arched off the bed as he came, cum spurting out so hard the first ribbon hit him in the chin. He didn't care, because everything was pleasure and Iggy and lights flashing. He was sure he made some noise as the orgasm racked his body, but who cared?

As he was coming back down, he felt Iggy tense. He moaned something unintelligible, and he stilled for a moment, and then he threw his head back in the purest look of ecstasy Matt had ever seen. Iggy might even have been smiling. He collapsed forward. He was still shaking when Matt pulled him into his arms.

"I can't think of the last time I came like that," Iggy said, panting.

"No, me neither."

They lay pressed together while their breathing evened out. Even then, Matt didn't especially want to move, but he was aware that his drying cum was getting sticky. Plus, Iggy had to be itchy inside the condom, his softening cock still inside Matt.

"Let's take a shower and go to bed," Matt suggested.

Iggy kissed his cheek. "That sounds like an excellent idea."

Chapter Eight

AFTER HIS turn at bat, Matt plopped down on the dugout bench next to Iggy. "Manning!" he said, pointing toward the pitcher. "He's been throwing meatballs all season, and now suddenly he's throwing ninety-five-mile-per-hour fastballs?"

Iggy patted his shoulder but then immediately withdrew his hand, hyperconscious now of anyone else in the dugout who might be watching them. Maybe Cruz was making innocent jokes, but once that idea was planted, one of their teammates might take it more literally, and then they were fucked, but not in the good way. Iggy cleared his throat and gestured at the mound. "And he added the changeup."

Matt groaned and rolled his shoulders. Iggy looked up in time to see Cruz trot from the on-deck circle to the plate. He did his typical prebatting dance, which mostly involved weighing the bat in his hands and digging his heels into the dirt. Cruz moved like a ballet dancer at times, with a quiet grace Iggy knew was a result of years of conditioning. Cruz's body was molded to do two things: run fast and hit baseballs. Iggy really liked watching him play.

Cruz took a few practice swings, then went up to bat. Someone in the stands called out, "Cruz is a faggot."

Iggy felt the words like a punch in the face. It was hardly the first homophobic thing he'd ever heard shouted from the stands, but he was already on edge. He looked at Matt, who shrugged. If Cruz heard it, he didn't acknowledge it, just went about batting. Matt mouthed *Shrug it off* to Iggy, but Iggy's stomach churned anyway.

The game didn't go well. The Eagles gave up four runs in the fifth inning, putting Philly solidly in the lead. The fans started getting restless, booing when a play went south. Iggy had heard from other players that he'd get used to the taunts, or at least he'd learn how to tune them out, but each time someone in the stands yelled, Iggy's heart rate spiked. Then, during the seventh-inning stretch, the audience changed the lyrics of the pop song that came over the loudspeaker from "Get out of the way" to "You are so gay!"

"Seriously?" Iggy said to whoever was standing nearby, which happened to be Matt and Roger.

"You get used to it," said Matt. "Don't let those assholes get to you."

"Used to it? Do the Eagles really condone that?" Iggy was about three seconds away from launching into a tirade about how it was hate speech, but Matt held up his hand and shook his head.

"You're in the big leagues now, kid," said Roger.

IN BED that night, Iggy said, "Do you really just let it all roll off your back?"

Not understanding what Iggy was asking, Matt ran his fingers through Iggy's hair and smiled. He felt pretty blissed out after Iggy had gotten him off with the sort of blowjob he bet more creative men than him wrote poems about. He was hard-pressed to get his synapses to fire—or to make his mouth form words, for that matter—but he managed to say, "What?"

"The homophobic bullshit the fans were shouting today, I mean. The 'You are so gay' bullshit." Iggy sang the last part.

Matt sighed, his bliss evaporating. Why couldn't he just lie back and enjoy the aftereffects of the orgasm? He didn't want to have a philosophical discussion about homophobia in baseball; he wanted to go to sleep. Why was Iggy hung up on this now? Had he not enjoyed the hand job Matt had provided earlier? Was he one of those guys who had to hop out of bed and run a marathon after sex? Matt stifled a groan and summoned all of his intellectual powers so he could make sentences through the thinning haze of his last orgasm.

"Go to sleep, Ig."

"I'm asking your advice. How do you deal with that shit? No one has accused me of anything, but anytime I hear the word 'fag,' I break out in a cold sweat."

"I ignore it." Matt coughed. "I don't see what choice I have. What am I going to do? Tell the fans I find that offensive? They're gonna ask why. And that's opening a whole new can of worms." Matt pulled Iggy close. "Seriously, there's this thing called sleep. Maybe you've heard of it?"

"You could just say you have gay friends and you don't appreciate the slurs. You don't have to actually tell anyone you're a big homo in order to make them shut up."

"I have no desire to get involved in the politics of all this. Fans say stupid shit all the fucking time. They're just idiots. This can't be the first time you've heard stuff like this, is it? You're not that naive."

"No, just... I wasn't expecting it, I guess. And I got scared for a minute, like someone had found out about us and was calling at us specifically."

"They weren't."

"I know, but it made me feel sick."

Matt kept on stroking Iggy's hair. "Me too, sometimes, but you just have to let it go. You can't control the fans. You can only control your reaction."

"Fans get away with saying shit like that because we let them. Surely the front office can take some kind of stand, maybe issue a press release…."

"Make pigs fly."

Iggy groaned. "You know, one of these days, there's going to be an out gay player in the majors. A couple of college players have already come out, and that guy in the minors. Plus the MLB hired Billy Bean to talk to teams about exactly this issue. I know we're not quite there yet, but we will be soon. And then everyone will think twice before spewing that shit from the stands."

"Don't even think about it."

"I'm not. I wasn't planning on doing anything. I just—"

"Iggy. Go. To. Sleep."

Iggy huffed. He laid his head on Matt's chest. "This is harder than I thought it would be."

Matt took a deep breath, awake now and irritated. He wanted back that sleepy bliss of a few minutes ago. "What is?"

"Playing in the majors. Being in the closet. Keeping everything with you a secret."

"That's life, kid. It's not always a walk in the park." Matt shifted his weight on the bed. He knew he'd spat out the words. He spared a thought for the tight circle of people he trusted: Iggy, Roger, his parents. "I know it's hard. And it's hard to know who you can trust. It… this sucks, if I'm honest. But it's life. We have what we have or we have nothing."

Iggy grunted but stopped talking. Matt closed his eyes and mentally pushed everything Iggy was saying out of his mind. He *was* still sleepy, it turned out, and he began to drift off. Just before everything stopped, he felt Iggy move away. He considered protesting, but sleep claimed him.

Chapter Nine

HE'D KNOWN it was coming, and still Iggy felt some dismay when he walked into the locker room and found a shopping bag on the bench in front of his locker. Someone had written *Rodriguez* in black marker on the front of the bag. There were four other bags around the room, each with the name of a rookie player inscribed on it. His bag contained an acid-green sequined dress and a matching feather boa.

Matt came in. He bypassed his own locker and started walking toward Iggy. "Hey, Ig, did you see the article in—whoa." He peered into the bag. "That time of the season, eh?"

"I can't wear a dress," Iggy said.

"The Eagles have a long-standing tradition of putting rookies in ridiculous costumes for the sake of the local media when we hit the mid-August doldrums." Matt spoke with an air of faux seriousness. "They made me dress as Big Bird."

Iggy fingered the sequins on the dress. "Not really the same. I…." Iggy started to feel a little dizzy. He sat on the bench.

"I get it, I do." Matt sat next to Iggy. "It's part of what you have to do, though."

In a whisper, Iggy said, "Right. And the minute someone finds out who I really am, guess which photo is going to end up on the front page of the *Post*."

Matt spoke with a lowered voice as well. "If you refuse, you'll just draw more attention to yourself."

"What are you girls whispering about?" Cruz said as he came into the locker room. "It's Haze Day, isn't it?" He laughed. "I thought that green would go well with your skin tone. We picked out a nice hot pink for Appleton."

Iggy pasted a smile on his face and tried to be a good sport. He changed out of his street clothes and eyed the dress. "What did Cruz have to wear?" he asked Matt.

Matt smirked. "That year, we had everyone dress up as characters from *The Wizard of Oz*. Cruz was the Scarecrow, if I remember correctly."

Cruz narrowed his eyes at Matt. "That was your idea, wasn't it?"

"What makes you think so?" Matt was so nonchalant as he asked the question that Iggy wondered if it bothered him. Or even if Cruz had some suspicions.

But Cruz just shrugged. "I know you like those old movies." He grabbed a towel from his locker and disappeared into the shower room.

"Was it your idea?" Iggy asked.

"Probably, but I don't really remember."

"Who was Dorothy?"

"Caballo." Matt chuckled. "He's got that pretty face. I do remember pushing for him to be Dorothy."

Greg Letum, another rookie, strolled through the locker room wearing a bright blue sequined gown identical to the green one Iggy held. "How do I look, gentlemen?" He posed. Someone in another part of the locker room whistled. "Come on, Iggy. Get dressed. I want to get these photos over with so I can get to batting practice."

Iggy sighed and pulled the dress on over his head. It was made of a cheap, stretchy material that hugged his very masculine body in ways he found problematic.

"Oof," said Matt. "I'd tell you that you look great, but you really don't. That's a terrible dress."

Iggy pulled on the dress to get it to lie straight and then draped the feather boa around his neck. "Thanks, asshole." To say he was uncomfortable would have been an understatement. He thought the dress stretched over his crotch area in a somewhat obscene way.

Greg laughed. "Roger put a box of cheap blond wigs in the dugout. Apparently they are meant to complete the look."

"Fan-fucking-tastic," said Iggy.

MATT HUNG around after the game to sign a few autographs. After he'd been outside for about ten minutes and talked to maybe a dozen kids, Iggy wandered out. Before he even opened his mouth, Iggy was swarmed.

Kids started shouting. "Rodriguez! Hey! Sign my ball? Iggy! Over here!" Iggy seemed to take it in stride, laughing and signing balls and gloves and baseball cards.

As all of the attention was diverted away from him, Matt became aware of two things. First, he was happy to see Iggy, plain and simple: happy to see his smiling face, happy when their eyes met however briefly, happy to just be around the man. He was further impressed by how charming and charismatic Iggy could be with the fans. But second, Matt realized that Iggy was garnering the attention that he used to get, and he suddenly felt like the opening act meant to keep the fans entertained until the band everyone was really there to see arrived. Iggy smiled and made jokes and teased the kids. Matt just felt old, like a has-been.

"Nice hit you got in the eighth," a kid said to Matt.

"Thanks."

"And that home run Rodriguez got in the ninth! Holy cow! That ball must have gone to the parking lot!"

Matt waved and retreated. It seemed like only a couple of people noticed.

He was already showered and most of the way into his street clothes when Iggy walked into the locker room. He was laughing. "Well, that was a day," he said.

"Sequins will do that to you," said Cruz.

"Don't let it confuse you," said Caballo. "The sequins can't be a regular thing."

"Aw, man," said Iggy, sitting on the bench. "And here I thought I'd sew some to my uniform. Don't you think the Eagles logo would look awesome if it were covered in glitter?"

Matt held his breath. He wondered where his teammates were going with this.

Caballo threw his towel at Iggy. "Next you'll be wanting to change the red to pink."

"Or," Jones said, dropping his wrist and adding a lisp, "he'll want to have slumber parties in the locker room after games where we paint our nails and talk about boys."

"Shut up, you guys" was Iggy's only rejoinder.

"Hey, as long as you don't touch my ass in the shower, we're cool," said Caballo.

The air stilled around Matt. Iggy froze too. But then Cruz said, "No one wants to touch your ass, Caballo," and the sudden tension dissipated.

Iggy stood and started peeling off his uniform. "Make fun of me all you want," he said as he pulled his undershirt off. "I just signed autographs until my hands hurt."

Caballo guffawed. "You sure that wasn't from jerking off at night thinking of me?"

"Nah, I was thinking of Blanco. He's much prettier than you are."

Matt almost passed out from the shock. "Can it with the gay stuff, guys," he said, not having to fake how uncomfortable he was.

Caballo chuckled. "Aw, now we're freaking out Blanco." Caballo walked over to Matt and slapped his ass. "What's the matter? Can't take a little teasing?"

"Just knock it off. It's not funny." Matt winced as he heard how whiny and defensive the words sounded.

"Jeez, Matt," said Jones. "How long have you been playing this game?"

Matt sighed and dug through his locker for a clean shirt. Sure, this had always been part of the game, but it made him think about what Iggy had said the other night. This would only go on as long as he let it. While he pulled his shirt on, he tried to come up with something witty to say. He couldn't come up with anything.

"Matt's right, though, you know," said Iggy. "One of these days, you'll have an openly gay teammate, and then you'll have nothing to razz him about."

Caballo sauntered back over to his locker. "Ha, that'll be the day. Like they'd ever let queers in the locker room."

"They will. A couple of those college players who came out will end up in the majors eventually. It's only a matter of time," said Iggy. "But good to know where you're at." He turned to Matt. "Did you have something you wanted to tell me about?"

Did he? "I don't think so."

"Before I sexified myself in that green dress, you asked me if I had seen something."

Matt remembered suddenly. "Oh, just this article I saw on Sports Net. Not a big deal."

"Wow, Blanco reads," said Caballo.

Matt rolled his eyes. He wanted to punch Caballo but settled for balling his hands into fists and squeezing a couple of times before letting it go.

"Can I get a ride home?" Iggy asked.

"Uh, yeah, sure, if you want."

"Good. We can talk about it in the car. I gotta shower first, though."

Twenty minutes later, they were sitting in Matt's car, pulling out of the staff parking lot.

"I'm sorry about before," Iggy said. "I didn't mean to—"

"That was actually probably the best thing you could have done. Those guys don't suspect anything. I'm sorry for being such a wimp about it, though."

Iggy laughed. "You, my friend, are no wimp. Besides, I told the truth. I did spend some time last night jerking off and thinking of you."

With that, Matt was instantly hard. He took a moment to adjust himself when they got to the next red light. Iggy laughed harder.

Once they were moving again, Iggy asked, "So what was this article?"

"You familiar with Cary Galvin? He writes for Sports Net."

Matt couldn't figure out why that was funny, but it sent Iggy into peals of laughter again. When he recovered, he said, "Sorry. Guess I never told you. I know Cary."

Matt didn't like the sound of that one bit. "You *know* him?"

"Oh God. No, not in the way you're thinking. Yikes, Matt. Cary and I played college ball together. He's my best friend."

"What?" Matt hit the brakes a little too hard at the next light. "Your best friend is a goddamned sports reporter? It never occurred to you to tell me that?"

"It never came up. It doesn't matter anyway. Cary's as gay as that green sequined dress, and he can keep a secret besides."

"He knows about you."

"Of course he does. But we never hooked up or anything."

Matt tightened his grip on the steering wheel. "He knows about me too, doesn't he?"

Iggy hesitated.

"He does. Shit."

"I honestly don't know. I asked him if he had heard anything when I first thought that you might... but I haven't told him about us yet."

"Okay."

"What article are you talking about?"

Matt pulled onto the BQE and took a deep breath. "Your friend Cary wrote an editorial that asked what it would take for there to be another openly gay athlete in one of the professional sports leagues. One who makes a bigger splash than the couple we've had already. Jason Collins, for example. I have a lot of respect for that guy, but his career was basically over when he came out."

"Did Cary come up with anything?"

"Probably nothing you haven't thought of before. He thought the league commissioners should take an interest, change the rules to pave the way for an openly gay player. More antidiscrimination policies, encouraging players and staff to avoid homophobic language, that kind of thing. Just the sort of stuff you were ranting about the other day, the kind of thing we just witnessed in the locker room. You were right, the MLB hiring Billy Bean sent a message, but obviously there hasn't been enough change yet. Cary thought there needed to be one high-profile gay player brave enough to risk the wrath of fans and the loss of endorsement deals by coming out and getting all up in everyone's faces. To be the gay Jackie Robinson, I guess."

"Huh."

"He's not talking about you, is he?"

"I doubt it. Cary's always telling me to be careful not to out myself."

"And yet you almost did today anyway."

Iggy rolled his eyes and looked out the window. Matt missed his laughter just then. "I didn't out myself. I saw a way out of the jokes Caballo and Jones were in on, and I took it. Hell, by calling you out, I deflected attention. And you got so squirrelly you've probably assured the whole damn team that you are completely heterosexual."

Iggy's tone was a little bitter. Matt felt like he'd disappointed both Iggy and himself with how he'd handled the situation. "I'm sorry."

"Stop apologizing. Look, if there's ever going to be an out gay baseball player, it won't be someone from your generation. But he might be of mine. Hell, he might be me eventually."

"It's too soon. No one's ready for it."

"I agree. Now is too soon. But in a few years, who knows?"

"Hmm."

AFTER A frustrating afternoon game the next day in which the Eagles lost because they all played like a bad Little League team, Iggy rode the subway home and called Cary.

"I saw the game," Cary said.

"Let's not talk about it. I have something else I have to tell you." Iggy walked into his apartment and dumped his bag near the door. "I just got home."

"Didn't the game end a couple of hours ago? Are you still taking the subway back from the stadium?"

"I don't have a car yet."

"What kind of celebrity athlete are you? Don't you know you're supposed to be blowing money on cars and women?"

Iggy laughed. He sat on his sofa. His apartment was still sparsely furnished, mostly because he'd barely had time to sleep since moving to New York, let alone pick out rugs and chairs to make his apartment more homey. He sat on the old sofa from his apartment in Rhode Island, which still had scratches from his landlord's dog and a coffee stain on one of the cushions.

"Are you alone?" Iggy asked.

"I am," Cary said. "Is it safe to assume that whatever you have to tell me has something to do with a certain first baseman?"

"Yeah," said Iggy. "I saw your article the other day. Matt is the one who brought it to my attention, actually."

"Oh, he's Matt now, not Matt Blanco?"

Iggy wanted to build up to the big reveal. It felt like a strange thing to blurt out loud. So he said, "He's still super skittish. Despite all the progress of the last couple of years, he still thinks it's a mistake for players to come out. The fans were shouting stupid homophobic shit from the stands the other day, and Matt told me to let it roll off my back. But that's basically exactly what your article was about, wasn't it? If a gay player were a reality and not just a hypothetical, everyone's attitudes would change."

"Well, probably not everyone's, but I think it would change some minds, yes. Why? What's all this about? Are you thinking about doing something?"

"No. Not really." Iggy didn't feel ready yet to make that kind of splash. He wanted to enjoy more of his time with the Eagles before he brought that kind of press attention to himself. "It was just on the brain. Because I discussed it with Matt last night." Iggy held his breath for a moment and then added, "In bed."

Cary gasped audibly. "You slept with him."

"Yes. That's what I wanted to tell you. And, uh, more than once, actually."

"Way to bury the lead." Cary paused for a long moment before he added, "You slept with Matt Blanco. More than once."

"We seem to have kind of a regular thing going. The only reason I'm not at his place now is that I wanted to talk to you."

"Jesus Christ. Matt Blanco. You slept with *the* Matt Blanco."

"That's what I'm telling you. That's what I wanted to tell you, because I keep thinking about what you said in your article about how attitudes are changing and how teams should be doing more to show support for gay athletes and what it would take to gain wider acceptance. Because I really like him. Not just because he's famous and hot, although that doesn't hurt, but because he's a really great guy too. And this situation is so complicated."

"Yeah. I'll say. When you first mentioned that you thought he might be gay, I just thought, 'Oh, wouldn't that be interesting,' but I never thought something would happen between you."

"Me neither."

"Holy shit, Ig. What the hell are you going to do?"

"Enjoy it while it lasts? I don't know." Iggy leaned back on the couch, fatigue from that day's game finally taking over. "All I know is that this is a crazy thing, and I had to tell *someone*. I know I can trust you, so." He pressed a hand to his forehead. "I have no idea what will happen. I don't know how we keep from getting caught. I don't even know if this will last longer than next week. It's kind of both a dream come true and a nightmare. I really like him, but it's so hard to keep this secret."

"Thanks for trusting me. You can, by the way. I know I've got the press pass and everything, but I won't tell. That's something you're going to have to work out how to do on your own, if you even want to."

"It's probably just a passing thing, you know? Like, we're both hot for each other. But we have nothing in common."

"That's not true. You both play for one of the biggest market baseball teams in the country. You both know what it's like to be a gay professional athlete. You both live and breathe baseball. I think you have a lot in common. This could be a good thing for you both, actually. I know it will be difficult, but like I told you before, it will be good to have an ally."

Iggy frowned. "When you said that, you thought I should befriend him."

Cary laughed softly. "It's true, I did not expect you to seduce him."

"Who says I'm the one who seduced him?" Heat flooded Iggy's face as he spoke, remembering the crazy brave streak that had compelled him to proposition Matt. He still wasn't entirely sure what had come over him, but he didn't regret anything he'd done for a moment.

"Be careful, okay?" Cary said. "Which I say because I want you to be happy. There are a lot of ways for this to go wrong."

"I know. Thanks, Cary. I'm glad I finally got to tell someone."

"As always, your secrets are safe with me."

Chapter Ten

IGGY THOUGHT a hard-fought-for victory was sweeter than an easy one. One of the sweetest of his first year with the Eagles was a marathon game in Kansas City that stretched to fourteen scoreless innings. At the top of the fourteenth, he stood in the hole and watched Manuel Cruz take a few practice swings in the on-deck circle. When Cruz went up to bat, there was already one out.

Iggy wondered if this game would just keep on going forever. It was the fourteenth inning, going on one in the morning, it was drizzling slightly, and Iggy felt the fatigue of the long game down in his bones. The Eagles couldn't seem to do anything against this phenom reliever from Kansas City. And Lord knew if Eagles reliever Jefferson Jones gave up the winning run, there'd be hell to pay.

Cruz made his bat connect with the ball hard enough to knock a line drive down the middle, and he took off for first, landing there seconds before the ball hit the first baseman's mitt. Safe. Iggy was up.

The first pitch went wild. The second looked like it was going to go high and outside but corrected itself in time to whoosh by Iggy and be called strike one. The third looked good, and Iggy swung, and he felt the bat vibrate as it collided with the ball and everything slowed down. The ball sailed through the air, and Iggy thought he'd just hit a fly ball that would be the second out of this already long inning, but he took off running for first. Then the ball kept going and....

It was gone, right into the edge of the right-field stands, and Iggy was too astonished to do anything but keep running those bases. Before he even made it home, his very tired team was surging onto the field. Iggy dug his cleat into home plate and was immediately pulled into grateful hugs, and he laughed, relieved the game had finally ended.

Matt sneaked into Iggy's hotel room afterward, but neither of them had the energy to do more than sleep. Still, it was nice to get a tight hug and a wet kiss and then a possessive hand on his thigh as he drifted off that night.

The next day was a travel day, and their flight got back into New York early enough that most of the team wanted to go out that night to toast

Iggy's big home run. He was reminded of his Little League days when the team would go out for ice cream after a win, and whoever hit a home run got a sundae on Coach. Iggy had eaten a lot of sundaes.

This particular home run was his thirty-fourth of the season, and when people asked, he sort of fell into a pattern of "Aw shucks, I was just doing my job" responses. Which was roughly what he said as he and the center fielders, plus Roger May and a few random hangers-on, gathered at a bar in Midtown.

Matt stood a few feet away and kept exchanging glances with Iggy. Cruz sidled up next to Iggy and leaned on the bar. "For a feat so pure and amazing, I'm thinking we need whiskey and big-bosomed blonde women, not necessarily in that order."

"What happened to your regular season celibacy pact?" Iggy asked.

"Oh, still in full effect. Sex throws me off my game. This is for you, my young friend."

Iggy sipped his beer. "Um, well. Big boobs and blonde hair aren't really my thing."

"Flat chests and dark hair, okay. I can work with that. See anyone here you like?"

Iggy glanced at Matt, who raised an eyebrow. Then he surveyed the bar, which was crowded. A few women had clued in to the fact that half the Brooklyn Eagles were milling around the place. Iggy said, "There are some nice-looking women here."

Cruz slapped him on the back. "You are the king of understatement, but that's the spirit. What about the girl talking to Jones. She your type?"

Iggy looked at the woman, who was twenty-two if she was a day. She had long black hair and was on the thin side but seemed pretty enough. Iggy shrugged.

"Wow, tough customer. Well, you need Uncle Manuel to help you out, you just holler, okay?"

"I think I'm capable of finding someone to hook up with all on my own."

Cruz laughed. "That's right. You're a goddamned Eagle, and you hit the game-winning home run last night. You could sleep with anyone in this bar. Including a few of the guys, I'd bet." He winked.

Iggy chuckled and sipped his beer to hide his embarrassment.

A little while later, he went to the men's room. As soon as he put a palm on one of the stall doors to nudge it open, a strong body pressed behind his and pushed him into the stall. He whirled around and found himself trapped against Matt.

Matt then proceeded to kiss the ever-loving shit out of him.

When Matt eased away, Iggy, feeling a little breathless, asked, "What was that for?"

"Turns out I have a jealous streak," Matt whispered, feathering his fingers over Iggy's shoulders and arms. "All that talk of looking for women with Cruz got me kind of worked up. So I figured I'd let you know that if you want someone to hook up with tonight, I'm happy to do the honors. I'll fuck you until you can't see straight. I'll do it right now."

Iggy bit his lip to keep from moaning. The mental image alone had him hard and throbbing. He took a deep breath. "You're the hottest guy in this bar. If I had a choice of anyone, I'd choose you."

"Convenient." Matt smirked. "You wanna get out of here?"

"Do you think it's smart to leave together? Particularly since Cruz is trying too hard to send me home with a woman."

"We'll have to slip out somehow. If no one sees you leave, they'll assume you found a girl to go home with." Matt leaned back against the stall door and gave Iggy a scorching look. The intensity of Matt's gaze was enough for Iggy to worry his pants might fall down of their own volition.

"I'll follow your lead."

Matt nodded. "You leave the restroom first. I'll follow in a minute."

Iggy gave Matt another kiss. It took some wrestling, but they managed to get out of the stall. Then Iggy washed his hands and left the room.

MATT WASN'T sure why Cruz's antics made his blood boil, but they sure as hell did. When he walked out of the men's room, he spotted Cruz with an arm slung around Iggy, nudging him toward a woman with freckles and a lot of brown hair. It surprised him to find he'd gotten so possessive where Iggy was concerned. They were just fucking. They weren't even really in a relationship.

Unless they were.

Fuck.

Matt walked up to the bar and ordered a beer. He considered the problem. He didn't date. He had sex, mostly one-night stands or the occasional regular arrangement, but rarely anything that ever lasted longer than it took to get off. Dating was too risky, too distracting from the game. And no one thought twice about a thirtysomething bachelor baseball player, so he'd never felt any particular pressure to find someone, except from his nonna. He laughed to himself, hearing her voice in his head. *"I know you love baseball, Matteo, but you'd be much happier if you loved a person too."*

He thought of Roger and Lauren, how cute they were together, how Roger had openly cried with joy at their wedding. Matt had felt a pang of longing watching them, knowing he'd never felt anything like that, doubting he ever would. He never got close enough to anyone to fall in love, and that was fine, because he had baseball. Baseball was the most important thing in his life. Falling in love risked taking it away.

Which, he knew, meant that when his career ended, he'd be left with nothing.

He watched Iggy, who was chatting with the freckled woman. Even Matt could see there was no spark between them. He sighed and sipped his beer, trying to work out how to get Iggy out of the bar and into his bed.

He could really fall for Iggy. It seemed so unlikely, but there it was.

Roger invaded his field of vision. He ordered a beer and then turned to Matt.

"I guess it's nice being the old man now, huh?"

Matt balked. "Hardly. Why do you say that?"

Roger pointed his bottle toward Iggy and Cruz. They had moved on to a redheaded woman with huge breasts. "No one's trying to get you laid. I think they've given up."

"I get laid plenty."

"*I* know that. Cruz thinks you're just a sad-luck case."

Feeling nervous now, Matt picked at the label on his beer bottle. Most of the team had started congregating around Iggy, and the bartender was at the other end of the bar, so Matt and Roger were effectively alone. He said, "You think there will come a time when a guy will sit in the wives' section of the stadium?"

Roger shrugged. "I think most players are more okay with it than you'd think. You know Rick Grayson? Played left field for Pittsburgh a couple of years ago?"

"Yeah, I met him once at a party. He bats for my team?"

"Yep. We played together on a Triple-A team in Pennsylvania for a couple of years before I met you. He had a 'friend' who came to all the games. We all knew what the deal really was, but no one ever said anything. And that's kind of how it is. Every last one of us has been on a team with a gay player at some point in our careers, whether we knew it or not. We all know this is true. But if you don't talk about it, don't draw attention to it, it's easy enough to pretend otherwise. I could not give less of a fuck about what my teammates do in their off time, but I'd be lying if I said there weren't some guys who were uncomfortable with it."

"You know, gay men are capable of being in a locker room without going into some kind of hormone-induced fugue state in which they try to stick their dick up every player's ass."

Roger laughed. "I know. Most of these guys know that. But most of these guys were also raised on apple pie and macho bullshit. I think we'll get there, but we're not there yet."

"Hmm. That seems to be the common refrain. Maybe someday but not yet." Matt sipped his beer. His stomach sank a little as he contemplated his impending fortieth birthday and wondered what he had to show for it. Normal guys his age had partners and families. He had a $2 million Manhattan apartment and Hall-of-Fame-worthy stats, and while those were nice things he'd worked his ass off for, they were empty. "What happened to Grayson?" he asked.

"He's retired. Arm turned to jelly, from what I heard. Stopped being able to throw the ball more than ten feet." Roger shifted his gaze over toward Iggy. "We exchange Christmas cards. He's still with the 'friend.' They bought a farm in western Pennsylvania somewhere."

"That's impressive." Matt knew of a lot of baseball marriages that had crashed and burned. He sighed. "When I retire, I'm gonna move somewhere warm."

"Nah, you'd miss New York."

Matt shrugged, but Roger was right. Matt loved the city, and more to the point, his family was here. He'd been avoiding his mother lately, not ready to talk about Iggy yet, but he knew she loved him unconditionally. She'd probably adore Iggy, come to think of it. But introducing Iggy to his big Italian family, or even just his mother, made the relationship feel... real. Matt liked Iggy a lot, but were they there yet?

Matt and Roger sat silently together for a few minutes. Matt looked over at Iggy. The redhead was obviously flirting with him, but Iggy was not quite succeeding at looking interested. Matt clenched his fists in an effort to avoid punching Cruz in the face to get him to knock it off.

"Do me a favor?" he said to Roger.

"Sure."

Matt grabbed a cocktail napkin and a pen someone had left on the bar. He scribbled out instructions for Iggy to sneak out and meet him back at his apartment. "Give this to Rodriguez," he said, handing Roger the napkin.

"Oh no. No. I'm not getting involved."

"All you have to do is walk up to him, say, 'Some chick told me to give this to you,' and walk away. If anyone asks what happened to me, make an old-man joke and tell them I went home to bed."

"You know that we're the same age, right?"

"You're five months older than me, actually." Matt grinned. "I'm gonna duck out. Say hi to Lauren for me."

"Later."

Chapter Eleven

IGGY WAS pulled out of a nap by the phone ringing. He looked around and realized he'd dozed off on his couch, the TV was still on, and it was dark outside. He cursed October and the sun setting earlier. He grabbed the phone and croaked out a "Hello?"

"Were you sleeping?" Cary asked.

"No." Iggy rubbed the crust out of his eyes. "Maybe."

"Well, wake up, because I've got a scoop that you very much need to hear."

Iggy sat up. "You've got my attention. What is it?"

"There's an Internet rumor about Marcell Timms. He's a point guard for New Jersey. Kind of a big deal."

"I know who he is." Everyone knew who Timms was. Despite being shy of his thirtieth birthday, he was routinely compared to Michael Jordan and LeBron James, destined to be remembered as one of the greats at his sport. Even people who didn't follow basketball knew who Marcell Timms was.

"It may be about to become public that Marcell Timms was seen in a gay bar last weekend."

"Oh" was all Iggy could say. He paused. "That's easily explained, I guess."

Cary laughed. "Well, it would be easier to dismiss if there hadn't been rumors circulating for weeks that he's gay. You can't tell anyone I told you this, but I have a source that says Timms has been begging his agent to let him come out, but the agent won't have it and wants him to deny the whole thing."

"He's gay? Wow. He's pretty hot. Do you think that…?"

"Focus, Iggy. Besides, I thought you only had eyes for a certain first baseman."

"I do. Doesn't mean a boy can't dream."

"Well, anyway. My guess is this will go away, but in the event it doesn't, it will be interesting to see how the American public reacts. There's never been a player with this kind of public profile who has come out before."

"Gauge how the public reacts in the event I get outed, you mean."

"That too." Cary paused. "You know as well as I do it only takes one of your ex-boyfriends to come forward. If there's even a whiff, you'll be guilty of being gay in the court of public opinion."

"I *am* gay, Cary."

"Not to the public. At least not right now."

Iggy grunted as a way to acknowledge the point.

"I thought you should know."

"Thanks, I guess."

"How are things with Number Three?" Three was Matt's jersey number.

"Good." Iggy didn't want to give details. "No one is onto us, if that's your next question."

"Keep it that way. Oh, by the way, I'm covering the Championship Series for Sports Net, so I'll be in New York next week. Wanna spend some of your ridiculous pile of money on me?"

"Sure. I mean, I have to play baseball, but you know."

"I'm staying in Times Square. That has the potential to be really wretched, but I've heard the gay scene in Hell's Kitchen is pretty great."

"I wouldn't know."

"I'm sorry, Ig."

Iggy lay back down on the couch. "What good is having a gay best friend in New York if he doesn't know what the good gay bars are, huh?"

"I didn't say that."

"I've never been to a gay bar in New York because it's too fucking risky."

"And now you've got a hunky boyfriend, so it's not like you even need to go out to meet men."

"He's not my boyfriend. We're just fucking." Although as soon as Iggy said it, he wondered if the words were true. He really liked Matt. He'd developed pretty strong feelings for him, in fact, but what good was any of it? It wasn't as if they could be together like a real couple. It wasn't like Matt really saw him as much more than a kid.

"I'm about to go through a tunnel, so I'm gonna lose you. Take care of yourself, Ig, all right? Be careful. I'll call you about making plans next week."

"Yeah. Thanks, Cary."

As soon as Iggy was off the phone with Cary, he called Matt, who answered right away.

"Can I come over?" Iggy asked.

"Yeah, okay. I was just watching TV. When are you coming?" Matt's voice was tempered. Iggy felt a brief wave of doubt but then reasoned that

Matt wouldn't have agreed to let him come over if he didn't really want him to. It wouldn't have been the first time Matt had begged off.

"Just as soon as my little feet can bike across the park," Iggy said.

Matt chuckled. "See you soon."

So Iggy stuffed his wallet and bike lock in a bag, grabbed his bike from the front hallway, and soon was pedaling across Seventy-Eighth Street and then through the park.

He still routinely got lost in Central Park, but in his months in New York, he had figured out that the most direct way to get to the West Side by bike was to take the Seventy-Second Street bike path. There was a decent amount of congestion from other bikers and people out for a night run. It was a lovely night, with a cool breeze that felt good against Iggy's skin as he sped down the path.

He walked up the stoop to Matt's building ten minutes later. He chained his bike to the rack just off the lobby and said hello to Raul the doorman. When he got up to the apartment, Matt stood at the door, looking a little wary. His hair was tousled, and he was wearing a faded Eagles T-shirt and sweatpants, and Iggy thought he looked downright delicious.

"Hi," Matt said as he let Iggy in.

"Hi," Iggy echoed. He waited for Matt to shut the door again before he leaned over and gave Matt a kiss on the cheek.

Matt smiled. "Well, I am not entirely heartbroken to see you. To what do I owe this visit?"

"I wanted to see you."

Matt narrowed his eyes but gestured to his sofa. "You want a beer?"

"No. Alcohol will just put me to sleep. Water?"

Matt disappeared into the kitchen and returned with two glasses of ice water. He handed one to Iggy, then sat next to him on the sofa. "What's up?"

"You were just on the brain. That, and my friend Cary tells me there's a rumor circulating Sports Media Land that Marcell Timms is gay."

"Marcell Timms? The basketball player?"

"Yep. Cary doesn't think the story has legs, but I thought it was kind of interesting."

"Hmm." Matt reached over and tugged on a lock of Iggy's hair. "I was sleeping when you called. I intend to go back to doing that. Care to join me?"

"I'd love to."

"We'll go to bed, but I suppose we may not only sleep."

"I figured."

Matt grinned. "Well. Come on, then."

They walked together to the bedroom, shedding clothes along the way. Iggy liked that there wasn't much preamble here. They were just going to get down to it. Which was what he wanted.

Right?

He wondered if Matt looked at him the same way he looked at Matt. Because sometimes he thought what they had was just sex, but sometimes he felt like he'd found a kindred spirit, a man who got him, who understood what he was about. And he certainly didn't want their relationship, whatever it was, to end anytime soon.

Matt's pale skin gleamed in the moonlit bedroom. When he reached for the light switch, Iggy said, "No, leave it. I like the moonlight."

Matt laughed. "You're kind of a cornball sometimes, Ig."

Iggy was glad Matt couldn't see his face, because he was sure he was blushing. "Whatever. Just get on the bed, mister."

Matt was still laughing when he lay on the bed. "For the record, that's not just the moonlight. Some of the glow in here comes from the security lights on the building across the street."

"You sure know how to kill the mood."

"You want to make love in the dark, that's fine with me. But don't keep a guy waiting."

Iggy climbed onto the bed and hovered over Matt. He dipped his head and kissed Matt deeply, tangling their tongues together, opening wide. He loved kissing Matt, loved how their mouths fit together. Matt lifted his hands and pushed his fingers through Iggy's hair. It was getting a little long and would probably soon be longer than Eagles regulations allowed, but Iggy loved it when Matt played with his hair.

Matt widened his legs and moved a little on the bed. He still had his underwear on, but Iggy dispensed with that quickly. With his hands, Matt slowly coaxed Iggy's body into wakefulness, and their bodies moved together while the arousal unfurled, desire mounting as he caressed Iggy's skin. A sleepy laziness tangled with the wanting. Being with Matt was fun and easy, and if unhurried lovemaking was on the agenda, that was fine with Iggy.

They laughed at nothing and rolled around on the bed, pressing their cocks together, rubbing skin against skin. Heat rose in a slow burn through Iggy's body, his need for Matt seeming to sneak up on him. He ran his palms over Matt's smooth skin, curled his fingers around the curves of Matt's body, pushed him down into the mattress. Matt groaned and thrust his hips up, meeting Iggy, challenging him.

"God, I want you," Matt said.

"How do you want me?"

Matt kissed him and shifted his hips. "Mmm. Inside me."

Iggy reached for the drawer beside the bed. He'd spent enough time at Matt's to know where things were, having been granted free rein of the apartment. This made it almost like they were a couple.

Iggy pushed the sudden pang of nerves away and focused on Matt, who was lying on the bed with his legs splayed. Iggy poured a healthy amount of lube on his fingers and then touched Matt. He loved this. He loved the way Matt's body pulled at him, closed around him, and he loved the way they just worked together. And how crazy was that? Who would have thought six months ago that he'd be here?

"What's so funny?" Matt asked, a smile on his face.

Iggy wasn't sure if he should say anything, but he said, "I was just thinking that I really like being with you."

"I like being with you too."

"It's just funny that we found each other in these weird circumstances."

Matt smiled and kissed Iggy. His lips were so soft and welcoming. Iggy could have kissed them all night. The kiss distracted him from what he was doing until Matt shifted his hips again and said, "Come on. Let's...."

Iggy kissed him and pushed his fingers inside.

Matt arched his back as Iggy prepared him. He explored inside Matt with one hand and used the other to rub his chest, pinch his nipples, make him writhe on the bed. Matt's reactions turned Iggy on an incredible amount. They were a strange mirror into what Iggy felt growing in his own body. But it wasn't just arousal coursing through him. It was affection too.

He was in so much trouble. Of all the men to fall for....

But there was no time for thought, because Matt reached for him, tugged him close, kissed him silly. Iggy stretched Matt and reached for a condom. Yeah, this was what he wanted, to be inside Matt, to make Matt *his*. And not Eagles First Baseman Matt Blanco, the man of his fantasies, his idol, but just plain old Matt, a hot guy he'd met a few months ago and was falling for hard.

Iggy stroked himself as he watched Matt move, as his skin began to tingle with anticipation and need. He *needed* Matt, needed to be inside him, needed to be with him, needed to come. He needed the mindlessness that came with orgasmic oblivion, needed to make his mind go quiet for a little while. When he was satisfied that Matt was ready for him, he held his pulsing, hard cock in his hand and pressed it to Matt's entrance. When Matt threw his head back and moaned, Iggy plunged inside.

Iggy began to move, accelerating quickly, needing the speed and friction against his cock to get to the white space he wanted. Matt reached for him and dug his fingers into Iggy's skin. He kissed Iggy's shoulder, his collarbone, his chest, murmuring how good it felt. "Good" was an understatement, because the way Matt's body squeezed him, pulled at him, that was sheer bliss, the greatest feeling there was, the kind of thing people made art to commemorate.

He thrust harder, and Matt encouraged him, pulling at his hair, urging him to move faster, harder, more. Then Matt was pushing at him, changing the angle, changing the position.

"Let me…," Matt said, breathless. He sighed. "Let me ride you. Roll over."

Oh God. Just the thought of Matt sitting on his cock, hovering above him, that pushed Iggy a long way toward orgasm. "Yes," he said. He pulled out and rolled onto his back.

Matt grinned and straddled him. He knelt and then moved back, grabbing Iggy's cock and stroking it before he repositioned himself. He shifted his legs a little and started to lower himself onto Iggy.

And then he screamed. But not in the good way. It was a scream laced with agony.

Before Iggy understood what was going on, Matt was on his back beside him. He held his left leg up and was rubbing his knee. "Shit," he said. "*Shit*."

"Are you okay?"

"My knee." Matt bit his lip. "God, it hurts." He closed his eyes tightly, and his breathing was labored.

Iggy had never seen Matt like this before. It was hard to figure out what to do through the haze of surprise and concern.

"I shouldn't have done that," Matt said. "It's been bugging me all day, but I thought it would be okay if we just… I mean, whoever thought that sex would…. Ah, Christ." He rolled onto his side, his back to Iggy. He jackknifed his legs, the bad knee closer to his body, and he rubbed at the side of it with his palm.

Iggy rolled over and touched Matt's back. "Is there something I can do? Get you some ice? Some pain meds?"

"Do you think the Wizard can give me a new knee?"

"Ha-ha."

Matt took a deep breath. "There's an ice pack in the freezer, and my meds are on the bathroom counter. I'm sorry, Ig. I think I'm out for the rest of the game."

"It's no problem. Make yourself comfortable. I'll go get the ice and your pills."

It wasn't the first time Iggy had noticed Matt nursing that knee. He wondered how bad the injury was if he had medication and an ice pack on hand for it. If it was a chronic thing, why did no one know about it?

He fetched the ice pack and a bottle of water from the fridge. Then he grabbed the prescription bottle on the counter.

"We're playing tomorrow," Iggy said as he sat on the bed. "You okay to take these?" The Eagles had been doing unannounced drug tests all season in an effort to prevent the use of performance-enhancing drugs. He shook the bottle of pills.

Matt reached for the bottle. "These slow me down and make me fall asleep. I don't think anyone would accuse me of using these to enhance my performance. Besides, I've got a note on file from Andy Su." He popped a couple of pills in his mouth and then chugged half the bottle of water in one go.

Iggy turned on the light. He helped Matt get into a more comfortable position and put the ice pack on the bad knee. He found his underwear and put them back on. He climbed on the bed and sat next to Matt.

"I'm sorry, Ig," Matt said.

"Is your knee really bad?" The question sounded stupid once it was out there.

Matt looked away. Quietly he said, "Su thinks I should get surgery done on it. It's a patellofemoral injury, or something like that. But I just…. If it's something worse than that and I have to have reconstructive surgery done on my knee, I might never play baseball again. So I get these flare-ups sometimes. It's manageable."

Iggy doubted that, but he didn't want to push Matt. Instead, he put an arm around Matt's shoulder and leaned into him. "You sure you're okay?"

"I'll be fine in a little bit. I probably just need to sleep. I'm…. You came all the way over here, but I can't…."

"Don't you dare apologize again. It's fine, Matt. We can just watch TV or something."

"Are you sure?"

"Yes. Are you comfortable?"

"Yeah, actually. I mean, my knee is on fire, but the pills will kick in any moment, and then I'll probably just fall asleep. The remote's on your side of the bed."

So Iggy and Matt sat leaning against each other and the headboard. Iggy flipped on the TV and started surfing. He watched a couple of minutes of *Baseball Tonight* before getting frustrated and finding a *Seinfeld* rerun. As he settled in to watch, Matt lost his fight with staying awake. He laid his head on Iggy's shoulder and drifted off. Iggy held him for a long time. He was worried for Matt, worried Matt was underplaying the extent of the injury, worried about what this meant for Matt's career.

Most of all, he worried what, if anything, this meant for Matt and Iggy's future.

THE RUMOR around the stadium was that the Eagles were interested in a hot fielder playing for Arizona, and management would do whatever they could to get him once trading opened, including trading good players.

That, Matt had to concede as he looked forlornly at his swollen knee, could mean him. For all the Eagles organization claimed to value him as a player, Teddy Rothschild and Bill Haverman wanted a younger, fresher team, and Matt was neither of those things.

As Matt pulled on a pair of pants, Iggy, Cruz, and Roger strolled into the locker room, yukking it up about something. When Iggy noticed Matt sitting on the bench, they made eye contact, but the moment was over before it really began.

Cruz said something Matt didn't hear, and then Roger and Iggy bumped fists. Roger turned to Matt and gave him an appraising look but walked to his locker without saying anything. On the way to his locker, Iggy walked by Matt and asked, "How's your knee?"

"Not bad," Matt replied, though it hurt like a motherfucker.

Iggy knew that, of course. Matt still regretted having to put the brakes on their session the night before, but it couldn't have been helped. He was embarrassed, too, that Iggy now knew about the knee. He hadn't wanted Iggy to know, hadn't wanted to lose face in front of him. He'd wanted to be a whole man for Iggy, a strong man. He wanted to live up to the image Iggy had worshipped for years. But now Iggy had seen his weakness.

Iggy raised an eyebrow but then turned silently to his locker.

Matt dug his sneakers out of his locker and eavesdropped on the conversations around him. A few more players trickled in and roamed around, some idly talking about plans for the evening. Matt mostly wanted to go home and ice his knee. And he wanted Iggy to come with him. Not for sex—Matt didn't think he could make his knee work well enough for that anyway—but just to hang out and talk with. The cat was really out of the bag now. It was kind of a relief not to have to pretend with Iggy that everything was hunky-dory.

"So the latest," Cruz said, addressing everyone in the locker room, "is that Teddy is flying to Phoenix his own self to do the early work on this deal with Arizona. He really wants Alvarez." Rothschild was fairly hands-off as far as general managers went. It was odd for him to get so directly involved in a trade.

"The season's not even over yet," said Caballo.

"I hope this guy's balls are made out of solid gold," said Roger. "I can't imagine any player being worth that much otherwise."

"I just hope he can hit a baseball," Matt commented.

"That too," said Cruz. "I was reading. His average this season was .342, seventy-some RBIs, thirty-five home runs, a couple dozen stolen bases. That in only a hundred games. He had a sprained wrist or something that kept him off the field for most of July."

There was a murmur among the ranks. "Jesus," said Matt. "How is it Arizona still finished out of the play-offs this season?"

"You're only as good as your worst player?" Cruz suggested.

"One good player can't carry a whole team," said Roger. "You know that. And Arizona can't afford Alvarez anymore, so he's on the market."

"The Eagles won't trade with a starter, will they?" asked Iggy. "They'd trade from the farm teams. Right?"

"Not if they want Alvarez," said Roger.

The sense of dread hanging over Matt made him think that taking Iggy home was maybe not the best idea he'd ever had. He didn't want Iggy to see him this low.

But then, once Iggy was dressed, he walked over to Matt and said quietly, "I have to run an errand, but can I come over later?"

"Yes." It was the only answer Matt could give.

Iggy smiled. "Later, guys," he said to the locker room at large before he left.

Chapter Twelve

A FREAK heat wave made the October air oppressive as Matt stood at first base, staring down the baseline at a Dallas batter he didn't recognize. The guy had a terrible goatee. Matt looked over at Iggy at third. Iggy pulled off his cap and used his wrist to wipe sweat from his brow. His dark hair was matted to his head. He looked miserable.

Matt couldn't decide if it was a blessing or a curse to be losing Game Six of the American League Championship Series with his lover on the field with him. Dallas had three games under its belt, the Eagles only two, meaning that losing this game would put them out of the World Series. They were at the top of the ninth and losing by three runs, and things felt pretty hopeless.

The batter with the bad goatee hit a pop fly toward third base, which Iggy deftly caught.

Maybe it was better for the season to be over. Matt and Iggy could spend the off-season together, out of the spotlight. Although that probably wasn't possible, not now that the tabloids had cottoned on to the fact that ladies found Iggy attractive and putting his face on the cover sold a lot of papers. Although Matt could have told them that.

In fact there were a couple of women in pink Eagles T-shirts in the field-level stands just to Matt's left. One of them held up a sign that said, *Marry me, Iggy Rodriguez.*

"Good luck with *that*, lady," Matt mumbled.

The next batter struck out, ending the inning. Matt felt sweaty and tired as he retreated to the dugout.

Before sending the next batter to the plate, Bill stood before them all and looked around. "Look, men, I know you're tired, and I know it's hot, and I know we're three runs behind, but we've triumphed over worse odds. Rodriguez, you're up. Letum, you're in the hole. The rest of you get your shit together and win this game."

Matt hated being in this position, down runs in the last inning of a crucial game. The batting order wasn't working in their favor either. The middle of the order would have worked best for circumstances like this.

Iggy got it done, hitting a homer over right field. The crowd in the stands went bonkers. Greg Letum hit a ground-rule double and thus was standing at second when the top of the order was up again. Haverman had put Overbey in the first slot, and he promptly struck out. Matt went up.

He was nervous, which was a rough spot to be in. The best way for him to get a hit would have been to clear his head, but there was too much going on. His mind was full of Iggy and his knee and newspaper headlines and the possibility he might get traded and the fact that they were losing.

He shook his head and lifted the bat. He tried to narrow his focus to just that white ball in the pitcher's hand. He lived for that slow-motion moment when the ball left the mound, and he had to make the bat connect with it. One, two, pitch, hit—that was how this went.

He whiffed the bat over the first pitch. The second one was low and inside, and he had to hop out of the way to avoid getting hit by the ball. He made his bat connect with the third pitch, though, so of course it popped up toward first base. The first baseman—that batter with the bad goatee—caught it and hurled it toward third, which took out Letum.

Game over.

To say that things were subdued in the locker room after the game would have been an understatement. Matt felt like the game had been lost by his hand, which was the first problem. The hangdog expressions on everyone's faces was the second. What a shitty way to end the season.

As if to emphasize how terrible the game had been, Bill pulled Matt into the postgame press conference. Matt's seniority on the team had made him something of a de facto captain, and Bill often made Matt represent the team when talking to the press, but Matt couldn't summon anything more to say than a few platitudes and monosyllables. Even he thought the bit about the team trying their best and looking forward to next season felt like bullshit.

Back in the locker room, Matt changed out of his uniform without bothering to shower. He could do that at home. He could wash away this whole fucking season and the knee pain and the threat of getting traded and watch all of it slip down the drain.

But then Iggy leaned on the locker next to Matt's and reminded him this season hadn't been all bad.

"You want to get a drink with me?" Iggy asked. "With us, I mean. Cruz and I are gonna go to that dive bar on Bedford and get completely shitfaced."

If anything, that just emphasized how young Iggy was. Matt had to work to hide his disappointment. "I was gonna go home and ice my knee and hide under the covers until next season."

"Aw, it wasn't that bad. Shit happens, Matt. You can't win 'em all."

"Says the man who hit the home run that made our loss just slightly less embarrassing."

"Don't be like that."

Matt had never felt older. He was so tired and sore that a night out drinking sounded about as pleasant as a root canal. But he thought Iggy should go party if that was what it took to get his mind off the game. Hell, Iggy should go party because he was young and beautiful, and Matt was old and broken. "I'll pass on the drink. I'm not up for much partying tonight. I'm sorry. Have fun, though."

Iggy nodded, though he looked disappointed. Under his breath, he said, "I'll ditch Cruz if you need me."

Did Matt really need Iggy in the way he was implying? He thought maybe he did, but that was too much to think about right then. He didn't want to hold Iggy back. "No, it's all right. I'm just tired. Go out with Cruz. I'll call you tomorrow."

"You sure?"

"Positive." Matt smiled to show he was serious.

"All right. Later, Matt."

Matt watched him leave, immediately regretting his decision. Of course, what he really wanted was for Iggy to come home with him, to hold him like he had that night Matt's knee had gone out during sex. He wanted them to sit and talk and laugh and just be together. He also wanted to fuck Iggy stupid, but his body wouldn't cooperate with that particular desire.

He was old. That was what Matt thought as he gathered his things and headed for the parking lot. He was too old for Iggy; that was for sure. Iggy was twenty-five and should have been doing things twenty-five-year-olds did, like going to bars and getting drunk and picking up inappropriate guys and having fun. He shouldn't be forced into taking care of Matt's old hide, shouldn't have to worry about Matt's bum knee, shouldn't be saddled with his old ass.

Matt chastised himself for getting too maudlin.

Roger caught up with Matt before he got to his car. "Hey, man," Roger said.

"Hey."

"You okay?"

Matt shrugged. He didn't think he could voice what he was feeling without having a breakdown, and *that* was the last thing he wanted to do. Media was still crawling all over the stadium, for one thing, but he needed Roger to think he was okay, needed Roger not to pry into what was going on in his head.

"I'm surprised you're not going out with Cruz and Rodriguez," Roger said.

"Likewise."

"Eh, I'm old and tired."

"That makes two of us." Matt rubbed his forehead.

Roger gestured toward his car, which was parked a couple of spaces down from Matt's on the far end of the lot. He said, "So having a young lover isn't making you feel younger?"

"Honestly? I feel older than ever. I'll never be that young again." Matt groaned. "God. He deserves so much better than me."

Roger stopped walking and turned toward him. He raised an eyebrow. "Is that what we're doing now? Pity party for Matt?"

"What do you want me to say?"

Roger started to walk again, so Matt stumbled after him. "You know, I wasn't really on board with this thing you've got going with our young friend at first, but you seemed to know what you were doing, so I let it go. Then I saw that, against all odds, he seemed to make you really happy. You've smiled more over the last couple of months than you have in a long time. I never thought I'd say this, but he's good for you. So what happened?"

"Nothing happened." Matt sighed. "My knee's bothering me. A lot."

"What does that have to do with what we're talking about?"

"Because it's a daily painful reminder that my days as a baseball player are numbered. And if I'm not a baseball player, what am I?"

"You're a lot of things."

"He's just getting started, and I'm on the way out. How can we ever make that work?"

"You know how you make it work? Shut the fuck up, go home, get a good night's sleep, and realize that this season's over but your career isn't, not yet. You've got a few more good years in you. You're just bummed out right now because we lost. Get a grip."

Matt sighed. "Yeah. Yeah, all right. I'm—"

"Don't fucking apologize. You spend half your damn life apologizing for things that aren't your fault."

Well, leave it to Roger to give him the kick in the pants he needed. "Thanks."

"Anytime. We'll go get a beer next week, all right? Or I'll have you over for dinner. Lauren keeps teasing me with promises of using your nonna's lasagna recipe. We need to have you tell us if it's authentic or not."

"Yeah, okay. That sounds good."

"Try not to sweat any of this. I know you're stressed. But you can't control any of it. Not the loss, not the off-season, not your knee, not the buzz about Alvarez. It's all out of your hands now. Just enjoy what you have, okay? And if you need anything, give me a call."

They had reached their cars. Weariness had sunk into Matt's bones, but he stretched and tried to shake it off. He waved at Roger. "Good season," he said.

Roger smiled. "Yeah. Good season. Good night, Blanco."

Chapter Thirteen

MATT WAS already awake when the phone rang. He'd been debating with himself about whether it was sweet or creepy to enjoy watching Iggy sleep. Iggy wasn't exactly a graceful sleeper; he tended to throw his limbs out and wound up in these awkward, uncomfortable-looking positions. As Matt watched him, his mouth was open slightly. Still, it was hard to deny how lovely he looked, how gorgeous every inch of that dark skin was, how much Matt liked his long eyelashes and his full lips and his hard body, even in repose.

Then the phone rang and pulled Matt out of his reverie.

Iggy winced and rolled over. "What the—" He didn't finish the thought before slipping back into sleep.

Matt grabbed the phone. "Hello?"

"Matt, it's A.J. Pierce."

And Matt knew. His agent could only be calling for one reason. "Tell me the bad news."

A.J. grunted. "Dallas. If the deal goes through, and it looks like it will, they're buying out the rest of your contract with the Eagles and offering a signing bonus and a bunch of incentives, including the option of signing on for two more years with Dallas."

"Two? That's an insult."

"Which is what I told them, but your numbers are down, Matt. You really think you're still going to be playing baseball when you're in your forties? This is a good offer."

Matt couldn't think of what to say.

"Look," said A.J. "You're contractually obligated to play baseball for one more year. You want to keep playing baseball, right?"

"Of course."

"The Eagles want a younger team. That Rodriguez kid, man. He's talented and the fans love him. He's the future."

Matt glanced at Iggy, who was awake now and rubbing his eyes. "I know."

"Rothschild and Haverman have been moving toward utilizing the farm system more effectively. In exchange for you and a couple of first-round draft picks, they're getting a couple of promising Double-A players plus Alvarez, whose on-base percentage is the best in the league."

Fucking Alvarez. "I get it," said Matt.

He lay flat on his back. It was all starting to sink in. A.J. didn't even need to spell it out. Matt was old. Nobody wanted old.

"The way I see it, you don't have much of a choice. You can hold out for another offer, but the one from Dallas is as good as it gets, and it looks like you're out of the Eagles either way. Besides, what have you got keeping you in New York? No wife and kids to worry about uprooting."

Matt glanced at Iggy again, who was now propped up on his elbows and shooting Matt concerned looks. His heart sank. "No, you're right."

"Great. So I'll call everyone and make the deal."

Matt didn't see an alternative. "Yeah."

"It's the right decision, Matt. I'll call you on Monday after I hammer out the details."

Matt hung up and placed the phone on his nightstand. He pressed the heels of his hands against his eyes. He felt a light touch on his stomach.

"What is it?" asked Iggy.

"Guess I gotta shine up my cowboy boots."

"Huh?"

"For when I move to the AL West."

"They're trading you." There was a gasp in Iggy's voice.

"Dallas."

"Oh my God." Iggy bolted to a sitting position. "Dallas. Fucking Dallas. They're trading Matt Blanco from the World Series champion Brooklyn team he helped build to *Dallas.*"

"We last won the Series four seasons ago."

"Still. You're… you're going to Dallas."

Matt sat up too. Knowing that this was a possibility hadn't softened the blow at all. It did hurt, getting traded. Still, that was baseball; that was always how the game worked. Old fogies like Matt got moved around like chess pieces while young prodigies like Iggy took over the game.

"This is hush-hush," Matt said. "Don't tell your friend Cary. At least not until the deal is official."

"I won't. Like I would even. God, Matt. Dallas."

Iggy repeating it made it worse somehow, like a hammer hit to the head. "I've got another year left on my contract. Dallas bought the end of it. After that, I have the option of signing on for two additional years in the Lone Star State or going free agent."

"Or retiring."

The *R* word. Matt wasn't ready to face that yet. Sure, his knee hurt, but retiring meant no more baseball. "I guess, yeah. I'd like to keep playing as long as they let me."

Iggy nodded. "So you're moving to Dallas. What does that mean for us?"

That was the question, wasn't it? While Matt had been thinking about the worst-case scenario for a while—it made sense to end things with Iggy if he was moving across the country—that thought made his chest hurt. Still, he and Iggy hadn't been seeing each other that long, and while what they had was sexy and satisfying, it was also convenient. Not to mention that an old guy like Matt would hold back a young guy like Iggy....

Iggy reached over and touched Matt's face. "I see the gears in your head turning. Just tell me what you're thinking."

"We don't have to decide right this minute."

"No, but tell me what your gut tells you."

"That it's probably best to break up."

Iggy winced but nodded. "Yeah."

"I mean, that's five months of the year we won't see each other. Six if you count spring training. Seven with the postseason. More than half a year that I'm on the other side of the country."

Iggy looked down. Matt ran a hand up his arm. How could this be happening? How would he ever be able to give up this beautiful man?

"I get what you're saying," said Iggy. "I agree, but it sucks."

"It does suck." Matt laughed ruefully.

"I guess if this is really going to happen, we'll have to make the most of the time we have left together."

"Yeah."

Iggy surprised Matt by pulling him into his arms. Matt closed his eyes and breathed in Iggy's scent. He wanted to commit it to memory so he'd be able to recall this moment when he was alone at night in Dallas.

"I'm going to miss you so much," Iggy said.

They hugged each other tightly. Matt knew he would miss this too, that he was already missing the years they could be spending together. But baseball was his life. He couldn't renege on a contract. Not for the sake of a relationship that was still so new. He'd gone whole seasons without sex and could do it again. He liked Iggy and cared about him a great deal, but there was baseball, and there was Iggy's whole career to think about.

Although it wasn't just Iggy. Matt had lived in New York City most of his life. His family was here; his parents still lived in Brooklyn. There were pieces of Matt imprinted on FSB Stadium, on his block of Manhattan, on the sidewalks of the Brooklyn neighborhood where he'd grown up. Being forced to move was like giving up whole chunks of himself.

Iggy pulled back a little and kissed Matt hard. The kiss was tender and strong and was really not helping Matt talk himself into leaving Iggy. Into not ever kissing Iggy again. Iggy was the best thing to happen to him in years. Was he really going to let it go?

Baseball. All he ever wanted in his whole life was to play baseball.

His throat closed up and his eyes were damp, but he swallowed, because he would not cry, not in front of Iggy. This was what he'd signed on for. This was the life that he'd chosen. It was foolish to think he really could have had it all.

Iggy deepened the kiss and pulled Matt back down onto the bed. They were done talking, clearly. Thank God. Matt needed Iggy to make him forget. But all this succeeded in doing was to remind him what he'd be giving up. As he drifted off to sleep that night, for the first time in his life, he wondered if he was making the wrong choice by picking baseball first.

WHEN CARY asked for something to drink, Iggy was somewhat surprised to find his refrigerator basically empty. "I guess I haven't been home much," he said. "I could go to the store or get something delivered."

"Nah, it's fine. I'll just avail myself of your tap water." Cary plucked a glass from the cabinet. "Dare I ask why you haven't been home?"

Iggy shrugged. "Matt and I are trying to make the most of the time we have left before he moves to Dallas."

Cary pushed past Iggy to the sink and filled his glass. "I thought you broke up."

"We plan to when he moves."

Cary shot Iggy one of his patented looks of disapproval, with his head cocked and an eyebrow raised. "Really?"

"I don't want to talk about it."

"When is he leaving?"

"First week of February. Says he wants time to settle into his house before spring training." Iggy realized he was rocking on his heels. He stopped. "Ugh, I hate this."

When Iggy looked up, Cary was staring at him with concern. Iggy hadn't planned to talk about this with anyone. He didn't want anyone to know how much Matt's leaving was tearing him up inside. When the trade had first been announced, Iggy's initial feeling was that it sucked that their arrangement would come to an end, but it was probably for the best. The more time he and Matt spent together, the better the odds were that they'd get caught. And it was just sex. Except it had stopped being about sex weeks ago; probably it had never really just been that. Because they also talked and laughed and spent time together, and Iggy genuinely enjoyed Matt's company even when they weren't having sex.

Iggy rubbed his face and hoped against hope that Cary would evaporate so he wouldn't have to explain himself.

"Well," Cary said. "You may be happy to hear that the Marcell Timms thing blew over."

"He's not gay?"

"No, he is. I've got it from a reliable source."

Iggy walked out of the kitchen and sat on his couch. He rubbed his forehead. "By reliable source, do you mean a guy you've slept with who also slept with Timms?"

"Maybe. But his agent issued a press release stating that there's no story here. I certainly don't want to report it. So my boss said to let it go."

"I can't decide if that's good or bad news."

Cary sat next to Iggy on the couch. "I'm not sure either."

They sat silently together for a moment. Iggy was happy to have him around. Cary had been staying at a hotel while he was covering a coaching shake-up with the Knicks, but he had that afternoon off, and he and Iggy were planning to spend it bumming around like they did in college. But Iggy was having a hard time relaxing.

"Can I make an observation?" Cary asked.

"I probably don't want to hear it, but go ahead."

"You haven't stopped fidgeting since we met up for lunch earlier. What's got you so tied up? Is it Matt?"

Iggy shrugged.

Cary put a hand on Iggy's knee. He whispered, "If you're this destroyed over his leaving, why are you breaking up?"

"What choice do I have?"

"Fight for him."

"I thought you didn't like that I was dating him."

"I was just worried about you. But he makes you happy, and I want you to be happy. And if you recall, I was the one who encouraged you to go after him to begin with."

"He's moving across the country. I won't be able to see him during the season. There's no way to make that work. Is there?" Iggy didn't expect

Cary to have the answer, but he couldn't help but hope that some viable solution would present itself.

"You're right, it's a tough situation."

Iggy leaned back on the couch. "I'm so tired of this." He'd started seeing Matt because it seemed so easy. It was convenient to have a lover on the team, someone he saw every day and had to spend time with anyway, someone who was just as invested in keeping things discreet as he was. But the longer things played out, the harder everything got. The everyday was easy. Talking to Matt, being with him, those things were easy. The pressure of keeping it a secret wasn't, and now the threat of baseball taking Matt away was making Iggy not so keen on baseball.

"I know," said Cary.

"I wonder sometimes if maybe you didn't have the right idea, getting out of the game."

Cary balked. "Nah. You're a star, Ig. You're goddamned Iggy Rodriguez. You just got declared Rookie of the Year! You're a great ballplayer. I wasn't much more than a benchwarmer. This gig with the Eagles, this is an amazing opportunity and everything you've wanted for your whole life. I know you're upset about Matt moving, but you've got your whole career ahead of you still."

Iggy nodded. He knew Cary was right.

"And in the meantime, fuck his brains out as often as you can."

Iggy laughed. "Thanks."

"Anytime. Now, let's see how well this fancy TV setup you've got here works. They're gonna have to pay me more before I can afford to watch any games in HD. I think the Bruins are playing this afternoon."

ROGER INSISTED on throwing a going-away party, and he insisted on using Matt's apartment, since it was the most centrally located. It was a relatively small party, filled with Matt's friends from the team, their wives and girlfriends, a handful of front office staff members, and a couple of former Eagles. It was a nice party, relaxed and low-key, and Matt had to admit it was great to be the center of attention and to get so much praise and gratitude from these guys he'd played with his whole career.

"Let's hear it for Blanco!" Roger said at one point, apropos of nothing in particular.

Everyone lifted their glasses and said, "Blanco."

"The team won't be the same without you," said Cruz.

"I can't imagine an Eagles lineup without Blanco in it," said Iggy.

"Eh, you guys will forget me five minutes after I land in Dallas."

"No!" someone shouted. Everyone else murmured assent.

"We're gonna miss you," said Roger.

The party wound down around midnight. After Matt let the last of his guests out, he turned around and saw Iggy leaning against the island in the kitchen. "Well," said Matt.

"So I've been thinking."

"I don't like the tone in your voice. If you've got some adventure planned for my last nights in town, I don't know if I'm up for it. I'm really tired."

"It's nothing like that. I just wanted to talk about what happens with us now that you're leaving."

Matt walked over to the fridge and pulled out a soda. He did not want to have this conversation again. It had been almost unbearable the first time. "We already decided."

"No, what *you* decided was that because we won't be able to see each other on a daily basis, we should just call it a day and get on with our lives. What *I* have decided is that you and me? We're pretty great together. And I can't just walk away from that."

"I don't see where there's a choice. I'm *moving*, Ig. And not just across town. I'm going to Texas."

"Well, but, so, here's the thing. You're playing for Dallas. We just spent four months together without any baseball to worry about. We'll have another four months starting in November. That's only, what, nine months from now. Not only that, but any time our teams play each other or even just when we're in the same city, we'll be able to see each other. And we'd have the All-Star break. And some time in the postseason. The way I see it, we'll see so much of each other we'll wish the distance was more of an obstacle."

"Iggy...."

Iggy looked down. For a moment his cocky swagger was gone, and Matt missed it. This was easier when they were joking around. This was easier when Iggy was just being Iggy, when Matt could dismiss his behavior as jokey or bratty. He couldn't deal with heartfelt speeches or shows of emotion. This was all devastating enough. Because the truth was, just when Matt had found something to hold on to, something to ground him and make him feel like he had a future, just when he thought he could be really happy, the rug had been pulled out from under him.

Matt cracked open the soda can and took a long gulp.

Matt had wondered recently if his heartbreak over having to move to Dallas was more a result of his having to leave a team he loved—and no doubt that was devastating enough by itself—or the city he'd grown up in, or if it was specifically because he'd have to leave Iggy.

"Matt," Iggy said quietly. "Look, the bottom line is that I'm in love with you. I know when we started this thing, whatever it is, we probably thought it would just be a sexy fling, but that's not what it is for me anymore, and I don't think that's what it is for you either. I want to keep seeing you. I know it will be hard, with the distance and all. The fact that we've had to treat this whole thing like a CIA op is not really helping matters. But I think we can find a way to make it work. It's tough, but you're worth it."

Matt put the soda can on the counter. He took a few steps forward and closed the distance between them before grabbing Iggy's head and pulling him in for a hot kiss. He didn't know how best to express what he was feeling, but it was a combination of longing and relief and anxiety and, yes, even love. He felt Iggy's hands on his shoulders and knew, above all else, that he didn't want to give this up. Maybe Iggy was right, and he wouldn't have to. "You really think we can make something work?"

"Of course." And the cocky swagger was back.

Matt smiled to himself. "I'm in love with you too," he said. He pulled Iggy into his arms. He really did love this man. He'd refused to let himself think about it, but saying it aloud now was like a revelation. What made him think he could ever be without Iggy? "I don't know what I'm gonna do when we can't be together."

"Test the limits of your cell phone's battery?"

Matt laughed. "Yeah, probably."

Iggy took his hand and started leading him toward the bedroom. "Come on, big guy. Let's go to bed. I'll give you a good reminder of why you never want to be without me."

Second

EAGLES LOOK GOOD OUT OF SPRING TRAINING

by Cary Galvin, Sports Net

This year's Eagles lineup is outstanding. Jake Caballo, Manuel Cruz, and Iggy Rodriguez are, I think, the gold standard. All three of them looked great at spring training. Nobody runs faster than Iggy Rodriguez. Nobody has quicker reflexes than Manuel Cruz. If this team doesn't at least make the postseason, I will be very surprised. And you can't count out Francisco Alvarez, the real coup of the off-season.

I'm interested to see how Alvarez does when he's not the only star on the team anymore. That's a lot of ego in one dugout. But it's also one of the best teams the Eagles have put up in years, so on paper they have the potential to go all the way this season.

I've been looking forward to tomorrow's home opener at FSB Stadium, but it's pretty strange to see an Eagles lineup that doesn't include Matt Blanco. It's hard not to get sentimental about that. But Blanco's best years are behind him. Which is to say, no doubt, Blanco is Hall-of-Fame material, but I don't think he's going to be breaking records anymore.

It'll be interesting also to see what Blanco does in a Dallas uniform. I still think he's got a couple of good seasons left in him, and he may yet surprise us all....

Chapter Fourteen

MATT HAD played thirteen seasons with the Eagles. He knew FSB Stadium like the back of his hand. He knew the staff, knew the players, had felt an ease there that came from long years of familiarity, of having the space be his second home. But Lone Star Field in Dallas was something else. He'd played in the stadium enough times that he went to the visiting team locker room more often than not in the first weeks, for one thing. Even once he found his way, the stadium was strange and unfamiliar. The staff knew him, but he couldn't remember anyone's name. The texture of the ground on the field was different, his locker was a different size than he was used to, the air was too dry, and everything smelled different. He felt like an outsider every time he went into the locker room.

Still, he felt respected. His teammates seemed to like him. He was still playing first base. He'd hit two home runs in preseason exhibition play. He felt optimistic.

But he sure missed the hell out of Iggy.

He missed everyone, though. Cruz, Roger, the whole team. He missed New York; he missed his family. The homesickness followed him around Dallas, on the trip between his house in the suburbs and the stadium, onto the field during practice, every time he had to walk through the foreign locker room.

His mother had called him more since he'd moved to Dallas than she had in all the years he'd lived in Manhattan; he supposed being in the same city made him accessible in a way he wasn't here. He rarely saw her in the last few years he lived in New York, even though she was right there in Brooklyn, but now he missed her too. He missed shooting the shit with Tony over a slice of pizza. He missed his father complaining about sports or city politics. He even missed family gatherings with all his aunts and uncles and cousins—and there were many—crammed into one house and all the chaos that ensued.

But his missing Iggy was a palpable longing, something that kept him awake at night imagining what it might be like to have Iggy there in bed next to him, something that plagued his mind through a great deal of each day.

He felt like an ass because he hadn't yet told his mother about Iggy. He didn't think he could without her saying something to one of her friends, and then the whole affair would be a part of neighborhood gossip. He loved his mother, and he knew she supported him no matter what, but didn't trust her to keep her mouth shut. And that was a hard thing. He was in love for the first time in his life, but he couldn't even tell his mother he was seeing someone because she could blow all of this for him with one word to the wrong person.

Jason Matarazzo, the Dallas shortstop, walked by and slapped his back. Jason was from the old neighborhood; his parents lived down the street from Matt's cousin Gina, so they'd become fast friends. It was nice to have a friend on the team, but it still all felt new and superficial.

"You ready for the home opener?" Jason asked.

"As ready as I'll ever be."

"You'll be fine. It's hot out there today, though."

That was the other thing about Texas. This April felt like an August did in New York. There was no gradual ease into summer; the hot weather just punched you in the face.

Jason waved and left the locker room, so Matt went through his routine. He'd had to develop a slightly different one in Dallas. He felt silly for doing it, but one of his superstitious things now was keeping one of Iggy's baseball cards in his pocket during games. He felt like it brought him a little bit of luck.

IGGY SURVEYED the field from the dugout. Opening day festivities had included a lot of pomp and circumstance, which had cut short batting practice. Iggy swung his arms, feeling stiff, wishing he'd had space for a few extra swings instead of what looked like an entire marching band playing on the field.

"So," Jake Caballo said, walking up next to Iggy, "there's a rookie playing for St. Louis that we gotta watch out for. They benched him for a lot of the exhibition games, but he's in the lineup tonight. Ronnie Smithfield. He's batting in the five-hole."

"Okay," said Iggy. "Why am I watching out for him?"

"Secret weapon." Jake tapped his nose. "This kid played ball for Rice, was part of that team that cleaned up the college play-offs a couple of years ago. Rumor has it he can hit pretty much anything but that he tends to hit 'em toward third base. When he's not hitting home runs, he hits into double plays."

Iggy nodded. "Good to know." He looked across at the opponents' dugout and scanned the names on the jerseys. *Smithfield* was on the back of a thin guy with a wispy blond beard.

Everything felt routine, but nothing did. So much was the same as last season, and the Eagles had played well during spring training, but being back at FSB Stadium highlighted for Iggy that Matt was no longer there. He wondered if everyone else felt Matt's absence in the same way, like a hole in the lineup. Based on the bits of commentary he'd been hearing through Cary, most people had decided Matt's career was over anyway, so the odds of him ever coming back seemed slim.

Dallas felt about a million miles away.

The weird thing was that no one talked about it. No one so much as acknowledged that Matt was gone. The only time Iggy had heard anyone even mention Matt was when a fight broke out between a couple of rookies in the locker room and Roger had said, "Matt would have put a stop to that but quick."

Iggy hadn't talked to Matt much since the season started because their schedules were so incompatible, and that was probably contributing to his irritability. So much for their separation being easy.

When the game started, Iggy decided to throw himself into it. His job was something he could focus on to get his mind off Matt. But, of course, every part of the game was tied to a memory. Iggy stared across the diamond at Alvarez and missed the simple camaraderie the infield had, missed seeing Matt standing there, missed the little winks and nods Matt would send his way over the course of a game. He looked out from the dugout during the bottom of the inning and kept seeing Matt walking up to the plate.

"You all right, Ig?" asked Greg Letum.

"Yeah," he said. "Just got the feeling this is going to be a long season."

Chapter Fifteen

THE EAGLES came to Dallas the third week of April.

Matt was thrilled, although he tried to keep his expectations tempered. The knee was a problem. By the time he'd arrived at the stadium that morning, the pain had morphed from a gentle throb to a slicing stab. But sitting out this game was not an option. The opportunity to just be on the same field as Iggy was too great to give up.

Yikes, when had he become such a sentimental fool?

Matt slathered on a thick layer of pain relief cream over his sore parts and then wrapped up his knee. He was so used to doing it now that he could put together an efficient brace in his sleep. It still hurt like hell, but the cream took the edge off. Experimentally he ran the length of the locker room and back, and his leg seemed to hold up pretty well, even if pain jolted through his leg every time his foot made impact. He definitely had to go see the staff doctor… after the game.

He went back to his locker and started the pregame routine. As he tucked Iggy's card into his pocket, he thought, *You'll see the real thing soon enough*, and felt a giddy thrill at that. He'd been hoping to see Iggy that morning, but the Eagles' flight had been delayed. He had gotten a text message about an hour before the game: *Dinner tonight. You pick the place. Can't wait. Love you.* So there was that.

O'Kelly, Dallas's left fielder, stuck his head in the locker room and said, "You coming, Blanco?"

"Be right there."

Although it wasn't unprecedented for players to have friends on other teams, most fraternizing happened after the game. That didn't stop Matt from thinking about sneaking over to the opposing team's locker room, although he ultimately decided against it. He was so anxious to see Iggy he practically shook with it.

As he walked out toward the field, he wondered idly if that made him pathetic. He didn't really care.

It was a sunny day, and the air was hot and dry. Matt thought that was one thing Dallas had over New York; yeah, it was hot, but it was much less muggy, and the air felt less oppressive.

He slipped into the dugout and looked across the field. He saw Iggy in the opponents' dugout, and as if summoned, Iggy turned his head. Their eyes met. Matt had to fight to keep the smile off his face.

"How's your knee?" asked Sam Jackson, Dallas's manager. "Heard it was bothering you last week."

"It feels great," said Matt. Nothing would keep him from playing this game.

IGGY HAD the sense that something awful was about to happen. He wasn't sure why. It was a gorgeous day. The Eagles were playing well. Matt was nearby, which was comforting. But his stomach churned with anxiety just the same.

Matt came up to bat in the sixth inning. Iggy watched from his vantage point at third base. He had thought he'd seen Matt limp the previous inning, but he wondered now if he'd imagined it. He was becoming such a mother hen. Matt looked solid now, going through his little prebatting dance, walking smoothly up to the plate, and then assuming a strong stance. He hit a double off the third pitch, then ran like he was completely free of pain, and Iggy felt his pulse kick up with the proximity.

This was exquisite torture, to be this close to Matt without being able to say anything.

He looked at Matt where he stood at second. They made eye contact, and Matt smiled. That was something, Iggy thought. He consoled himself with the fact that they were having dinner in just a few hours, and then he'd have Matt all to himself for a night.

The batter who was up then hit a line drive toward left field. Everyone took off running, including Matt, who was headed right for Iggy. He stepped on the bag and adjusted his hat.

"Well, hello, stranger," Matt said. His grin was so wide and so deliriously happy-looking that Iggy couldn't help but grin back.

"Hello yourself."

But they couldn't speak much. For one thing, the Dallas base coach was within earshot. Also, there was a game to play. Matt stepped off the bag and started to get a bit of a lead toward home. And that was strange, because it should have been Iggy's job to keep him from doing that, to get him out. He didn't especially want to.

Iggy looked around and tried to refocus on the game. The play had gone toward first, so the batter was out and a new batter was up. There was only one out. The batter hit a pop-up, which Roger moved to catch. Matt ran toward home.

Then suddenly he was on the ground.

Silence descended over the field, although Iggy wasn't sure if it was in his imagination or if everyone really had gone quiet. Since he was the closest, Iggy ran over to Matt and knelt beside him. He looked unconscious. Iggy saw he was breathing, but his eyes were closed. Then he groaned, and his eyes fluttered open.

"Iggy?"

"What happened?"

"My knee."

"Are you okay?"

"Hurts like a motherfucker."

Iggy looked at Matt's knee and could tell even through the uniform pants that it was already starting to swell.

"Iggy?" Matt's hand started to snake up.

"I'm here, baby," he said, softly. "Help is coming."

Matt seemed to understand what Iggy was implying and dropped his hand. "Don't leave," he said.

"I can't stay."

The medic got to Matt just then and ordered Iggy away, so Iggy backed up toward third base, not knowing what else to do.

Game play stopped while the medic and a couple of other medical personnel saw to Matt. Iggy watched, unable to breathe as they examined him. Then the medic and a guy in scrubs helped Matt up. He leaned on both men and hopped off the field on one foot.

All Iggy knew once Matt was escorted off the field was that Dallas put in a pinch runner to take over for him and that the game went on as if he'd never been there. But Iggy's heart was somewhere in the depths of the stadium, his mind on a man he loved more than maybe any other person in the world. He had to keep playing as if nothing had happened. He didn't know if he could.

PAIN RADIATED out of his knee and through his whole body. That was mostly what Matt was aware of, although the nurse who couldn't seem to put in an IV kept buzzing around him like a fly in his periphery.

"Torn ACL," the doctor said. "Among other things. That knee is a mess. How long has it been bothering you?"

Matt tried to focus on the doctor. They'd given him something for the pain, but that had only succeeded in making his head foggy. His knee still hurt like someone had shoved a knife through it. "Um. A while." At the doctor's raised eyebrow, he added, "Maybe a year?"

"You've been walking around on that knee for a year?" The doctor scribbled something on his clipboard. "Why didn't you get it checked out sooner?"

"I did. My physical therapist in New York said he wanted to send me to a surgeon, but I refused."

"Well, I'm not giving you a choice. I know how you sports types are, but I will tell you this. You get reconstructive surgery on that knee, or you'll never be able to walk again, let alone play baseball. It's a pretty standard procedure, and it will seriously reduce your pain."

"Will I be able to play again?"

"Next season. Maybe." There wasn't much optimism in the doctor's voice.

"If I'd gotten surgery sooner, would that have made a difference?"

The doctor dropped his arm and slid the clipboard into its slot. "Don't play that game with yourself. It doesn't matter. Would it have made a difference? Maybe so, but it might have ended your career sooner as well. It sure as hell doesn't make a difference now, though, does it?"

"Are you always this much of an asshole?"

"Yep. I'm going to try to get your surgery scheduled as soon as possible, but that will probably be tomorrow morning. In the meantime, Hailey will keep you in pain meds. You have any allergies we should know about? You're not on other medications? Or anything else?"

"Are you asking about steroids?"

"You take any?"

"No, of course not."

"Because I'd rather you be honest and avoid an unpleasant reaction than for you to uphold your position."

"I just take the pain meds, and only when the knee is really bad. The only thing I've taken in the last forty-eight hours is what the paramedics gave me." He hadn't taken anything in anticipation of Iggy's visit, because he wanted to be awake and lucid for it. He wasn't sure if it upset him more that his career was effectively over or that he wouldn't be able to spend tonight with Iggy.

What had happened to his priorities?

"You have visitors," the doctor said. "I'll be back in a little while. If you get tired, signal Hailey, and she'll make everyone leave."

Matt had to assume that Hailey was the buzzing nurse who had, thank God, finally inserted an IV in his arm. They were alone briefly, and she smiled at him. He supposed she was pretty, if you were into small, pale women with delicate faces, and not burly Latino men.

Matt sighed and rested on the pillow. He hoped the pain meds would kick in soon and at least put him to sleep or something.

Matarazzo and O'Kelly and a couple of other guys from the Dallas team strolled in.

"How did the game go?" Matt asked.

Matarazzo and O'Kelly glanced at each other. Matarazzo said, "Rodriguez hit a three-run homer in the eighth, and we never came back from that. Final score was 6–2."

Matt wondered if it was blasphemous to be proud of Iggy at the expense of his new team.

"How are you doing?" O'Kelly asked.

"It hurts like a bitch. I'm, uh, probably out the rest of the season."

Matarazzo and O'Kelly murmured sympathetically, but then things turned awkward. These guys were his teammates, but they still barely knew each other.

When things wound down, O'Kelly said, "So basically the whole Eagles team is in the waiting room. I'll send them in."

That perked up Matt's spirits. He decided to postpone summoning Hailey back with more drugs.

Roger, Cruz, Iggy, and five other guys filed into the room. Matt couldn't remember when he'd been happier to see any of them.

"Man, are you guys a sight for sore eyes," Matt said.

"How is the knee?" asked Roger.

Matt looked at Iggy, and their eyes met. He tried to convey what he could in a glance, but it was hard with the rest of the guys standing around.

"Surgery," Matt said. "We should maybe keep this quick, because the only things standing between me and a whole lot of narcotics are you guys."

"Thanks, man," said Cruz. "We love you too."

"How are things back in New York?"

"Alvarez is playing well," Iggy said.

"Yeah, but he's a dick," said Roger. "Any guy who becomes the center of a bidding war like that is bound to be."

Cruz laughed. "Leave it to Roger to tell it like it is."

"I asked Bill if we could borrow the bus to come over here to see you," Caballo said, "but Alvarez put up this big stink. I was like, whatever, dude, you don't have to come."

"Why would he give a shit if we took the bus?" Iggy asked.

"That's what I wanted to know," said Caballo. "I told him, 'Hey, Blanco is our friend, and he got hurt, and we're gonna go see him. *You* can go fuck yourself.'"

"That *is* the proper response," said Jones.

"How long are you going to be on the DL?" Iggy stood at the foot of the bed, and he lifted his hand as if he were about to touch Matt's foot, but then shoved both hands in his pockets.

Realizing belatedly that Iggy had asked him a question, he said, "Don't know. Depends how the surgery goes." Although Matt was pretty sure the answer to that question was *forever.*

God, he wanted to touch Iggy. He would have settled for just a hug, but even that felt loaded. Dudes hugging each other were too, well, gay. But his arms ached to be wrapped around Iggy, and his heart pounded whenever he looked at him, and he wanted too much to seek comfort in those arms, to feel his soft skin under his hands, to just be near him. He had to work hard to school his face not to show any of that.

"Well, for our sakes, I hope you do sit out the rest of the season," said Cruz.

Iggy rolled his eyes and elbowed Cruz in the stomach. "That's a terrible thing to say."

"Do you really want to spend the ALCS playing against this guy?"

"No, but Matt, I really do hope you get better soon. I know we'd all like to see you in the field again."

"Yeah, man," said Roger. "It's fucking weird to be playing against you, but I'd rather have you on the field than off."

Matt nodded. "Me too." But did he really feel that way? He was starting to wonder. More than anything, he felt tired. Tired of being away from New York, tired of the pain, tired of missing Iggy, tired of pretending they were just buddies. Was baseball really worth sacrificing everything else?

"You okay?" Iggy asked.

"Yeah, I'm just tired. It's really great to see you guys, and I'm happy you came by, but I gotta catch some z's. The doc is trying to get my surgery scheduled for first thing tomorrow."

"We'll leave you, then," said Roger.

"Feel better," said Iggy.

After everyone filed out—Iggy was the last to go, and he gave Matt a sad little wave on his way out the door—Matt pushed the button to summon Hailey. At least the meds would put him to sleep so he could forget all this pain for a while. And he knew the pain wasn't just physical.

Chapter Sixteen

THE EAGLES won the second game of the series, but the heat seemed to be wearing everyone out, so rather than celebrating, the team went back to the hotel to go to bed early. Iggy stood in his room, trying to decide if he wanted to get room service or just go to sleep. Before he decided, someone knocked on the door. Iggy opened it to find Roger. He stood wringing his hands for a long moment before he spoke. "He's out of surgery. I'm going to the hospital. You want to come?"

"Yes," Iggy said. He grabbed his wallet and followed Roger down to the lobby.

"I already called a cab," Roger said.

"We're not going with the whole team?"

Roger sighed and stopped walking abruptly. He leaned close to Iggy and whispered, "Look, I know about you and Matt." This was news to Iggy, who had to fight to keep the reaction off his face now that they were in the lobby. "I invited you to come along because I think seeing you would do him some good. Plus, if we go together…."

"It looks less suspicious."

Roger nodded.

A bellhop signaled toward the approaching cab, and they got in. The ride to the hospital was tense. Iggy wondered how long Roger had known about the relationship between him and Matt. He wondered what Roger thought. In an effort to make nice, Iggy said, "I appreciate your taking me with you."

Roger nodded. "Sorry for all the silence," he said under his breath. "I'm just worried."

Iggy was too, more so when they got to the hospital and a nurse let them into Matt's room. Matt's eyes were closed, but Iggy knew from the strained expression on his face that he wasn't asleep.

At least he had a private room. Iggy supposed all of Matt's money at least afforded him this much. This hospital had a lot of security as well, more guards than Iggy suspected would have been there otherwise.

As Iggy and Roger approached the bed, Roger pulled the door closed.

"Hey, Matt," Roger said.

Matt opened his eyes. He looked first at Roger and then at Iggy. His gaze met Iggy's.

Roger said, "Just us this time. I thought you'd be more comfortable with less of a crowd."

Matt nodded and worked to sit up. Iggy sat in the chair next to the bed. He glanced behind him to ascertain whether he could be seen through the narrow window in the door. He looked up at Roger, who nodded almost imperceptibly.

Roger took Matt's hand, and they did some kind of improvised handshake. When Roger moved to grab a chair from across the room, Iggy took Matt's hand in his own, intertwined their fingers. He leaned down and kissed Matt's knuckles. Matt murmured something nonsensical, but it sounded like appreciation. "Iggy," he whispered.

"How was the surgery?"

Matt shrugged. Then he blinked and looked away.

"Matt?"

When Matt looked back at Iggy, there were tears in his eyes.

Not knowing what else he could do, Iggy pulled Matt into his arms. Matt's arms came around him, and Iggy felt him sob in earnest, his body shaking with it. Roger looked on but kept his distance.

"You're okay," Iggy said, stroking his back. He kept repeating that and just held him. He felt Matt pull at a fistful of his shirt. They stayed like that for a long time.

Roger settled into his chair and frowned.

The little breakdown was a lot like a flash thunderstorm. Matt eased up and lay back down, wiping at his eyes. He inhaled deeply and then let out a shaky breath. He pinched the bridge of his nose. "Sorry for losing it like that. I don't know what the hell is wrong with me."

"Totally understandable," Iggy said.

"Yeah, man," said Roger. "It's been a rough couple of days."

Matt looked at his knee. "Surgery went okay, but they want to go back in tomorrow. I guess the damage is even worse than they thought. So I'm out of the game for the rest of the season."

"That sucks," said Iggy, taking Matt's hand again. "Are you in a lot of pain?"

"I think my career is over." He stared unfocused at the wall behind Roger.

"Come on," Roger said. "I know your knee's been bothering you for a while, but you get it fixed up, do some rehab, you'll be good as new next season."

Matt shook his head. "No." He looked at the window. "I've been thinking about it ever since I woke up in the hospital. The doctors are sure I'll be able to walk, maybe even run, with no problem, but I'm pretty sure my ball-playing days are over. Plus, I can't—" He stopped and coughed. "I can't do this shit anymore. I miss New York. I miss both of you. This season has been completely awful. The Dallas players are fine, but I'm so…." He shook his head and swallowed. "I think this is it. I hang up my cleats at the end of the season. Then I'll come home."

"Are you sure?" Iggy asked.

Matt looked at him. "I wake up every goddamned morning missing you. I thought we could do this. I really thought you were right and we could make a relationship work during the season, but it's so hard."

Iggy shook his head. "Please don't quit baseball on my account. I know how much it means to you."

"I'm done, Ig. I want to come home. I want to be with you. I want to be back in New York. Me and baseball, I think we're over."

"Come on, that's the injury talking," said Roger.

"No." Matt wiped at his eyes again. "God, Iggy. I've been looking forward to seeing you for weeks, and then when I finally do, all these other people are around, and I can't…." He stole a glance at the window in the door. "I couldn't do this." He reached up and cupped a hand behind Iggy's head and then pulled him down for a kiss.

And what a kiss it was. They'd hardly seen each other in three months, and this simple meeting of lips felt like everything. Matt's mouth was dry, his lips chapped, but Iggy didn't care. He'd missed this so much. He hadn't been letting himself feel it, hadn't let himself think about it, but his longing for Matt was like a stone sitting in his chest. Suddenly that stone burst open, and Iggy felt everything, from the last time they'd made love before Matt moved to Dallas, to every late-night phone call or text message, to all the times he woke up in the middle of the night because he'd reached for someone who wasn't there.

Roger cleared his throat.

Iggy reluctantly lifted his head, breaking the kiss. Matt closed his eyes and frowned. He looked so tired, and he wondered how much of that was just the pain from the knee injury. Unable to help himself, Iggy smoothed Matt's hair away from his face. He hoped Matt found it soothing.

"Are you in a lot of pain?" Iggy asked, since Matt hadn't answered the first time.

"It does hurt, but not as bad as yesterday. Of course, they put some kind of local anesthetic on it."

"Should we get a nurse in here to give you more medication?"

"Not yet. It'll make me sleepy, and then I'll miss this." He reached up and caressed Iggy's face.

It was nice, but Iggy was hyperconscious of Roger, who just sat there looking at them.

"Are you staying in Dallas to recuperate?" Roger asked.

"I don't know. I've thought about flying home. Maybe let my mother take care of me for a couple of weeks and then move back into my old place. It's just sitting there empty since I never got around to leasing it." He squeezed Iggy's hand. "I'm renting a house in Fort Worth that I like well enough, but I have trouble sleeping at night. There's not enough noise."

Roger laughed. "You can take the Brooklyn boy out of the city...."

Matt smiled. "Thank you for coming down. Thanks, Roger, for bringing Iggy."

"What are friends for?"

There was a knock on the door. Iggy let go of Matt's hand. A nurse came in. "Visiting hours are ending, gentlemen."

"How long are you in for?" asked Iggy, standing.

"At least a couple more days."

Roger said, "We'll come back tomorrow before we fly back East."

Matt nodded. "I'd like that." He yawned. "You win today at least?"

"Yup," said Iggy. "3–2."

"Sweep 'em."

That made everyone laugh.

In the cab back to the hotel, Iggy said, "Thank you for doing that. It means a lot."

"I know. That was weird, though. He's never... I mean, I've never met one of his significant others. He keeps everything so private. And seeing it was just... it caught me off guard, I guess. Made it real in a way it wasn't before. Not that it was bad. Just weird."

"Okay."

"I hope you're not offended."

"No."

"We can go back tomorrow. Make sure you see him before we leave."

"Thank you. It does mean a lot to me." Iggy took a deep breath. "How long have you known?"

"A while."

Iggy didn't push further, conscious of the cabdriver eavesdropping on their conversation. He supposed it was good that someone knew, that Matt had a friend he could trust.

He gazed out the window and thought about the situation. He wondered if it was selfish of him to look forward to Matt coming home.

THE SECOND surgery got postponed, so Matt had nothing to do the next day besides sleep and watch TV. He got so bored he even called his mother.

"I looked at flights. Your father has to stay here for a work thing, but I can be out there tomorrow morning," she said.

"You don't have to do that."

"Who else is going to take care of you in Dallas?"

There were shades of an old argument that Matt didn't want to bring up in the question. "Ma, I'll be fine."

"You have a secret boyfriend, don't you? You won't tell your old mother who you're seeing."

"I don't have…." He sighed. A nurse came in to check his vitals. "There's no one in Dallas."

"You lead this lonely life, Matteo. I worry for you."

"I'll come home, all right? Just as soon as they clear me to travel. You can fawn over me all you want when I'm back in New York."

When that didn't get him anywhere, he begged off, telling his mother he was tired. He really didn't want her in Dallas. He was almost forty years old; he didn't need his mother to take care of him. But that was the old argument, wasn't it? All through his early twenties, his mother had nagged him about finding a wife so he'd have someone at home to take care of him. When he was twenty-five, he'd finally broken down and told her there would be no wife. "A husband, then," she'd said without missing a beat.

He loved his mother, he did, but he did not want to deal with her right then. What he wanted was to wallow in his pain alone for a while, to privately mourn the loss of his career. Or, really, what he wanted was a week alone with Iggy, but that certainly wasn't in the cards.

The doctor came in while he was watching a news report on himself.

"Dallas management expects Blanco to be out for at least a month," the sports reporter said.

"Did you tell them that?" Matt asked the doctor.

"I have taken a firm stance against talking to either the media or your bosses. I have no desire to break the HIPAA rules. How do you feel today?"

"Better. So what you're telling me is my bosses just made that up."

The doctor lifted the sheet and took a look at Matt's knee. "Given your age and the extent of the injury, I'd say you shouldn't play for three months. You don't even realize it, but I would guess you've been walking on that leg wrong for as long as it's been injured. You're not one of those young guys— what was that kid's name? Burns? The one who had his appendix removed and then went back to playing the next day."

"Yeah, I heard about that."

"That's nuts. Maybe I'm too conservative, but it's much better to get everything back in working order before you go back to putting stress on your body. You go back too soon, you risk a graver injury."

"Understood."

The doctor replaced the sheet. "Huh. You're much more agreeable today."

"I decided to do my recovery back in New York, if that's okay with you."

"Yeah, that should be fine. I'll look into rehab facilities there. I have a buddy in sports medicine at one of the hospitals there. He might know of the best place for you. Any special reason?"

"If I can't play baseball, I'd rather spend the time with my family."

"Good. That might help speed along your recovery." The doctor picked up the chart. "Well, everything looks as good as can be expected. We're going to open up your knee again tomorrow afternoon. Ring the nurse if the pain gets worse or you start to feel feverish."

"Gotcha."

An hour later, he settled in to watch the Eagles-Dallas game. It was a pretty tight game, but Iggy was on fire, and Alvarez proved pretty agile on his feet. The Eagles won by two runs.

At the end, a local reporter interviewed an out-of-breath Iggy at the edge of the field. A thrill went through Matt as he watched the interview. It was just so wonderful to see Iggy's face, even if he couldn't touch it. Iggy panted out some platitudes about hard work and working together as a team, and Matt was so proud that Iggy was doing well.

He really was a sentimental old fool.

CRUZ HAD insisted on coming along, which put a serious crimp on Iggy's plans. Matt seemed happy enough to see Cruz, but the longer he remained in the room, cracking jokes and chatting away, the more distressed Iggy became that his last meeting with Matt was going to be distant and casual, when all he really wanted to do was hold Matt and kiss him silly and make a happy memory for when he went back home.

He'd gotten Matt a gift, and now it felt heavy in his pocket. But he couldn't give it to Matt without giving himself away, could he?

Matt seemed to notice his agitation. "Ig? Are you all right?"

Everyone turned and looked at him. "I'm fine."

He tried to make eye contact with Roger in a futile attempt to mentally communicate that he would like a few moments alone with Matt, but Cruz kept distracting everyone.

This was torture.

Iggy fingered the box in his pocket. He worried that if he opened his mouth, just the tone of his voice would give him away. Why was this so hard? It never had been before.

Probably because he had to leave Matt again. That was hard enough the first time, and they'd had the entire night before to spend alone together. Now he just felt like he would lose it if he so much as moved.

Iggy didn't listen to Cruz's yammering and instead mostly stared at the floor, but he heard Cruz say, "Right, Iggy?"

"Huh?"

"Wow, where the hell are you?"

Iggy grunted. "I'm here. Sorry, I'm tired. I guess I spaced out."

"I was just telling Matt that Roger said you had a little gift for him."

Iggy panicked. How was he going to play this off? He swallowed and said, "Well, I do, but it's just a stupid small thing. It's not…." He sighed.

"When is your flight?" Matt asked.

"In three hours," Iggy said miserably. "Haverman wanted to use the travel day for extra batting practice."

When Iggy looked up, Matt was smiling. He looked tired, and his skin was a little puffy, but he looked so much himself too, handsome and a little disheveled, and Iggy found just looking at him to be such a comfort. Was this what love was like all the time?

Fuck it, he thought. He squared his shoulders and walked toward the bed. He pulled the box from his pocket. After he handed it to Matt, he stood by the bed, bracing himself for whatever would happen.

Matt opened it. The box held a silver charm that Iggy had found, oddly enough, in a sports store. It was a replica of a masculine leg bent at an angle, as if it were running. It was a strange piece, but Iggy thought Matt would get the joke.

Matt let out a little gasp. "The Wizard brought me a new knee," he said softly.

"Yeah. If only that little charm would let you play baseball again."

Matt smiled and gazed at the box. Feeling like he needed to fill the silence, Iggy added, "I mean, I saw it, and I thought of you, and…." Then he dropped his arms.

"It's wonderful, thank you." Matt rubbed at his eye with the butt of his hand. "It sucks that you have to leave so soon." He looked up and met Iggy's gaze. Iggy wanted to stand there and look at Matt forever, but he turned away. It was too much.

"Oh, just kiss already," said Cruz.

Iggy's attention snapped toward him. "What?"

Cruz rolled his eyes. "You're fucking, right? That's why the tension in this room is so thick?"

"Wha-what makes you say that?"

Cruz crossed his arms over his chest. "That night we went out last year. When both of you so conveniently disappeared. Roger hands me this note that some chick had allegedly asked him to pass to you, but Blanco was the only person he talked to most of the night."

Iggy said, "That's not—"

"Look, it's fine. So you're gay? What do I care? My brother's gay. We get along great."

"You want to maybe not say it so loud?" said Matt.

"How long?" Cruz asked.

Matt shifted so he was sitting up a little straighter on the bed. He glanced toward the door, which was closed. "How long have I been gay, or how long have Iggy and I been together?"

"Both, neither, I don't care."

Matt sighed. "Well, I've been gay my whole life, as it happens. The giveaway was the awful crush I had on this kid Robbie in my ninth-grade biology class. The only people who know are my immediate family, Iggy, Roger, and now you, so I assume you can keep this under wraps?"

Cruz mimed zipping his lips.

"I think you left every dude you ever slept with off that list," Roger said.

"Do you make them sign nondisclosure agreements when you hand them cab fare?" asked Cruz.

"I've been very discreet. But let's not talk about past conquests in front of my current boyfriend, okay?"

"It'll be a year at the end of July," Iggy blurted.

"You certainly didn't waste any time," said Cruz. "Well, congratulations. You can count on me to guard your secret." He turned to Matt. "He's a little young for you, Blanco."

"I'm twenty-six," said Iggy. "Why does everybody treat me like I'm an infant?"

"Because we're senior citizens in baseball years," said Roger. "So you *are* an infant."

"Ig?"

Iggy looked down at Matt, who was still holding the little box with the charm.

"Kiss me."

Mindful of Cruz, Iggy bent down and gave Matt a peck on the lips.

"Weak," said Cruz. "If you're gonna bother, at least really kiss him."

So Iggy rolled his eyes, but he couldn't keep the smile off his face as he bent to kiss Matt again. This time he parted his lips and slipped his tongue into Matt's mouth and *really* kissed him. It was nice to be able to show their affection in front of other people.

"Love you," Iggy whispered before he stood back up again.

"Love you too," said Matt. "Thanks for the gift."

"The *Wizard of Oz* thing was a giveaway also," said Cruz. "I always kind of wondered if you were a friend of Dorothy, Blanco."

"You did not," said Roger. "Matt, I think we have to get going. Gotta catch that flight."

"Thanks for coming by, guys. It means a lot."

"Thanks for humoring us," said Cruz. "We know you really wanted to see Iggy."

Matt shrugged but didn't deny it.

Iggy risked one last peck on Matt's cheek. Then he left Matt there with his new knee.

Chapter Seventeen

BEING BACK in his own apartment was a relief.

After being away for four months, Matt decided that one of the smartest things he'd ever done was to keep paying his cleaning lady, because the place was spotless.

Raul the doorman came in behind him, carrying his luggage. On crutches, Matt propelled himself farther into the apartment—his *home* in the way Dallas was never going to be—and directed Raul to drop the bags near the couch. In the three weeks since Matt had gotten out of the hospital, he'd talked O'Kelly and Matarazzo into coming over and helping him pack up all of his stuff. Then he shipped everything home and sublet his house to a rookie pitcher. He was never going back to Dallas if he could help it.

"You just here for a visit?" asked Raul.

"Nope. Back for good."

"I saw on the TV that you were injured." Raul pointed to the crutches. "But you get better, yes? Play for the Eagles again?"

"I don't think so."

Raul nodded gravely. "You be okay, though. New York is glad to have you back."

Matt felt that deep in his gut. The moment he'd touched down at LaGuardia, a sense of comfort and ease drifted over him. "I belong here."

"Yes. You need help, you call the desk, okay?"

"Yeah." Matt fished a few bills from his pocket and handed them to Raul. "I appreciate the help."

"Thank you, sir."

When Raul was gone, Matt surveyed his kingdom. The apartment was neat as a pin and a little impersonal-looking—Iggy had said something to that effect once, hadn't he?—but he knew every nook and cranny in it. He knew where the nicks in the hardwood floor were, knew which hinges were a little sticky, knew which lights flickered before they went on. He also had visceral memories of making out with Iggy on that sofa, of tearing off Iggy's clothes in the hallway, of having Iggy in his bed.

He looked around and sighed happily. He was home.

IGGY CAME by that night, and it was like old times in some ways, and yet it wasn't.

Raul called to let Matt know Iggy was on the way up, just as he had dozens of times before. Matt hadn't always waited by the door, although sometimes he did. This time he had the crutches, which were new. He unlocked the door and then shuffled back a little. His heart pounded. When Iggy knocked, he yelled, "It's open!"

The door opened slowly, and Iggy poked his head around it. A thrill went through Matt as each delicious inch of him was revealed, from his dark hair to his dark skin to the curves of the muscles on his arms. Iggy came in and frowned, pointing to Matt's crutches. "What are you doing standing there like that?"

"Waiting for you."

"You shouldn't be putting your weight on your legs. Go sit down. Come on, I'll help you."

"Kiss me."

One of the things Matt loved about Iggy was that he wasn't shy once they were alone. He let the door slam shut behind him, and then he stepped forward and took Matt's face in his hands. There was nothing reticent or careful about the kiss; it was hard and forceful. To Matt, Iggy's lips seemed to be saying, *Hello. I missed you. Don't ever leave me again.*

Iggy pulled back a little and grinned. "Happy now?"

"Very. Now take me to bed."

Iggy's grin turned wry. "What, no dinner? No wine or flowers? Just, 'Kiss me. Take me to bed'?"

"Ig, I have missed you something awful. We haven't been together in almost four very long months. I'm going out of my mind with wanting you. We can eat later."

Iggy's smile wavered a little. He gestured toward Matt's bad knee. "Can you even?"

"I assure you, my dick works just fine."

"I'm sure. But I don't want to hurt you."

"So we'll be careful. Don't make me beg."

Iggy sighed. "You're a hard man to say no to, Matt Blanco."

"I'm hard in other ways too."

Iggy rolled his eyes. "Fine. Come on, big guy."

Iggy led Matt to the bedroom as Matt hobbled behind him. Once they were in the room, Iggy paused and looked around.

"It's a little weird being back here."

Matt leaned his crutches against the wall and hopped on one foot over to the bed. "There will be time for reflection later." He sat down and wiggled back so his legs rested on the mattress. He pulled his T-shirt off with one hand.

"Matt...."

"You won't hurt me. I'll tell you if you bother the knee." Matt shimmied out of his sweatpants.

Iggy nodded and pulled off his own clothes. Matt sat back, leaning on his hands, and watched the show. Iggy did have a delicious body, finely honed, sculpted as the baseball elite had to be. His arms were really incredible—had they gotten bigger, or was Matt only just noticing?—and he looked strong and powerful and athletic and so beautiful.

When Iggy was down to his briefs, he crawled on the bed. He pushed Matt onto his back and then settled between Matt's legs. He hovered for a moment and then lowered himself until he was lying on Matt, until their growing erections met.

Iggy's skin was so familiar: the color and texture of it, the way Matt's hands fit over the muscle, the way everything felt under Matt's palms. Matt hadn't realized he'd memorized Iggy's body, but he was struck again by that same feeling he'd had when he'd come into the apartment and known where everything was. This was like coming home.

Matt lifted his head and kissed Iggy. He started slow, parting his lips slightly, dipping his tongue out to taste. Then he opened his mouth to let Iggy in. Iggy reciprocated, plunging his tongue into Matt's mouth, sliding it along Matt's teeth. Even Iggy's taste was familiar; his smell was comforting.

"God, I missed you," Iggy said when their lips parted for a second. Then he dove back in.

Iggy's cock was hard and pressing against Matt's thigh as they shifted their hips and tried to find the right position. Matt ran his hands down Iggy's back, aroused by the strength he found there. Iggy moved his mouth and began to nibble on Matt's jaw, skimmed his tongue down the length of Matt's neck, planted a kiss right on his Adam's apple. Matt bucked up to meet him, trying to press their bodies together.

Had it really been four months since they'd had sex? Matt still knew all of Iggy's secret places, still knew where his scars were, and still knew how to please him. He moved his hands into Iggy's briefs and cupped his ass. He knew the shape and texture of that too, surprisingly supple for a man who worked out as much as Iggy did, the skin there soft. Matt lifted his hands and slid the briefs down. Iggy shifted up to let him, and Matt looked down to see Iggy's hard cock revealed.

"You are so goddamned beautiful," Matt said. He kissed Iggy's mouth again and then wrapped his hand around Iggy's cock. Even *that* was familiar, the shape of it, the texture of it, the way it felt in Matt's hand.

But familiar certainly did not mean boring.

Iggy bit Matt's shoulder and then began to trail kisses all along his collarbone. He propped himself up on one hand and used the other to tweak Matt's nipples. Heat and arousal flooded Matt's body as he stopped trying to recount all of Iggy's features and started to just feel, to sink into the sensation of their bodies rubbing together, of the arousal pooling in his abdomen.

Iggy thrust his hips against Matt's hand, against Matt's cock. He backed away again. He hooked his fingers into Matt's briefs and dragged them down, careful when he got to Matt's knee. He bowed and kissed the bandage that still hid surgery scars and stitches. He tossed Matt's underwear somewhere behind him.

Then he was back, and they were fully naked and pressed together. Matt put his arms around Iggy and spread his legs as much as he could without bothering the knee. Iggy pushed his cock against Matt's and then took them both in his hand. He thrust and stroked.

Four months it had been. Matt went from zero to sixty in a heartbeat, it seemed. Because now he was hot and panting, and though he wanted to make love to Iggy slowly, he was dangerously close already.

"Ig…," he said.

Iggy moved his hand and pulled on Matt's balls, temporarily stopping the tide of orgasm from sweeping over him. Matt closed his eyes and put his arms around Iggy and held them together. He loved this man so much, wanted to show him how intense that love was, but this was going to be quick and dirty like teenagers did it.

There'd be time later.

Iggy lined them up again. He stroked their cocks together with his warm, calloused hands. The sensation of Matt's cock against Iggy's felt incredible. They fit together so well, Matt thought, their bodies so different— Matt was broad where Iggy was compact; Matt was soft from not working out much recently, but Iggy's body was all hard muscle—and yet still they just fit together. And the simple act of joining their bodies, of pressing them together, of searching out pleasure in each other, was everything. Matt kissed Iggy and shifted his hips up until their balls touched, and Iggy started to stroke faster, and all of it was hot and hard.

"Come for me like this," Iggy said.

"Yes," Matt whispered.

"I'm gonna come soon too."

Yes, that was what Matt wanted. He wanted friction and heat; he wanted dirty sex and sweet love; he wanted Iggy, in his life, in his bed, for always. And that was his last thought as his reptile brain took over. He thrust up against Iggy, struggling to get the right angle that would get him off. Iggy squeezed harder, thrust again, and then let out a moan. As soon as the first shot was fired, Matt surrendered to everything and let the orgasm power through him. He closed his eyes and arched his back, and then he was coming, shooting onto Iggy, onto himself, into the air. It didn't matter. None of it mattered, because he was back with Iggy, and that was where he belonged.

Iggy collapsed on top of him. Matt put his arms around him and held him close for a long time, savoring the sensation of having his lover back in his arms. When Iggy's breathing slowed, Matt thought he might be falling asleep, but then Iggy said, "I love you."

"I love you too. It's nice to be able to tell you that in person." After all those weeks of only being able to speak by phone or e-mail or text message, it really was wonderful to express how he felt with Iggy right there.

Iggy lifted his head and dropped a kiss on Matt's nose. He smiled. "How's your knee?"

"Feels wonderful."

"Pain meds?"

"Endorphins, I think. It'll probably start to hurt again soon. Although, actually, now that the surgery scars are healing, it feels better than it has in a long time. I haven't been taking the pain meds that often."

"Good. But what I hear you saying is your knee feels better because of the postorgasmic haze."

"Well, you know. The healing powers of good sex are legendary. Having an orgasm is supposed to help with headaches. I know I feel better now than I did before you got here. So I think if we have sex a few more times, I might be cured."

Iggy laughed. "Nice try."

"We'd have to have a lot of sex to make my knee better, I think."

"What a hardship."

"You can tell how upset I am by the prospect of that."

"I suppose I'll have to help you out. But I want you to know it's a sacrifice I'm willing to make."

Matt laughed and squeezed Iggy closer to him. He was content to just lie there, but then Iggy's stomach grumbled.

"I suppose I have to feed you," Matt said.

"Mmm. It's the least you can do if I'm expected to have all this sex with you to fix your knee. Gotta keep my strength up somehow."

GOING OVER to Matt's felt routine almost right away. Iggy wanted to spend as much time at Matt's as he could work into his schedule, which made him wonder how much longer he should keep his own apartment. It seemed like a lot of money to spend on something for the sake of appearances.

He waved at Raul on his way into the building and then headed up to Matt's floor. The door was locked when he got to the apartment, so Matt had to open it. Iggy felt a wave of guilt as he helped Matt back over to the sofa.

"Maybe I should just give you a key so I don't have to get off the couch when you come here," Matt said as he eased himself back down into the cushions.

"I'm sorry, baby," Iggy said. "Is the knee bad today?"

"It's all right. A little sore."

When Matt was settled, Iggy nodded and moved to go into the kitchen.

"Hey, where are you going?"

"I'm dying of thirst. I'm stealing water from your fridge."

"C'mere."

Iggy stood obediently in front of Matt.

Matt ran his hands up Iggy's sides and planted kisses on his stomach before he wrapped his arms around Iggy's waist. "I missed you."

"Since yesterday?"

"In general."

Iggy couldn't resist. He put his hands around Matt's head and hugged him close. They were clearly still recovering from Matt being in Dallas. "I missed you too. So much." It was amazing to be able to hold Matt again. He worried about Matt, about his knee and his state of mind, but he was so elated to just be able to touch Matt again that a lot of his worries drifted away.

The buzzer sounded. Iggy walked over to the intercom to answer it. When he picked up the receiver, Raul said, "Mr. and Mrs. Blanco are here. They're—ma'am, I can't let you up there until Mr. Blanco says it's okay."

"I'm his mother!" A woman's voice rang clearly through the speaker.

"It's fine, Raul. Send them up."

Matt shifted and winced as he tried to reposition his leg on the couch. "What's going on?"

"Apparently your parents are here."

Matt frowned. "Of course they are."

A few minutes later, there was a knock at the door. Iggy answered. A short, round woman pushed her way inside. She had blonde hair with dark roots and was holding a large pan. Hot on her heels was a tall man who looked a lot like Matt but with graying temples and sun-damaged skin. Mrs. Blanco bustled into the kitchen. "I brought you a lasagna," she said.

Matt met Iggy's gaze and raised an eyebrow. "No hello, Ma? No 'we're so glad you're back home'?"

Mr. Blanco walked over to the couch and shook Matt's hand. "We're glad you're back. You know your mother. She shows her love with food."

"I got sausage from that place on Avenue U!" she called.

Matt's father turned toward Iggy. "Ignacio Rodriguez. I saw that two-run homer you got in the game yesterday. Really great stuff. How many home runs is that this season? Twenty-three?"

"Twenty-seven. Sir. It's nice to meet you. I was just—" Iggy tried to concoct a way out of the conversation, or even out of the apartment. Had they just gotten caught? Could Iggy explain away his reasons for being in Matt's apartment?

"Ig, it's fine," said Matt.

Iggy wondered what was fine until Mrs. Blanco walked over and looked him up and down. "So you are the boyfriend. Of course, leave it to Matteo to find a baseball player. Always with this boy is baseball." She turned to Matt. "He's not Italian."

"I know, Ma."

"Rodriguez. Are you Puerto Rican?" she asked Iggy.

"Dominican."

She nodded. To Matt, she said, "At least he's not Irish."

Matt rolled his eyes.

"What do you think of the Yankees this season?" Mr. Blanco asked.

"Uh, well. There are a lot of injuries."

"Dad, don't give Iggy the third degree."

"Matteo, don't use that tone with your father."

Matt's parents took over the kitchen. Iggy turned to Matt and said softly, "I thought you weren't telling your parents about me."

"Ma was trying to set me up with every eligible bachelor in Bensonhurst. She thought I was all sad and lonely sitting here in the apartment by myself. So I felt like I had to come clean. She's on warning not to tell a soul."

Iggy supposed that was something. Meeting his boyfriend's parents seemed like such a normal thing in the otherwise not-so-normal life he was leading. Iggy thought about his own mother, still in the house he'd grown up in outside of Phoenix. Iggy had told her about Matt one night, and she was similarly sworn to secrecy, although she'd never been especially prone to gossip.

Matt's parents, however, provided a steady stream of commentary on everything from sports to people they all knew to city politics. Iggy felt overwhelmed by how loud the Blancos were, how fast they talked. They sat around the little table in Matt's kitchen and ate lasagna. Iggy felt a great deal of relief that Mr. and Mrs. Blanco seemed completely unfazed by him, so he put forth a good-faith effort to impress them. He smiled, he was polite, he ate a second helping of lasagna.

"So now," Mr. Blanco said as his wife cleared the plates. "The Eagles are a game out of first place. You're playing Oakland tomorrow?"

"Yes, sir."

"Enough with the sir! Call me Johnny. Now, this Oakland pitcher, Johansen? I read in *Sports Illustrated* that he has a wicked curveball, and—"

"Dad. Knock it off."

"He's sorry," Mrs. Blanco said. "We're sorry. It's just that we haven't met one of Matt's boyfriends in… well, ever. This is kind of a new experience."

"Is that why you came by unannounced?" Matt asked. "To ambush him?"

Mrs. Blanco frowned. "No, not to ambush. I'm not that ruthless. I will admit that I hoped he would be here."

"We knew the Eagles weren't playing today."

"But we wanted to see you too." She reached over and caressed Matt's face. "I wanted to make sure you were all right. I worry." She glanced at Iggy. She stage-whispered to Matt, "He's very handsome."

"I know," said Matt.

"Of course you do."

"Look," said Mr. Blanco, "you call us, you tell us you've blown out your knee, and you probably won't play baseball again. That's a hard thing to deal with. We just wanted to make sure you were okay with everything."

"I am," said Matt. "It was the right decision to move back here. There's nothing for me in Dallas."

"Does Dallas know that?" asked Iggy.

"They own me until the end of the season, I guess, but I'm not extending my contract. And my doctor says I can't play until October at the earliest, so what's the point?"

"The postseason?"

"Nah. Dallas is in rougher shape this season than anyone realizes. If they even make the play-offs, they'll probably fall apart in the Division Series."

"And now you are at least not alone anymore," said Mrs. Blanco.

Matt smiled at Iggy. "That's true."

Mr. Blanco nodded. To Iggy, he said, "I will admit, I had a hard time with Matt and…." He moved his hands in a circular motion as if that would generate the words he wanted to say. "The gay thing."

"Here we go," said Matt.

"Hush," said Mrs. Blanco.

"But we love him," said Mr. Blanco. "God saw fit to bring us three children, and all of them are wonderful. Matt is just as deserving of love as our daughters are."

"So now that he's done with baseball, he can have a family," Mrs. Blanco said.

"Ma."

"Matteo."

Iggy found himself giggling. He could just imagine Thanksgiving dinners with this crew, with everyone fighting for attention and talking over each other. But he felt how much they all loved each other too.

"Are you happy, Matt?" Mrs. Blanco asked.

"I wish I could still play baseball." He took Iggy's hand under the table. "But I'm at peace with that decision now. And yeah, I'm happy."

"That's all we can ask for. Now finish your lasagna."

Chapter Eighteen

MATT AND Iggy made out on the sofa, with Matt's bad leg dangling off the couch. It throbbed a little, but the pleasure he found at Iggy's hands, in the way their lips moved together, completely outweighed any twinge in his knee. Things were just getting really good when the phone rang.

"Don't answer it," Iggy said against his mouth.

"Can I at least see who is calling? If it's my mother, she's going to keep calling until I assure her I haven't died."

Iggy groaned. "Fine."

Matt grabbed his phone from the coffee table. The caller ID indicated it wasn't Matt's mother, but was his agent. He wasn't sure which was worse. "This can only be bad news," he said aloud.

Iggy kissed his neck and mumbled, "So don't answer it."

He almost didn't, but curiosity got the better of him. "Hi, A.J."

"I have news."

"Good or bad?"

The pause led Matt to believe it was bad, but then A.J. said, "I think you'll like it. I've got the paperwork on my desk for another trade."

Matt sat up and nudged Iggy away. "Wait, what? A.J., I already told you, I can't play any more this season, and I plan to retire at the end of it anyway. Can't I just get to the end of my contract without any more upheaval? Who the hell wants me?"

"The Eagles."

Matt nearly dropped the phone. "Huh?"

"The trading deadline is a week from now. If we expedite this, that puts you back on their lineup long enough to have a ceremony in which Matt Blanco gets to be an Eagle one last time and jersey number three gets retired."

"Are you kidding me?"

"No, not at all. I just got off the phone with Teddy Rothschild. I know that what happened in the off-season was awful, but apparently Eagles management thought it was the best move in order for them to have the team they wanted and for you to keep playing baseball. But everyone loves you, Matt. The fans, your old teammates, they all want this to happen. And it's hardly unprecedented. They did it for Nomar so he could retire from the Red Sox."

"I…. Wow."

"This is good, right?"

Matt hadn't had time to process it. But the more he thought about it, the more thrilled he became. It felt… right. "It is good. I'm…. That's really great. If you're behind this, I can't thank you enough."

"Great. I need you to sign some papers. I'll have a messenger bring them over to your place. How's your knee?"

"Better. Stiff, but it hurts less."

"Fantastic. Congratulations, Matt. I know deciding to retire was hard for you, but you can hardly look back at a career like yours and have any regrets."

Deciding to retire. It sounded strange when A.J. said it. But this was it, wasn't it? The end of his career. Soon he'd be retired. At the age of thirty-nine. How odd was that?

"No, I suppose not. No regrets."

When he got off the phone, Iggy was staring at him expectantly. "Sounded like good news," he said.

"My retirement has been moved up," Matt said.

"Aw, shit."

Matt held up his hand. "So that I can retire as an Eagle."

Iggy's face lit up. "That's wonderful!" He threw his arms around Matt.

"Yeah, I'm happy."

Iggy pulled away again. "Then why do you look upset?"

"I'm not upset."

"Something is bothering you."

Matt narrowed his eyes at Iggy. "You know me too well, I think."

"Talk to me, Matt."

He sighed. "Hearing the actual word 'retire' hit me in a strange way, I guess. I mean, this was my decision, and I've been thinking about it for a while, but now that it's official, it just really hit me that my baseball career is over."

"You're not having regrets, are you?"

He shook his head. No, he still felt like he'd made the right decision. "No regrets," he repeated. "But I guess I'm sad that it's the end."

Iggy nodded. "I can imagine."

But how could he know, really? Iggy was still so young. His career was just getting off the ground, and he had a promising one ahead of him. He was still at the beginning, still had so much to look forward to. Everything for Matt was ending.

"What will I do?" Matt asked.

Iggy ran his hands through Matt's hair. "We'll think of something. You can coach, maybe. Or be a TV commentator. Or, I don't know, what do retired people do? Go to the beach? Play golf?"

"I hate golf."

Iggy laughed. "You know what I mean. But take it one day at a time. You're still recovering from your surgery, and then you've got your whole life ahead of you. The possibilities are endless."

Matt admired Iggy's enthusiasm, but he couldn't quite get there himself. At least not yet. He needed more time to mourn his baseball career. A.J. was right, of course, that it was hard to look back at a career like that and have any regrets. And yet....

But Matt didn't want to think about it just yet. "This is weird, but I'm glad that team rules obligate you to be at my retirement ceremony. It will be nice to have you there even under the circumstances."

"Yeah," Iggy agreed. "Otherwise, I'd find a way."

"Really?"

"Of course. I love you. I want to be there for you, and this is a big deal."

Matt leaned back on the couch. It was sad that he'd gotten so used to hiding his relationship with Iggy that it was almost a habit. "Wouldn't it be great if you could be there as my boyfriend? Players bring their wives to events like this all the time. I'm glad you'll be there, but I'll have to pretend I'm there alone."

Iggy laid his head on Matt's shoulder. "It sucks."

Matt put his arm around Iggy. "I've never been much of an activist, you know? I didn't feel like I could be. My sister sent me a biography of Walt Whitman, and there's all this stuff in it about how Whitman didn't even have a name for what he was feeling when he looked at other men. As I read it, I keep thinking, 'I know what this is. But I can't even say it out loud.'"

"Cary keeps saying it's like Don't Ask, Don't Tell."

"Yeah, feels that way sometimes."

"Wait, you're reading a biography of Walt Whitman?"

"*Leaves of Grass* is one of my favorite books."

"Really?"

Matt rolled his eyes and stood up. "I know it's kind of a literary choice for a jock, but I read it for English class in eleventh grade or something, and it just spoke to me." He hobbled over to the bookcase and pulled off a leather-bound book. He opened it and flipped through the pages. "Have you read it?"

"I don't think so."

"Whitman was a Brooklyn boy, you know. So we had that in common, first of all. Some of these poems are about Whitman struggling to find the words to explain how he feels about other men, and when you're a gay kid from a big Italian Catholic family, you spend a lot of time with that too. When I was sixteen, I didn't know how to explain what I was feeling. I guess I empathized with him." He settled on a page and read silently for a moment. "I don't know if this was what Whitman meant, but I always thought that 'Song of Myself' was about self-expression more than anything else. It's about wanting the freedom to just stand there and say, 'This is who I am.' I never really got to do that. With my family, with you, yeah, but not with everyone. I have friends, close friends, guys I've known for years, and I've never told them I'm gay. They probably know, but I never said, and it...." He shook his head and put the book on the shelf.

"You have all these depths to you I keep stumbling upon. I.... That's amazing."

"Yeah. Well."

"I mean, what you just said was beautiful. And painful. And I know exactly how that feels."

"I lie every day to people I care about. I see couples walking down the street—straight, gay, they're all here in New York—and they'll just... hold hands. And I think, 'That'll never be me. I'll never get to do that.' I'll never be able to just walk down the street with my boyfriend and do something casual like take his hand, because then my life will end. And I hate that feeling, Iggy. I hate it. It eats at me. But I don't have any fucking choice."

Iggy motioned for Matt to come closer. Matt limped over to the couch and sat back down. Iggy took his hand and wove their fingers together. "I understand."

"I know you do." Matt sighed. "That's kind of what I like about you. You get me the way no one else I've ever been with gets me."

"It's not hopeless, you know. Tides are changing. There are gay characters on TV, gay politicians in elected office. Gay marriage is legal across the country. Could be soon, none of this will matter. No one will give a shit if there's a gay player on a professional sports team. You can walk down the street and proudly hold your boyfriend's hand."

Matt smiled, though he was still a little sad. He admired Iggy's optimism. "I hope that if that day comes, you're my boyfriend."

"I hope that too." Iggy leaned over and kissed his cheek.

Matt settled back into the couch and threw an arm around Iggy. "I do love you, Ig. I'm happy you will be there. I'm happy I'll have you to come home to when it's all over."

IGGY WENT with Cruz and Roger to get a drink after an especially awful loss to the Red Sox. Iggy hadn't played well—he got strikes on balls he should have hit, he got an error in the third inning when he completely flubbed a catch, and everything had just spiraled out of control. So when Cruz had said, "God, I need a drink," Iggy had said, "Amen," and now they were at Plucky's, a sports bar across the street from the stadium.

"I've never actually been in here before," Iggy said as Cruz led him inside.

"Yeah, I only come here after a bad loss. The area totally clears out. After a win, people tend to want to stick around and celebrate."

Not that the bar was even empty. Iggy estimated that about three-quarters of the seats were taken. Plus, when they walked in, they were recognized and mobbed.

"That's why we never come here," said Roger before a fan stuck a ball in his face to sign.

Cruz was genial enough that he secured the three of them seats at the bar before he held court, telling stories to the fans, making jokes, and gleefully signing autographs. Iggy signed a few balls as well, though he felt like an ass doing so. One fan came up to him and handed him the ball he'd hit foul into the stands during the fifth inning.

As it got later, the buzz died down. Iggy bought a third round for everyone and quietly sipped his beer while Cruz told some story and Roger interrupted with sarcastic comments. He was only half listening and realized too late that his small dinner plus three hours of sweating on the field meant all the beer was going right to his head. And his bladder. He watched the room spin for a moment and then got up to find the men's room.

Once that was taken care of, a man stopped him in the little hallway outside the restrooms.

"Rodriguez," said the man.

"Oh, hey. You want an autograph? I left my pen up at the bar."

The man put a hand on Iggy's chest. "Tell me something, *Ignacio*. What's it like to be a big fat liar?" The man had a crisp voice with the tiniest bit of a lisp.

"I beg your pardon?"

"Because you're a big fag, aren't you? You're the fag baseball player."

"What are you talking about?"

"Look, don't bother to deny it. I have excellent gaydar, and honey, I spotted you from a mile away."

Heat came to Iggy's face. He knew he had to deny it. He almost didn't want to. "You're mistaken. I'm not—"

"You're even hotter in person than you are in pictures. I would give anything to get my hands on you."

"I'm flattered, really, but—"

"Go back in the men's room and I'll give you the best blowjob of your life."

Iggy couldn't speak for a moment. The odd thing was that he saw through his panic that this guy was quite good-looking. He had Matt's coloring: dark hair, olive skin, deep brown eyes. But where Matt's face was composed mostly of straight lines, this guy had curly hair and a round face and features that looked a little squished. But attractive or not, he made Iggy's heart race, and not in the good way.

"I'm not gay." There was a pang in his chest as Iggy said the words. He hated lying. But there were dozens of baseball fans with big mouths standing not five feet away. "I mean, it's cool that you are. But you're wrong about me. Thanks, I guess, but no thanks." He didn't think it was possible to hate himself more than he did right then.

Iggy turned on his heel and walked back to Cruz and Roger. He picked up his pint glass and downed the rest of his beer.

"Slow down, Ig," said Cruz.

"What's got into you?" asked Roger.

"Some guy offered me a blowjob outside the restroom."

"Um. What?" asked Cruz.

Under his breath, Iggy added, "Called me a fag and said he could spot one a mile away."

"What did you do?" asked Roger.

"Told him I wasn't gay and got out of there." Iggy leaned forward and pressed a hand to his forehead. "You know, I think I need to go home."

"I'll help you get a cab," said Roger.

Roger and Iggy walked outside, leaving Cruz to entertain fans at the bar. Iggy knew yellow cabs were rare this long after a game, but Roger seemed determined to flag one down. Once it became clear one wouldn't be coming, he relented and called a car service.

"You all right?" Roger asked while they waited.

"Yeah. Rough day, though."

"What was worse? The game or almost getting outed?"

"Not sure. Maybe not being able to say I couldn't accept the blowjob because I have a boyfriend." Iggy sighed. He thought about what Matt had told him recently about lying every day. "I hate this, Roger. At the end of the day, I just want to be honest. I think a little part of me dies every time I have to lie like that. But I just don't see another way."

Roger nodded but didn't say anything. A black sedan pulled up; it had a sticker in the rear window advertising the car service Roger had called.

"You're gonna be at Matt's thing Friday, right? There's a reception at the Third Avenue Hotel after the game."

"Yeah. I'll be there."

"Good. See you tomorrow, Ig."

Iggy got in the car. Before he pulled the door shut, he said, "Night, Roger."

He considered telling the cab to take him to Matt's, but the way the man's eyes widened in the rearview-mirror reflection gave Iggy pause.

"Iggy Rodriguez! Man, I can't believe it!" The cabbie had a familiar accent. In Dominican-inflected Spanish, he said, "You're the best thing to happen to the Eagles in five years, and you just got in my cab."

Iggy answered back in Spanish. "Yes. Thank you." He rattled off his Upper East Side address. As the cab pulled away from the bar, Iggy said, "You're Dominican?"

"Yes. I read in the papers that you are too."

"Yes, my parents are. My mother lives in Arizona now. That's where I was born. My father is with God."

"Bless him." There was a pause. "Your Spanish is very good."

"Yes, thank you."

"Could you sign something for me?"

"Yes, of course." Iggy leaned back in his seat, praying the ride would be a short one.

MATT GAZED out from his place on top of the dais and spotted Iggy. He was dressed in a throwback uniform designed for this occasion, based on the Eagles' uniform from the 1930s. The rest of the current Eagles roster was standing along the first-base line wearing similar uniforms, waiting for the pomp to be over so they could start the game. Matt had been to a number of these ceremonies and knew exactly how boring they were, which was why he'd planned a short speech.

Teddy Rothschild stood at the podium. Bill Haverman stood behind him, his hands clasped behind his back, waiting for the speeches to be over, no doubt. Jack Keaton, the Eagles' owner, sat in his own chair too, apparently content not to say anything. Keaton had always been a hands-off owner, trusting Teddy completely to run his team, so even though Matt had played fourteen seasons with the Eagles, he'd only met Keaton maybe a dozen times.

Teddy said, "Ladies and gentlemen, we're here today to pay tribute to one of the greatest players to ever wear the red and blue. With him, we retire his jersey number, and it will forever be a part of Eagles lore. Please welcome Number Three, Matt Blanco!"

The roar of the crowd was deafening. Matt stood from his chair. He used the cane Iggy had helped him pick out and managed to walk toward the podium without too much trouble. He took a deep breath. He wasn't really nervous, but he was uncomfortable. His knee throbbed, the sun was beating down on him, and he was sweating like a pig under his suit.

"Thank you, everyone!" he said. "I know you all are really here for the game, so I'll keep this short." He paused for the laughter. Then he said, "I spent fourteen years of my life with the Eagles organization, and I love everyone here like family. Every one of you—management, my teammates, the fans—has made my career wonderful beyond my greatest imaginings. To retire as an Eagle is the greatest blessing of all, perhaps, because it means that I will always be a part of this organization, and for that I am grateful. While I'm sad that my career is ending, I'm happy that I can look back at it and be proud of what I achieved. I want to thank everyone here today"—he sought out Iggy as he spoke, and their eyes met—"and I want to thank my family and my close friends for making this day so wonderful. I will miss you all, and I will miss baseball, but I thank you for this. I am truly a lucky man. Thank you for everything."

He took a step back from the podium to signal that he was done speaking. Teddy walked back up to the microphone.

"As you may know, we have a tradition here at FSB Stadium. When we retire a jersey, we add the number to the crown of the stadium. Please direct your attention to left field."

And there they were. Numbers 5, 8, 9, 17, 42, and 66. Each number was represented by a lit-up number at the edge of a wall next to the scoreboard. Teddy made a signal with his hand, and right there at the beginning of the row, number 3 lit up.

Matt's chest swelled. It was impossible not to feel pride at that accomplishment, not to think back on his childhood in Brooklyn when his greatest desire was to be a good enough ballplayer just to make it to the majors. He thought about everything he'd done, all the work he'd put in, the sacrifices he made, the good times, the bad; everything passed through him. His heart pounded as he looked at that number 3, at once so insignificant and yet meaning everything. He felt sadness too, the sense that this was all ending, that he was only thirty-nine years old and yet out of a job.

He realized belatedly that the crowd was cheering again. He lifted his hand and waved. The cheers crescendoed. Matt closed his eyes for a moment and let it all soak in. He couldn't keep the smile off his face as he waved, as he was escorted off the dais, as that afternoon's game began.

And this, he thought as he took his seat in the VIP box to watch the game, was the end of Eagles First Baseman Matt Blanco. Let the life of Matt Blanco, regular guy, begin.

Chapter Nineteen

EVERY COMPANY wanted Iggy to endorse them. Or that was how it felt, anyway, as offers poured in. A lot of the companies that wanted Iggy to be the face of their products made high-end luxury items of the sort Iggy had never dreamed he'd get near. He got offers from car companies—Iggy had laughed when his agent, Chris McGrath, had told him that; Iggy still didn't even own a car—from jewelry manufacturers, from fashion designers. A vineyard in Napa wanted him to endorse their wine and a maker of champagne wanted him in their ads. All that paled in comparison to the offers he had from sports equipment manufacturers. These companies wanted him to hawk everything from bats and gloves to T-shirts and jockstraps.

The most absurd thing was all the money he was offered.

"You can say no to all of these," Chris said when he and Iggy met one afternoon. "You can afford to be choosy. Pick the products you think you'd do well with. Maybe do a few ads for this sporting-goods store but don't explicitly endorse any products. Or go ahead and let this toy company put your face on their bat and ball set for toddlers. Or, actually, here's my favorite of the bunch." He moved paper around on his desk and came back with a brochure. "This is the ad campaign for Field Motors. Have you seen the ads on TV?"

"Are those the weird ones where the athletes morph into wild animals? Because that's kind of freaky."

"Yes, they did those too, but in the new ad campaign, they want four athletes, two men and two women, and in the ad you get stripped down to your underwear. The point is to show all the strength underneath."

"To compare me to a car?"

"Well, yeah, but I think it's a cool concept. Look at the mock-ups they sent me." He pointed to the brochure.

The ad featured a woman Iggy recognized as being from the World Cup-winning American soccer team. There were three photos of her. In the first, she was in a soccer uniform. In the second, she was in a slinky gown. In the third, she was wearing a sports bra and tiny spandex shorts. The ad copy said, *No matter how you dress it up, the same strength looms beneath.*

"Clever," said Iggy, "but I can't be in my underwear in front of a camera."

"Why not?"

The flush came to Iggy's face before he could stop it.

"Don't be embarrassed," said Chris. "You're a handsome man; you're in excellent shape. There's no shame in that."

Iggy rubbed his head. "This was easier when the hardest decision I had to make was whether or not I'd pose holding a bat in my baseball card photo."

"I know, but these are all excellent opportunities. You'll gain more visibility with fans, which puts more of those fans in the stadium, which gets you more favorable treatment from the Eagles front office. Everything is linked."

"With money."

Chris scoffed. "Don't be like that. It's part of the game, Ig. You signed your name on that contract knowing that."

"I know. I'm sorry. I'm really grateful for all this. It's just completely overwhelming." Although now that he'd said it, he wasn't sure "grateful" was really the right word. He supposed he was happy enough that people wanted to give him money. And really, if having too much money was his only problem, he was happy to take it.

"You're kind of a sex symbol, you know," Chris said. "You could be cultivating your female fans."

Iggy sighed. "Is it a cliché to say I just want to play baseball?"

"You're young and attractive. Take advantage of it. You can be humble after you've been on top for ten years. Retire in grace like Matt Blanco. Then you can say that all you ever wanted to do was play baseball."

"Right."

He ultimately let Chris talk him into the car ad, though he felt deeply uncomfortable about it. He also signed the paperwork to allow his likeness to appear at some stores of a sporting-goods chain in the New York City area. He had a dozen other offers that Chris made him take with him to consider.

When he left Chris's office, Iggy decided to walk the thirty or so blocks uptown to his apartment. On the way, he called Matt.

"They want me to pose in my underwear," Iggy said when Matt picked up.

"Who does?"

"Field Motors."

"Uh-huh. When I worked for them, all they made me do was drive a car around the streets of Manhattan very early in the morning. Will you be driving a car in your underwear?"

"No." Iggy explained the ad concept.

"That's kind of interesting. I understand why they want you."

"Because I'm a famous baseball player."

"You're a beautiful man, Iggy. I never had a body like yours, even when I was in the best shape of my life."

"What do you think about endorsements?"

"Well, it can get dicey if you lend your name to a product that ends up being unpopular or dangerous. That happened to Horatio Estevez a few years ago. Remember?"

Estevez had been a player for Cleveland who had endorsed a line of baseball helmets that turned out to be defective. Although he still played, his career hadn't quite recovered from that blow.

"But you did endorsements."

"Of course. In the early days, I was mostly amazed by them. Like, 'You really want to pay me money just to say I like this brand of cleats? Where do I sign?' But A.J. was good at helping me make smart decisions."

"Chris said it's good for visibility."

"Sure. You're working for people like Rothschild, who believes winning is the only way to keep fans in the stands, but it looks good for you if there are a lot of people in the stands wearing Rodriguez jerseys. And man, you do an ad like the one you're describing? The stores are going to sell out of Rodriguez jerseys in women's sizes."

"I don't know if I like all this attention."

"Part of the game, babe."

"Yeah. That's what Chris said. Without the babe."

Matt laughed. "Do the ad. I, for one, would be happy to see you in your underwear."

"Yeah, but you get that show for free."

"True."

Iggy stretched out his arms as he walked. He was feeling a little stiff today. He'd skipped practice to go meet with Chris, which he was kind of regretting now. "I think I'm gonna go to the gym after I get home," he said to Matt.

"To do extra crunches to make your abs even hotter for the ad?"

Iggy groaned. "I give up."

"Have fun. I promised my mother I'd go out to Bensonhurst tonight for my uncle Dante's birthday."

"You mentioned. You know, your family sounds like the list of characters in a mob movie. Do you really have an uncle Dante?"

"I really do. He's my mother's brother. Comes from being purebred Brooklyn Italian."

"I'll say. I'll see you tomorrow?"

"Yeah. Love you."

"Love you too."

IGGY WAS in awe of his mother's intuitiveness, although he supposed that, after he took a phone call in the middle of dinner, it wasn't too crazy to assume it was his boyfriend.

And still Iggy sat back down and said, "How did you know?"

"You think you can hide things from me, Ignacio?" his mother said in Spanish.

"Of course not, Mama. But we're keeping the relationship a secret so that I don't lose my place on the team."

Iggy's mother waved her hand dismissively. "You would not keep a secret from your mother."

Iggy looked down at his plate full of tamales. The evening had begun with him attempting to make an authentic meal for his mother—though he lived primarily on whatever the team chef provided during the season and had forgotten some of the basics—and his mother shooing him out of the way to fix his mistakes. Iggy had enjoyed their old rapport; they didn't see each other as much as he would like. The meal was delicious, but his mother's gaze felt like hot lasers.

She glared at him. "So you are seeing a man. Is it serious?"

Iggy shrugged. "How serious can it be if we have to keep it a secret?"

After a pause, she said, "So yes."

So Iggy decided to finally just tell her. "All right, fine. I'm seeing Matt Blanco."

Iggy's mother looked at him blankly for a moment. He knew she knew who Matt was, because she watched as many of Iggy's games on TV as she could. Her eyes went wide as the realization hit. "Your old teammate?" she asked.

"Yes. I've been with him about a year. And I love him, Mama."

"He's so much older than you."

"I know, but he's not taking advantage of me, if that's what you're thinking. He understands me. And I understand him. I've never had that in a relationship before, not on this level. The age doesn't matter. Not to me."

Iggy's mother looked at him for a long moment. Iggy felt a bit like he'd worn the wrong thing to go to church and she was about to send him to his room to change.

"I must meet him at once," she said.

"I'm with him, Mama. I don't need your approval."

Switching to English, she said, "Not approval. You have important man in your life, I should meet him."

"Are you practicing your English for when that happens?"

Iggy's mother picked his phone up off the table and handed it to Iggy. "You call him. Tell him to come tomorrow night. I cook."

And so the next night, after an afternoon game that the Eagles handily won while Iggy's mother cheered on from the stands, Matt came over. Iggy greeted him at the door and said, "Just so you know, my mother swears she only wants to meet the man who is an important part of her son's life. She claims she won't be judgmental. But I've seen her in action. Not to scare you."

"I'm sure it will be fine. I'm only a little scared." Matt grinned.

Iggy let him into the apartment and made introductions. His mother gave Matt a once-over, then walked to the table and said, "Your leg hurts. Sit."

"Thank you," said Matt. "What's for dinner?"

"Carne mechada," Iggy's mother said, "y arroz con maíz."

"Sounds delicious."

"You have no idea what she just said, do you?"

Matt grinned again. "It *smells* delicious, anyway." He carefully lowered himself into a chair at Iggy's little table. He left his cane near the wall. "So?"

"Braised beef tenderloin with rice and corn. There are some plantain fritters too, although Mama will tell you they are not authentic because I don't have the right cooking equipment."

"You don't! I buy for you."

"I never cook, Mama."

"You should cook. Your boyfriend has hurt leg."

Iggy rolled his eyes. "I tried cooking yesterday, but you said I was doing it wrong."

"You were. You should know better. I teach you well."

Matt laughed. "Gracias, Señora Rodriguez. I look forward to eating it all."

The meal *was* very good. There was a little coconut milk in the *arroz con maíz*, which gave it a sweet tang that paired nicely with the beef. Matt ate everything with gusto, complimenting Mrs. Rodriguez on the meal.

"So what do you plan to do now that you do not play baseball?" she asked in halting English.

"Not sure yet," said Matt. He'd endeared himself to Iggy by speaking slowly enough to be understood but not otherwise demeaning Mama or assuming she was stupid because her English wasn't very good. He'd been polite and friendly all evening, never betraying any lost patience when she forgot a word or had to pause to recall what to say. "I may coach or write for a sports website or something. I'll see what strikes me when I'm better recovered."

She nodded and continued to eat. Iggy waited to see if she would say anything further. When she didn't, he kept eating. When he reached for his glass and found it empty, Matt poured him a little more wine. "Not too much, though," Matt said. "You have a game tomorrow night, right?"

"Yes." Iggy looked up and met Matt's gaze. Some understanding passed between them, borne of a year of working and being together, some intuitive understanding of how much or little Iggy could indulge if he had to play the next day. Matt probably knew Iggy's limits better than Iggy did.

Mama nodded as if she were satisfied with what had just transpired. "You take good care of Ignacio," she said to Matt. It wasn't a question.

RETIREMENT WAS boring. That was all Matt had figured out so far.

By September, his knee was much better, enough so that he didn't need crutches or a cane to walk much anymore, but he wasn't any closer to figuring out what to do with the rest of his life.

Worse, his convalescence had made not going out a habit, so now each day he had trouble digging up the motivation to do much beyond domestic chores. He really only went out to buy groceries or for his physical therapy appointments.

Iggy accused him of being depressed, but that wasn't quite the problem.

Like Iggy would even know. Sure, Matt saw him a few times a week, but Iggy was still mostly preoccupied with the baseball season. As well he should have been, but still, it wasn't like he was around for Matt's everyday routine. They weren't even sleeping together much lately.

He didn't want to be bitter. He still felt deep down that he'd made the right decision, but man, he missed baseball. He missed being outside every day, he missed the physical activity, he missed his leg having its full range of motion. He was jealous that Iggy still got to do these things. And for all that he felt like he'd done the right thing, he sure as hell hadn't expected to have so little to do. And he could only clean his apartment so many times.

In the middle of the month, he went to a charity banquet that was raising money for childhood leukemia. The date fell during the middle of an Eagles road trip, so he couldn't talk Iggy into coming with him, even on the pretense of them going together because they were friends. So he pulled on a tux and went to the banquet by himself, attempting to live his life as Matt Blanco, regular guy. Although he suspected that not too many regular guys went to banquets like this.

The charity held the banquet at a ritzy hotel in Midtown, everything done up to beaux arts extremes. The ballroom was ostentatious and a little garish, but it had some Old New York charm that Matt admired.

As he walked in, people swarmed him, which hadn't happened in a while. Rationally he knew he'd only been out of the game for a few months, not long enough to be forgotten, so he didn't know why he'd assumed no one would know who he was. Half the reason he was invited was because of who he was.

Maybe he *was* depressed. He'd have to talk to his doctor about his apparent recent inability to think rationally.

As it turned out, plenty of people recognized him. A dozen or so other men dressed in tuxedos asked for autographs or shook his hand, and for a brief moment, he felt on top of the world again.

Not that he'd been after fame, he reminded himself. He'd just wanted to play baseball.

He recognized Dale Forrester, the longtime Eagles right fielder who had retired five or six years before. He made his way over to him and shook the man's hand.

"Ah, Blanco," said Dale. "Nice to see you. How's the knee?"

Matt had brought his cane just in case, and he lifted it now. "Much better. I don't normally need the cane, but I don't like being away from home without it. I tried that a couple of times and had to be helped home. Somehow this is slightly less embarrassing. Plus it makes me look dapper."

Dale laughed. "Yeah. I pulled my Achilles once. Was on the DL for six weeks, could hardly walk. Getting used to being on my feet again took more time than I would have expected."

"Yeah, I remember when that happened."

Dale slapped him on the back. "Well, I'm glad to see you out. The rumor was you'd holed up in your apartment. I figured that meant you were either shacked up with some bosomy blonde thing, or you were having a hard time of it."

Matt shrugged. "Not really either. Recovery just took a long time. I'm much better now."

"That's how it is when you get older. Here, come with me, there are some people you should meet."

Matt wound up having a perfectly delightful time with several retired Eagles players, all of whom had gone on to interesting careers postretirement, if you counted coaching college ball or playing in celebrity golf tournaments as work. Although he enjoyed talking with everyone, Matt didn't feel much better about his prospects once it was over.

Did he even want to coach? He had a fair amount of patience. That was something his mother had always remarked upon; she said once that she had first clued in to the fact that he was different when she noticed he was the calm one in an otherwise hotheaded Italian family. He figured he could channel that into being patient with students or other players.

At some point, the conversation turned to a book written by an ex-Yankee about his years on the team. The book had been widely panned for being too dishy and negative—the player was accused of being bitter because he'd been traded in the twilight of his career—but some people at Matt's table had read it and thought it was actually pretty insightful.

"There's so much that happens that nobody knows about," one of the ex-Eagles said.

"You can say that again," Matt said. He reflected on that a little. Not for the first time, he wondered what would happen if he came out publicly, or if he just told his friends and let the rumor mill do what it would, or hell, if he simply let his guard down more often. He didn't feel like he could— the fans would turn on him in a hot second, wouldn't they? But sometimes he only wanted to stop lying. And it would have been nice to talk about Iggy when all the other guys at his table started going on about how wonderful their wives were.

As dinner was winding down, Matt decided to test the waters a little. He turned to Dale. "Hey, you know that batting coach for Baltimore? What's his name? Del Rey?"

"Delano. Nice guy. He's the gay one, right?"

There didn't seem to be any judgment in Dale's voice, so Matt said, "Yeah, I think so. There was a story about him on *Baseball Tonight* a couple of weeks ago, but I was only half paying attention to it." This wasn't true. The whole theme of the story was that this guy, who was the brother of a major-league outfielder, was, as far as anyone knew, the only openly gay staff member of any Major League Baseball team. "I only bring it up because I was thinking about coaching as something to do now that I'm retired. Did he ever play?"

"No, not that I know of. His brother plays for Colorado."

"Right, right."

"You might be a good coach. You were always good with the rookies."

"Yeah, thanks." Matt smiled and drank his wine.

"I mean, unofficial captain and all that. You're a great leader. I'd bet you'd be pretty good at coaching."

"I appreciate that. It's definitely something to look into." Matt put some thought into how best to phrase his next question. "Delano, though. Must be weird for the players to work with an openly gay coach."

Dale shrugged. "From what I've heard, nobody cares. And Delano stays out of the locker room most of the time."

"Huh." Matt decided that was good to know. He tucked that knowledge away for later.

"If I hear of any openings, I'll let you know," said Dale. "There's a rumor that San Diego is shuffling some staff around again."

"Wow, thanks."

"Sure thing."

Of course, that was the other problem. The coaching staffs at all of the New York teams were so entrenched that working for a team in the majors would mean traveling or moving to another city, which meant more time away from Iggy. At least now that Matt was back in New York, he got to see Iggy whenever the Eagles were in town. Dallas had been miserable. But he doubted the Eagles would hire him anyway, and the fans would surely consider his coaching for the Yankees or the Mets as some kind of betrayal.

And yet, the idea of living openly and still having something to do with baseball certainly had its appeal.

Not in this lifetime, he thought sadly during the cab ride home that night. But it was food for thought.

FIELD MOTORS filmed their commercial at the end of the regular season, after the Eagles had clinched their spot in the Division Series but before postseason play had begun. To say Iggy was nervous as he walked onto the set was understating the case.

For the first set of scenes, the director had him stand perfectly still in front of a black screen. He wore a crisp Eagles uniform. Then the director had him pose more aggressively, flexing his muscles, posing with a bat, tossing a ball in the air. He changed into a beat-up uniform, and the makeup people made him up to look like he'd been in a fight.

"What's going to happen," one of the people from the ad agency said, "is that you're going to morph from clean uniform to messy uniform, then we're going to show you in the suit, then we're going to show you stripped down. It's all going to be done with a lot of cuts and sped-up animation. It'll be really cool in the end."

Iggy admired himself in the suit. It was really nice and very expensive from the feel of the fabric. A male PA smoothed down his lapels before he went on camera, and his fingers lingered a little too long on Iggy's chest.

"My, my," the PA said.

Iggy could do nothing but laugh nervously. He felt like all attention was on him as the PA continued to feel him up. He wanted to put the guy off, but he didn't want to be rude, and his embarrassment paralyzed him. He thought of poor Matt lying around at home. Matt, who hadn't felt up for sex much since the end of the regular season. Matt, who had nonetheless talked him into doing this ad.

"Sorry," the PA said. "You're irresistible. I don't watch a lot of baseball, but you can bet I will now."

"I—"

"And you're flattered but you're totally straight. I know. Story of my life." The PA waved his hand.

Iggy sighed but didn't say anything. The PA pushed him back in front of the camera, so he posed in the suit.

The next part of the ad involved Iggy in his underwear. Another PA handed him a pair of black boxer briefs and told him to change into them. A robe hung in the changing area, so he slipped it on before walking back out to the soundstage, but he still felt deeply uncomfortable, naked in a way he didn't like.

"You have any tattoos?" the director asked.

"No."

"Good. Take off the robe. I want to see what we're dealing with."

Iggy slid out of the robe and held his breath the whole time. He draped the robe over a chair.

"Nice," said the director dispassionately.

The gay PA practically swooned.

"Just stand in front of the screen and pose the way you did before, with your arms down like this." The director demonstrated.

Iggy stood in front of the screen and posed in his underwear, feeling completely mortified the whole time.

"You have *nothing* to be embarrassed about," the gay PA told him when it was over. "God. What's your workout routine like? I'll have to tell my boyfriend to do whatever you do."

"I play baseball professionally?" said Iggy.

"Ah, so that's the key." The guy grinned. "You're handsome and modest and a delight to work with. You have a lifelong fan, Mr. Rodriguez."

"Ah, thanks."

Could his life get any weirder?

IGGY TRIED to focus. He was preoccupied by the upcoming Division Series against Tampa, but something was irking Matt and he wasn't talking about whatever it was that was bothering him.

Iggy felt bad for not being around much lately, but it couldn't be helped. The push into the postseason and all the extra practice the Eagles' coaching staff had demanded ate up a lot of his time, not to mention filming commercials and meeting with his agent. Terry, the Eagles' batting coach, had been working with him to hit curveballs with more accuracy, and he was improving, but all that extra work meant less time with Matt.

The man in question had been pacing around the apartment all day. Iggy had been worried something like this would happen, that too much idle time for a man who had until now been busy almost constantly would cause depression. The fact that Matt hardly ever left the apartment anymore hadn't done much to back up Matt's continued assertions that he was fine.

They were sitting at the table in the kitchen with sandwiches. Matt wasn't really eating.

"You have to tell me what's going on," Iggy said.

Matt sat back a little, his eyes wide. "Nothing's going on."

"You've been mopey for weeks. What the hell is up with you?"

"Nothing!"

"I don't believe you."

Matt sighed. He looked toward the window. "Look, it really is not a big deal. I just am having some trouble deciding what I should do now that I'm no longer playing baseball. I haven't settled on anything, so I'm restless. I'm a little bored. That's all."

"Are you sure that's it?" Iggy didn't like being this combative, but he was tired of the silence, of the continued assurances that Matt was okay when he clearly wasn't.

Granted, Iggy had been out of town more often than not in the last month, and now that it was October, if the Eagles played well in the play-offs, he'd be out of town more in the coming weeks. He hated leaving Matt alone, wondered what he got up to when he had all that time by himself to think.

Matt shrugged.

Iggy reached over and rubbed the back of Matt's hand. "Please, baby. I'm worried about you. Talk to me."

Matt glanced at Iggy and then went back to looking out the window. "It's just that… I don't know. I can't figure out what to do with myself, and the longer I take to decide, the longer I just sit here not doing anything."

"You don't want to rush into a decision. I get that."

"And now, look at you. You're the new hot thing on the scene. The sports media is talking about you almost constantly, and you're filming sexy new commercials, and everything's coming up Iggy. I guess I kind of… feel like a waste. That I'm just a waste of space." He leaned forward and put his elbows on the table. Then he put his head down.

Bingo. "You're not…." He looked down at where Matt sat with his head in his hands. "You're not a waste of space. There are lots of things you can do. You can't tell me that your life is over before you turn forty just because you've retired from baseball. You can still coach, for example."

"Coach what? I don't want to coach in the majors because I'll have to move out of New York, and we all know how well that went the last time. So what's left? Coach high school? College? What are the odds I could even get a job here?"

"You're being too negative."

"Next you'll tell me to play in the old-timers' league."

"Well, why not?"

"Iggy, get real. I'm still not allowed to do more than limited physical activity, according to Dr. Fishbauer. I can't play right now. That's the whole fucking reason I retired, remember?"

Iggy grunted. He hated arguing with Matt, but this was getting ridiculous. He hated seeing Matt like this.

So he decided to mention the idea that had popped into his head a few days before. He wasn't sure how well it would go over, but he was running out of things to say. And this funk could not continue. Iggy had tried initiating sex the night before, and Matt had put him off, not seeming interested. He hadn't seemed interested in anything. Iggy was determined to bring him out of it.

But first he had to call Matt on some of his shit. "I know this is hard, but the way things are? It can't continue."

Matt stared sullenly at his sandwich.

"I know I haven't been around much," Iggy continued. "I'm flying again Thursday for the ALDS. Which sucks, because honestly? I'd rather stay here with you. Help you feel better. I know you're really struggling with retirement."

Matt closed his eyes and dipped his head forward again.

Iggy reached over and rubbed his back. "You haven't been around much either, you know. I mean, you've been here, but you haven't been present. You're always spacing out. I say we do something, and you say you're tired and don't want to. I know this is not how you wanted all this to go, but I can't watch you shut down like this anymore. I want to help you fix this so I can get my old Matt back."

"The old Matt is gone," Matt whispered.

"No. I don't believe that's true. I think you're upset because your career is over, and if you could just find something to engage you the way baseball used to, you would get better. I gave you space because I knew you needed to lick your wounds and recover. Now it's time to figure out what to do with the next phase of your life." Iggy took a deep breath. "It's killing me to watch you like this. But don't do it for my sake. Do something for yourself."

Matt bit his lip and shook his head. Then he looked up and met Iggy's gaze. "What would you have me do, Ig? What marketable skills do I have that aren't baseball?"

"Plenty. You're a smart guy. You could learn how to do anything. What do you want to do?"

Matt threw his hands in the air. "I don't know!" he shouted. "I don't know. That's the whole fucking problem."

Iggy felt encouraged by Matt's outburst. Anger was good. Emotion was good. It wasn't the flat silence of the past couple of weeks. So Iggy gave Matt his idea. "You could write a book."

Matt stared at Iggy. "A book?"

"Sure. Like a memoir. You're done with Major League Baseball now, right? So there's no risk in being honest. You could write a memoir about being gay in the major leagues."

Matt looked unconvinced. He leaned back in his chair and shook his head. "Right," he said. "A fucking memoir. Okay. And then when I write it, everybody will hate me. I'll be that fag baseball player, and then everything I've worked so hard for, all of it goes away. No one will respect me; the fans will turn on me. It's all over. No, I just want to retire quietly and live my life."

"Is that really what you want?"

"I'm not Eagles First Baseman Matt Blanco anymore. I'm just Matt, regular guy."

"That's not true. You'll never be just a regular guy. I think you're proving that pretty well with your retirement."

"It's too risky to come out publicly. I've thought about it, and I can't see any way that it will work out. You want me to write a whole goddamned book? So everyone will hate me?"

Iggy's frustration bubbled over. "No one will hate you. Stop saying that." He regretted raising his voice immediately, but then he decided, *Fuck it*. Matt needed to hear this. "Even if they do, it doesn't matter. *I* love you. Your friends, Roger, Lauren, Cruz, they all love you. The people who matter are on your side. If some former teammates turn on you, well, they're just homophobic assholes, and you never have to speak to any of them again. Besides, being honest about who you are won't erase your record. You are still one of the greatest men to ever play the game, and I'm not just saying that. It's fact. Numbers don't lie. But you could be honest and tell people about your experiences and maybe change the game for everyone, for people like me, for every gay kid who ever picked up a bat but didn't think he'd be allowed in the majors."

Matt stared at Iggy, his eyes wide.

"Or don't write the fucking memoir. You need something to do. I gave you a suggestion. Whatever, Matt." Iggy stood up and turned to leave the room.

"No, wait."

Iggy turned around.

"I'm sorry, I didn't mean to...." He sighed. "I don't know what to do with all the time on my hands."

"I know. I'm not saying you have to write a book. I just thought... I mean, you were always one of my heroes, Matt. You still are. And I keep thinking about the kid I was and how I would have felt if one of my heroes came out and said, 'Hey, I'm just like you.' It would have meant a lot. And you keep saying that you hate having to lie every day. I do too. You want something to do with your time now. I think you could make a big difference, maybe change some minds. You can talk about your experiences, what staying in the closet did to you, how it made you feel. You could pave the way for an active player to come out, to give all of us more freedom. You could stop lying."

Matt leaned back in his chair. His chest rose and fell as he took a deep breath. "Maybe I could… I mean, it's an idea. I don't know. I've never been much of a writer."

"Yeah," Iggy said, not knowing what else there was to say. He didn't know how to help Matt get over his depression or whatever this funk was. And the more he thought about it, the more it seemed like a good idea. "Just think about it, okay? That's all I ask."

"Yeah. I will."

"I love you, Matt. I want you to be happy."

"I know. You make me happy, Iggy."

Iggy smiled, but he didn't think he was quite enough. "I'm glad."

He reached over and took Matt's hand. Matt turned his hand over and threaded his fingers together with Iggy's.

"I will think about it," Matt said. "I'll find something. I'll figure this out."

Third

EAGLES LOOK GOOD GOING INTO THE ALL-STAR BREAK

by Cary Galvin, Sports Net

The Eagles just won their seventh game in a row, sweeping Colorado in the process. Such a great story, this team. The front office is making really smart decisions. Reminds me of Oakland in the early aughts. The World Series has eluded them the last few seasons, but this really feels like the year for the Eagles. I know I'm not exactly impartial, but can I just say, Iggy Rodriguez is on fire. This is his third season with the Eagles, so it shouldn't be news, but it's hard to deny that he's been playing very well all season.

Rodriguez seemed to be all over the place in the off-season too. The ads and endorsements are still piling up, and between you and me, he looked hot in those Field Motors commercials.

And can we talk for a moment about the late-career resurgence of Roger May? He's been looking great all season. So it's not just young players who are cleaning up this season. Keeping May in the rotation wouldn't have been my first instinct, but it has proved to be a good choice. He may continue to pitch well into his forties. That's nice to see, especially since so many pitchers ten years younger than May have killed their pitching arms and were forced into early retirement.

The Eagles are about to start a nine-game homestay that should be pretty enjoyable to watch. There have been a lot of home runs hit in FSB Stadium this season, and that's a pretty awesome thing to behold....

Chapter Twenty

WITHOUT TELLING Iggy, Matt spent months thinking about the book. He thought about it while he asked around about coaching gigs, he thought about it as he watched the Eagles fizzle and lose in the League Championship Series, he thought about it during every physical therapy session, he thought about it through the off-season, and he thought about it when Iggy left for spring training. The more he thought about it, the better he felt, the more it felt like a thing he should do.

He thought about Brian Delano, the batting coach in Baltimore who got along just fine despite the fact he was gay. He thought about what Iggy had said about wanting his hero to say something simple like *I'm just like you*. He thought about the kid he'd once been, watching baseball games on TV or flipping through his card collection for comfort when things were the worst, when he didn't think he'd ever meet another kid like himself, when he was sure he'd be banned from baseball for telling a simple truth about himself. He thought about wanting to have Iggy with him at public events, he thought about having to laugh or joke about dating hot women, he thought about how sad it was that he'd been in a relationship for two years but everyone still thought of him as a confirmed bachelor. He thought about every kid in the news who had killed himself and how hypocritical he was for saying it would get better in public while not making things better for himself.

The more he thought about it, the more it became clear what he had to do.

On a weekend when the Eagles were out of town, he called up A.J. and said, "I want to write a book."

A.J. clucked his tongue. "Of course you do. Can you write?"

"Well, I'd probably need some help with that. But I think I have a story worth telling."

"Ex-player memoirs are a dime a dozen. What's your hook?"

Matt took a deep breath. "I want to write a book about what it's like to be a closeted gay Major League Baseball player."

Matt let that hang there and waited for it to sink in. A.J. started to speak a couple of times before cutting himself off. The longer A.J.'s silence stretched on, though, the more nervous Matt got. Was it really okay to tell his agent? If he couldn't tell his agent, who could he tell?

Eventually A.J. sputtered and said, "Are you fucking kidding me?"

"No. That's the book I want to write."

"You're gay. You, Matt Blanco, are a gay man."

"Yes. That is what I just said." Though, had he really said it? No, he hadn't really said it out loud. He swallowed and said, "I'm gay." It made him nervous to say it to someone he'd never told before, but he trusted A.J.

"I never would have guessed in a million years."

"I didn't want you to. I've been very careful. No one knows, really, except my immediate family. Well, and my boyfriend."

"Jesus H. Christ, Matt. That is a hell of a hook. There have been a couple of memoirs by ex-players in which they came out of the closet, but those guys were nobodies, small potatoes. Not a Hall-of-Fame-bound player. Not a name laypeople know. I mean, you think contemporary baseball, you think Derek Jeter, Albert Pujols, Matt Blanco. This book, man. If this is what you really want to do, it could blow the roof off the sport."

"I know. That's why I want to write it. I want to come out, A.J. I'm done lying."

A.J. agreed to represent him when trying to sell the book. In the weeks following the initial conversation, A.J. made inquiries with editors he knew, and he told Matt he'd been careful to keep Matt's name out of the conversation. A.J. wanted the book to drop like a bomb, he kept saying. There seemed to be enough interest. A.J. then sent Gus, who had ghostwritten the memoir of a gospel singer who had come out a few years previously.

Or rather, A.J. just showed up one day with Gus in tow.

Matt hadn't been expecting company. He was thankful Iggy was out of town, but he still felt caught when he opened his apartment door to let them in. He wore one of Iggy's old T-shirts and a pair of warm-up pants, and his hair was disheveled because he hadn't planned to see anyone.

A.J. gave him a once-over and frowned. "Is this how you live now?"

"Why are you here?" Matt asked.

"Allow me to introduce August Lockwood. Goes by Gus. He's your ghostwriter."

Gus was a good-looking guy, younger than Matt had expected based on A.J.'s descriptions. He was maybe thirty and well-groomed, though he dressed like an aging college professor in tweed pants and a button-down shirt.

"I can help make your story really compelling," Gus said at A.J.'s prompt. "We'll work together to find the best way to tell it."

Matt still felt ambushed, but Gus smiled brightly, and he thought he might be all right. He took a deep breath, trying to calm down, and said, "Well, come in. Can I get you something to drink?"

Matt, A.J., and Gus talked over coffee and cookies about exactly what Matt wanted to do with this book. Matt said, "It's too late for me, since I don't play in the majors anymore, but I know for certain there are active gay players."

Gus clicked the pen in his hand a couple of times. "But you don't want to gossip?"

"No. I don't want to name names. This will just be about my experience. We might have to come up with code names for some players, though, I guess." Matt thought about Iggy, who probably wouldn't appreciate getting outed in Matt's autobiography.

Or maybe he would, given how he'd been talking lately.

But no, Iggy would come out on his own terms when he was ready. Matt knew there was a certain inevitability to it, that it wasn't an *if* but a *when*.

Gus grinned. "Code names. I like it. Like a spy novel."

Matt laughed. "Well, not quite."

"Sure it is. You spent, what, fifteen years fiercely protecting a secret? There's quite a bit of espionage involved there."

Matt liked Gus well enough; he was amiable and had a wicked sense of humor. A.J. seemed to agree. He said, "Well, this seems to be going well. I have a meeting downtown in a half hour, so I'll leave you to it."

Matt saw A.J. out and returned to the table, where Gus was still making notes. When Matt sat down again, Gus said, "Must have been hard, keeping that secret so long. I can't even imagine."

"That's part of my motivation for the book. It... sucked. A lot."

Gus smiled and trailed a finger up Matt's arm. "Bet it sucks less now. Bet I could help with that."

Heat flooded Matt's face. "I have a boyfriend."

"Sure you do."

"I'm faithful to him. I'm not going to work with you if you're just going to hit on me. I'm sure there are a thousand writers in New York who would love to help me write my memoir."

Gus looked suitably chastened. "Oh. I'm sorry. I didn't mean—"

"It's okay. But you and I have a professional relationship. You're helping me write this book. That's it."

"Okay. Agreed. I promise to take this seriously."

Gus behaved after that. And they were off to the races.

Matt started the book as a pretty straightforward memoir of his life. He wrote while Gus coached him, or he dictated while Gus transcribed what he said. He talked about playing baseball, what it was like to get drafted, what it was like to move up to the majors, what it was like to get his first World Series ring. Often he typed up what he wanted to say at night and then worked with Gus the next day to clean up the prose. This system seemed to work pretty well, and within two weeks, they had the first few chapters done.

Then one afternoon, Gus said, "You know, you're avoiding the juicy stuff."

"What are you talking about? This is good, don't you think? You told me last week that not many people really know about what things are like in the major leagues. That's interesting, right?"

"Yeah, most people don't give a shit about the inner workings of their favorite sports team. It ruins the magic. You know what these people really want to know about, though? When did you first know you were gay?"

That was the thing Matt dreaded talking about. He still had a hard time discussing that part of himself, particularly with Gus, whom he still didn't quite trust. Not committing it to paper—or screen, in this case, since Gus was working primarily on a laptop—still gave Matt the option to change his mind, or that was how Matt viewed it.

"I was probably twelve, I guess, when I figured out I was gay," Matt said after stalling for a few minutes.

"See, this is the good stuff. That's what belongs in your memoir. The baseball stuff is good, but the way to make people read your book is to show them something they haven't read about before. So you're a gay kid who grew up in Brooklyn in the seventies and eighties. What was that like? Did your parents accept it?"

Matt started talking, and Gus transcribed everything he said. Matt talked about fearing his parents' reaction, about keeping it a secret for as long as he did, about sneaking around in college, about coming out to his mother, about the lengths he went to to keep his secret.

Next Gus asked, "So, like, how do you feel about homophobia in sports? Did anyone ever say anything really awful to you? How did you keep it a secret from the tabloid media in New York? What is your boyfriend like?"

Matt answered all of those questions too and started writing passages about the strategies he took to ensure his secret, about ugly things people had said to him, about how homophobic baseball audiences were. He wrote about Iggy but of course kept his identity a secret. He wrote about falling in love, wrote about how it changed his perspective.

"I could have probably gone on keeping it a secret forever if it hadn't been for him," Matt said. "He made me realize how much this secret was hurting me."

Gus ate it up and helped Matt make a compelling narrative, or that was what he kept saying.

Matt was a slow writer. It took four months to get the first draft done. That was longer than Matt would have guessed, but he liked having a project. Because it wasn't just that Iggy was on the road a lot; all of his closest friends were still playing baseball too. Without something else to occupy his mind, Matt got bored, lonely, and yes, depressed, despite what he told Iggy. But working on the book gave him something to do, a reason to get up in the morning. And Iggy was supportive, encouraging him to be honest in the storytelling and always listening when Matt complained about getting stuck or working with Gus.

Matt and Gus worked out of Matt's apartment a few hours each day. Everything went fine, or it did until Iggy came by one afternoon while Matt was working with Gus. Matt had forgotten he'd invited Iggy over after that afternoon's game. When the buzzer sounded, he spat out a curse, catching Gus's attention.

Matt hopped up and hit the intercom button.

"It's Iggy." His voice crackled through the speaker.

That definitely caught Gus's attention. Matt sighed and hit the speaker button. "Come on up. Gus is here."

Matt hit the lock button, but then the buzzer sounded again. When Matt hit the intercom, Iggy said, "Should I come back later?"

"Damage done, I think." He hit the lock again.

Iggy showed up on Matt's doorstep a few minutes later with a huge duffel bag slung over his shoulder. He took a cautious step into the apartment.

Gus gasped. "Ignacio Rodriguez."

Matt took Iggy's stuff and dropped the duffel in the bedroom, happy enough to avoid the standoff between Iggy and Gus. It wasn't much of a standoff, though; mostly Gus gaped and Iggy stood in the living room, shifting his weight from one foot to the other. Matt walked over and stood near Iggy.

"You're not going to say anything," Matt said to Gus, "because you signed a nondisclosure agreement, so if you breathe a word about Iggy so much as being here, I will sue the hell out of you." He grinned and threw an arm around Iggy.

Iggy stiffened but didn't move away. He crossed his arms and glared at Gus, though.

Gus shrugged. "Hey, I don't care. Your secret is safe with me."

Iggy spent the next hour nervously moving around the apartment, apparently unable to keep still for longer than three minutes at a time. He tried watching TV, then he went into the bedroom, and then he came back out and helped himself to a snack from the fridge, which he only ate half of. He paced, he sat, he stood. Matt found it distracting but tried to ignore him. Gus didn't seem to notice.

Gus finally left, by which time Iggy was in a near frenzy. He was in the kitchen, poking at half a sandwich. Matt walked over and hugged him.

"Did you cheat on me with a swarm of bees?" Matt asked.

"What?"

"I've never seen you this agitated."

Iggy frowned. "I know you trust him, and I know I should too, since the media hasn't caught wind of the fact that you're writing a book, but he made me nervous."

"I can see that."

"I'm sorry."

"Don't be." Matt kissed Iggy. He let the kiss play out long and lazily, and he could practically feel Iggy's muscles relax under his lips and hands. "He made me nervous at first. You get used to it."

"Sure you do."

"You wanted me to write this book, didn't you? I need Gus's help to write it. So we have to put up with him a little while longer."

"Yeah. All right."

A TENSE couple of days followed while Iggy waited for Gus to spill the beans, but nothing came of it, so Iggy started becoming a regular fixture during Gus's hours with Matt. He tried to stay out of the way while they were working, though he didn't like Gus much and wanted to keep an eye on him.

He was happy Matt had something to occupy his time, genuinely so, and he was glad this book was being written, but he was getting tired of having to share what little time he had with Matt with Gus too.

Iggy sat on the couch watching TV one afternoon when his commercial came on. He was about to switch channels—he still found the ad mildly embarrassing—when Gus whistled.

"Really, dude?" said Iggy.

"What? You look hot in the ad."

"I'll thank you not to hit on Iggy," Matt said.

"Wow, you guys are no fun," said Gus. "You're all shacked up and monogamous."

"We're not 'shacked up,'" Matt said. "Can we finish this, please?"

Iggy found something dumb to watch but wound up brooding instead. Maybe that was half the problem. They *weren't* shacked up. Iggy had started thinking lately that their relationship would be better if he weren't constantly going between their apartments. He didn't trust his doorman enough to let Matt be more than an occasional visitor to his place, so he almost always came to Matt's. He paid a hefty sum every month to keep that apartment on the other side of the island, but if he was pretty much living with Matt, what was the point? Every time he brought it up, Matt shrugged him off and mumbled something about continuing to be discreet. It could all be rationalized, Iggy had argued. It wouldn't be strange for players to live in the same building. Hell, three of the Yankees lived in the same Trump luxury building on the West Side. "The same *apartment*, though?" Matt had said the last time they'd had this argument.

Wasn't the whole point of this book to make it easier for Matt to live openly?

Gus finally left around the time the evening news came on. Matt sat next to Iggy on the couch. "How was the game today?" he asked.

"Fine. We won, no thanks to me. I hit a double in the seventh but couldn't get my bat on the ball otherwise."

"You score a run?"

"Yeah."

Matt put an arm around Iggy. "You're so modest. There are some members of that starting lineup who haven't gotten so much as a hit in two weeks, and you think you played badly because all you did was hit a double."

Iggy shrugged.

"Is that what got up your ass?" Matt asked. "You've been sitting here sulking since you got here."

"I don't like Gus."

"I know. You haven't made a secret of that."

"And I was thinking again that you should really consider just letting me move in here. I'm so sick of going back and forth."

"Iggy, we've talked about this."

"And you decided that we had to keep up appearances and blah blah."

"I'm right, you know."

Iggy huffed out a breath. "I know." He leaned his head on Matt's shoulder. "I'm just tired. I'm sorry."

Matt hugged him. "It's all right."

It wasn't all right, but Iggy didn't feel like he could comment on that. Their relationship was good, a solid presence in Iggy's life, but at the same time, it was stagnant. If it continued to be a secret, did it have any hope of ever moving forward, developing into a lasting commitment? Or would it always be something dirty to be hidden behind closed doors?

He buried his face in Matt's neck. He loved Matt and should have been happy with what they had, and for the most part, he was. But every now and then he got a restless feeling.

Matt pulled him into his arms, and they sat like that for a long moment. Iggy rested his cheek on the soft fabric of Matt's T-shirt and became aware suddenly of Matt's warmth, of his presence. He didn't like for there to be strain between them, but it felt like that sometimes lately, like there was something not quite right.

He wanted to make it right.

"I'm sorry, baby," he said, kissing Matt's neck. "It's been a rough few weeks, I guess. I want to be with you is all. I want to find the best way to keep us together."

"I know. Maybe someday we can live together, but I don't think we're there yet."

"Yeah. Matt?"

"What?"

"Make love to me."

Matt answered the request with a hungry kiss, and Iggy was reminded why he took risks and made sacrifices. He was tied in knots lately over this man he loved so much. Maybe he couldn't have his cake and eat it too, but he could have this.

Matt stood up slowly. "Come to the bedroom with me."

Iggy followed Matt through the apartment. When they were in the bedroom, Matt put his hands on either side of Iggy's face and kissed him. Their mouths opened to each other; their tongues tasted. Love and arousal zipped through Iggy's body, a heady combination. He wanted Matt to press him down into the mattress, wanted to touch Matt's skin, wanted Matt to make him forget his sadness.

"How do you want me?" Matt asked.

"Inside me."

Matt smiled against Iggy's cheek. "I think that can be arranged."

Iggy tugged Matt over to the bed. He pulled off his T-shirt and shucked his warm-up pants. He lay down on his back and waited for Matt to join him.

Matt's body was maybe not as toned as it once had been, but it was still solid, his strength maintained through physical therapy and trips to the gym a few times a week. As Matt peeled off his clothes, Iggy admired that body. He gazed at the long lines of it, the dusting of dark hair over his chest, the way the muscles in his arms and thighs were sculpted. Even the scars on Matt's knee were a part of him, a reminder of what he'd given up and how hard he'd fought to keep it for as long as he had. Matt was so strong and sexy, and Iggy loved every inch of him.

Matt knelt on the bed, and Iggy ogled him, appreciating the way his hard cock tented his briefs. Anticipation and excitement started to move through Iggy, arousal uncoiling, heat spreading. He pulled off his own underwear and gave his cock a few strokes, wanting to show Matt what he did to him.

"I want you bad," Iggy said.

"I can see that." Matt pulled off his briefs and then reached for the drawer with the lube. "You're gorgeous, you know that? So fucking sexy."

"Back at you. God, Matt, hurry up. I want you to fuck me."

"Yeah?"

Matt poured some lube on his fingers and then dipped his head. He licked the skin over Iggy's left nipple before pulling the nipple into his mouth with his teeth. Iggy hissed as sparks of pain and pleasure went through him. He clutched Matt's head and tangled his fingers in Matt's hair. Matt pinched Iggy's other nipple with one hand while he slowly explored the space between Iggy's legs with his other. Lubed-up fingers slid over his cock and then closed around his balls, squeezing gently. Iggy squirmed as his pulse kicked up. He bucked his hips, trying to press his cock against Matt, but Matt moved, planting kisses down the line of Iggy's chest, licking at the muscles. The texture of Matt's tongue and mouth and teeth made Iggy's skin light up, made him arch his back and strain for more.

Matt reached the space where Iggy's legs met his hips, and he pressed his nose into the crease. Matt inhaled, and the movement of air tickled Iggy's skin.

"God, the way you smell is such a turn-on," Matt said. "Even after all this time, I'm still so hot for you."

"Me too. Hot for you, I mean. Want you inside me so bad."

Matt took one of Iggy's balls into his mouth. Matt's lips were smooth, his mouth warm, and Iggy's blood felt like it was pumping hot through his body.

"You're such a tease," Iggy said.

"You like it."

"I do, but I need you closer."

"Mmm."

Matt shifted again. He enveloped Iggy's cock in his mouth. Iggy thrust his hips up and watched as Matt's lips closed around the head of his cock again, as they slid down the length of it. Matt moved his tongue in a zigzag motion up and down the whole shaft, and then he stroked Iggy's cock as he licked the head, slid his tongue into the slit. Lightning bolts of arousal burst through Iggy's body.

"Fuck!" he cried out.

"Getting there. Give me a hand, will you?"

Matt moved his body so his ass was closer to Iggy's face. He went down on Iggy again. Iggy couldn't get his body to bend in a way that would allow him to return the favor, but he could reach Matt's cock with his hand just fine. He wrapped his fingers around it and stroked Matt. Matt rocked his hips, started to fuck Iggy's fist. With awe, Iggy watched the red length of Matt's cock slide through his fingers.

While he was distracted by that, Matt slid his fingers over Iggy's entrance and then plunged a lubed-up finger inside. *Finally*, Iggy thought, wanting more, wanting pain and pleasure. He stroked Matt's cock while Matt sucked him, and all of it made him forget everything but Matt's cock in his hand, Matt's mouth on his cock, Matt's fingers up his ass. It was heady and overwhelming and so fucking hot, Iggy thought he might just float right out of his body.

Matt tossed the lube up toward Iggy. "Slick me up," he said.

"Yes," said Iggy. He poured lube on his hand and then stroked Matt's cock until it was shiny.

"That feels amazing," Matt murmured. "Can't wait to be inside you."

"Now, Matt. Do it now."

"Yeah. Now."

Matt shifted again. He moved carefully now, obviously trying not to put too much of his weight on his knee. He settled between Iggy's legs and gave Iggy's cock a few strokes. "Are you ready?"

"Yes."

Matt positioned the head of his cock at Iggy's entrance but didn't push forward. Iggy tried shifting his hips to encourage him. He wanted nothing more in that moment than for Matt to be inside him. He was half-crazy with anticipation.

Matt kissed him and then said, "Will you still love me when I'm old and gray? Will you still love me when you retire at forty and I'm fifty-three? When we retire to Key West and spend our days on the beach?"

"Yes," Iggy said. "Matt, I want—"

"Will you still love me when I'm out of the closet?"

"Of course."

"Forever, Iggy. You're mine forever."

"Always."

Matt plunged forward.

Pain mingled with satisfaction as Matt finally moved inside Iggy. Iggy dug his fingers into Matt's back and wrapped his legs around him. He dug his heels into Matt's butt to pull him forward. They moved like that for several minutes, their bodies in perfect synchronicity as they glided together. Matt's body pulled sparks and heat and pure pleasure right out of Iggy, made everything bubble and come to the surface, arousal and emotion and so much love for this man he held in his arms, this man who moved inside him. Iggy moved his hips up to allow Matt a better angle, and the head of Matt's cock started to press against his prostate on every thrust inside, making Iggy see stars, making his cock even harder.

"I love you," Iggy said, warmth spreading through his chest.

"Love you too. Forever, Iggy."

"Yes."

Iggy pressed his lips into Matt's neck and loved kissing the stubbly skin. Matt put a hand between them and started tugging on Iggy's cock, which made Iggy forget everything except for the dual sensation of Matt pushing into him while he pulled on Iggy.

Iggy's balls began to tingle, and he knew he was close. He kissed Matt, ran his fingers through Matt's hair, tried touching Matt everywhere. Matt kissed every part of Iggy's face and kept pumping inside him, his pace becoming erratic, his breath uneven, and his movements a little desperate.

"I'm close, Ig," he whispered against Iggy's skin.

"Me too. Harder, Matt. Give me more."

Matt shifted a little and then started thrusting hard and fast into Iggy. He stroked Iggy's cock swiftly, his hand dancing over it.

That was exactly what Iggy needed. He arched into Matt, seeking the last bit of pressure he needed to topple over the edge. And then it hit him, a powerful orgasm, one that seemed to burst through his whole body. He came spurting into Matt's hand, digging his nails into the skin of Matt's arms as he held on for dear life while he flew apart.

Matt followed a split second later, groaning and stiffening and then letting everything go. He threw his head back when he came, and Iggy felt Matt come inside him.

They lay together for a long time afterward, holding each other. But as blissful as this was, some of Iggy's doubts and fears came creeping back as he fell asleep that night.

MATT AND Gus were just finishing up the second draft of the book when the Eagles played their first postseason game.

By Game 4 of the American League Division Series, Iggy was exhausted. Matt seemed thrilled to be so close to finishing his book, and Iggy was grateful that Matt had been able to keep busy for most of the season, but everything seemed to be wearing on him now. The Eagles squeaked out a victory in the game, which ensured that there would be a Game 5. Everyone on the team seemed giddy with the victory, and Iggy had played pretty well, but he had a lot on his mind. He went home after that game instead of going to Matt's.

Matt called him about an hour after he got there. "Why didn't you come over tonight?"

"I'm beat, Matt. If I have any hope of being functional tomorrow, I have to get some rest."

"You can sleep here."

That was true enough, though Matt would be a distraction. "Not tonight, all right? I need some alone time."

"What's wrong?"

"Nothing. I'm just really fucking tired. Let it go so I can sleep and do my job tomorrow, all right?"

"Yeah, all right."

Iggy dragged himself to bed after he got off the phone. It was like everything hit him all at once: he was tired from going back and forth between his and Matt's apartments, tired from extra practice, tired from a long game, tired of all the pressure put on the Eagles to win the World Series.

Teddy Rothschild had paid for a World Series victory this season; that was what the press was saying. It didn't matter that the players were working their asses off, that they'd learned how to work together to make the team a well-oiled machine. The only thing that seemed to matter was the payroll. Not that Iggy could have said anything; his salary was nothing to sneeze at.

But he was tired of all of it.

It shouldn't have been this hard. That was what he thought as he lay awake that night. Being with Matt, having a relationship, it shouldn't have been the struggle it was becoming. Hell, playing baseball shouldn't have been as hard as it was. The game itself was one thing, and Iggy still loved it, still loved going out there every day and playing. He loved the friends he'd made on the team, loved running and hitting the ball, loved the thrill he got when he crossed home plate. But he hated getting mobbed when he went out in public and was tired of sorting through all the offers of endorsement deals.

When he and Matt had first started hooking up, it seemed so ideal, so easy. Matt got him; Matt understood. But lately it felt like they were drifting apart. They loved each other, Iggy didn't doubt that. But Matt was absorbed in writing the book, and Iggy was still playing baseball, worrying about winning and money and bullshit.

Even just being with Matt felt overwhelming and difficult lately. And Iggy had no idea what to do about that.

Chapter Twenty-One

WHEN IGGY came in, Matt was sitting at the table in the kitchen, tapping away at his laptop.

"Is Gus here?" Iggy asked.

"Nope. Didn't come today. I'm just making a couple of revisions. Then it's off to my new editor." Matt grinned.

"That's great." Iggy dropped his bag in the living room.

"You want to get dinner out tonight? Now that this thing is almost done, I feel like celebrating."

"Are you sure?"

Matt shrugged. "We're friends, everyone knows that."

"Okay. Maybe someplace close by. I'm really tired."

"Mmm."

Matt kept typing, so Iggy went about putting his stuff away and washing up for dinner. It struck him as he cleaned up that this was an awfully domestic thing to be doing. He had clean clothes in Matt's dresser, a spare uniform hanging right there in his closet, a toothbrush and a razor and a full set of the rest of his accoutrements. And yet this was still definitely Matt's place. Maybe it was a symptom of Iggy's general fatigue, but even thinking about picking the argument about moving in with Matt made him feel tired.

"Hey, Matt?" he said as he walked back into the kitchen.

"What?"

Iggy stretched. "When the season is done, maybe we should, I don't know, go somewhere together."

"Go somewhere?"

"Like Europe. Asia. A private Caribbean island. Someplace no one will recognize us."

Matt looked up with his eyebrows raised. "Like a vacation?"

"Yeah. If the Eagles win the World Series and I get a nice bonus, then we can go any damn place in the world we want. I don't even care where, as long as I'm there with you."

"I like the sound of that." Matt smiled. "Yeah. Let's do it."

"Excellent. It'll be nice not to have to move between our two apartments for a little while."

Matt stopped what he was doing and dropped his hands. Iggy regretted bringing it up almost immediately.

"You're not still going on about that, are you?" Matt asked. "I thought we discussed it."

Iggy got angry. Something in Matt's voice really grated on him. "We did. And I get it. Just, you know, do we keep living in separate apartments indefinitely?"

"I suppose so."

"No, that's nuts. You have a new opportunity now. When this book comes out, you can live out in the open. There's no reason to keep up the pretense."

"For me, maybe not. But for you, there is. And I think you should spend less time here after the book comes out."

"What?" That tipped Iggy's irritation into fury. "Are you kidding me?"

"You can't risk your whole goddamned career by getting caught with me. When this book comes out, everyone's going to know about me. People will be watching me, paying attention to me again. If you're seen here a lot, people are going to start thinking twice about you."

"So you want to see less of me?"

"That's not what I said. Of course I don't want to see less of you."

"So you're 'looking out for me' by not letting me choose where I spend my time? You know, last time I checked, you were not my boss. I'm not a child."

"I never said you were. Come on, you're twisting what I said. All I meant was I think that once the book comes out, we should be smart about how much time we spend together so there's less risk of you getting exposed."

"Will you listen to yourself? Stop pushing me out!"

"I'm not. This is the best thing for you."

Anger pooled in Iggy's gut. He fisted his hands. "Stop telling me what's best for me. Let me decide that. What I don't want is for you to push me away."

"You said yourself, playing with the Eagles has been your dream since you were a kid. I won't let you throw that away."

Iggy groaned. "You know what was also my dream? To meet and fall in love with a really great guy. Yeah, the Eagles, I've been wanting that most of my life, but it's not worth it to me if I can only have it without you."

Matt sat back, clearly stunned. He furrowed his brow. "So you would give up all of it? For me? No, don't do that. I'm not worth it."

Iggy plopped into a chair and rubbed his forehead, his anger diffusing. "Of course you're worth it. Matt, you're the greatest guy I've ever known.

I want to strangle you right now, but you make me really happy otherwise. Happier than I am when I'm playing baseball. But if all that means nothing to you, then maybe you're right and I should leave."

"I don't…." Matt looked at the ceiling. "I don't want you to leave. You…. Of course you make me happy. You mean a lot to me. You've changed my whole life. I want to be with you. Why can't you do both? Be with me and play baseball?"

"Well, sure, that's the question. Except the way you're proposing I do that is to have half a relationship with you, and that's just not how I operate. I'm tired of sneaking around. I'm tired of the stress of wondering who is going to find out."

Matt raised his eyebrows. "You're not saying…. You're not thinking of coming out publicly, are you?"

"Why the hell shouldn't I?"

"It'll end your career!"

"Will it?" Iggy realized he was shrieking, so he took a deep breath and tried to calm down. "Yeah, you're right, it might. But let's see how your book is received. If the public is willing to accept a gay ex-baseball player, maybe they're ready to accept a gay active player."

"Not just the public. Everyone on the team. I mean, I love those guys, but they're not an open-minded bunch, not all of them anyway, and they could really make your life difficult, and—"

"Yeah, maybe. But maybe it's time to stop dealing in what-ifs."

"You're not going to do anything rash, are you?"

Iggy sighed. "No, of course not. Just…. Don't you get tired of this?"

"I did all the time when I was playing, yeah. You know I did." Matt closed his laptop. "I get what you're going through. But you just had an amazing season, and I don't want to see you do anything to jeopardize your career."

"Yeah."

Matt reached over and rubbed Iggy's knee. "I love you, Ig. I want good things for you."

Iggy nodded. "Things between us, they've been weird lately. Feels more like a routine than a relationship sometimes."

"Yeah, I noticed that too."

"It's as much my fault as yours."

Matt stood up. "I'm not trying to push you out. Hell, if I had my way, you'd move in here tomorrow, damn everyone. I'm just trying to be smart about the risks we take."

Iggy stood as well. "I chose to take this risk, Matt. I chose to be with you. I knew the whole time that the wrong person could catch us. If something happens, we deal with it. And you know what? If the league is so shortsighted that all they can see is my sexuality and not my record, well, fuck 'em. I'll retire with you, and we can be together publicly, and everyone can go fuck themselves."

Matt smiled. "That's a foolish thing to say, but I do adore you."

"I meant every word."

"I know." Matt took a step closer to Iggy. He reached over and traced a line along the edge of Iggy's jaw. "Maybe we need a reminder that we, together, are worth the risk," he said before pressing a sweet kiss to Iggy's lips.

And there it was. The connection, the thing he'd been missing from Matt the past few weeks—hell, the past months. Iggy had liked having his old Matt back while he worked on the book, and surely this was better than the sad, surly Matt of the year before, but distance remained between them that Iggy didn't know how to close.

Now he put his arms around Matt and pressed his palms into Matt's back and thought that maybe they could get back what was missing. They could close the distance.

Matt pulled back a little. "Come on, let's go get something to eat. We can go to the Italian place on Amsterdam that has the gnocchi you like."

"Okay. And while we're there, we can talk about where we're going on vacation."

"Yeah. Someplace really exotic, I think. We'll have your World Series victory to celebrate."

Iggy pulled away and grabbed his jacket. "Yeah, let's not count those chickens yet."

"I predict Eagles in five games."

"Matt?"

"Hmm?" Matt shrugged into his coat.

"Let's talk about anything but baseball tonight."

"MY MOTHER'S flying to New York next week," Iggy said as he pushed gnocchi around his plate.

"Yeah?"

"For the World Series, I mean. I thought maybe you could come have dinner with us one night or something."

"I'd love to."

Iggy nodded and then, thankfully, resumed eating instead of playing with his food.

Matt had spent a little bit of time with Iggy's mother over the past year. In addition to the time he'd met her in New York, he and Iggy had flown to visit her in Arizona during the off-season. From their first meeting, Matt had liked her, and enjoyed both her company and her cooking. She obviously adored her son, which made Matt like her even more.

"What do you think about Barcelona?" Matt asked. "As our vacation destination, I mean. I've always wanted to go to Spain."

Iggy glanced around. They'd been seated in a quiet little corner. Matt had slipped the maître d' extra money to put them somewhere inconspicuous on the pretense, he'd said, of not wanting to be mobbed by fans. The maître d', clearly an Eagles fan, had shown them to this fairly private table.

"Yeah, maybe. I wonder…."

"What?"

Iggy let out a heavy sigh. "Should we hire a plane or something? Is it going to look fishy if we're at the airport together?"

"Probably."

"I've always wanted to go to Spain too. Barcelona is supposed to be a beautiful city."

"I love those old European cities. My sister and I did a tour of Italy a few winters ago, you know that? We went to Venice, Florence, Rome, and Milan over the course of three weeks. I loved Florence the most, I think. We spent a whole week there looking at art. It was wonderful."

Iggy perked up a little at that. "How is Dina these days?"

"Good. She's dating a guy named Pete O'Riordon, so my mother is having fits, going on about how he's one of those *other* Catholics. It's pretty fun to watch, actually. I've talked to him on the phone a couple of times. He seems like a good guy."

"Good, I'm happy for her."

"She's trying to get me to buy art again. Apparently there's an artist out of San Francisco who does the cityscapes that she really likes. Says they're very much my taste. I might fly out there in December and take a look. You can come with if you want."

Iggy seemed to sink into his chair.

"It's easy enough to charter a flight," Matt said. "Keep it all on the down low."

"I know. Just…."

"I know."

Iggy nodded. "How's your chicken?"

"It's good. This sauce is incredible. You want to try it?"

"Okay."

Matt loaded up his fork and was about to feed it to Iggy when he thought better of it and just handed Iggy the whole fork.

"Roger and Lauren went to Vienna a few years ago," Matt said. "They said it's a lovely city."

"That's another idea. By the way, Lauren invited us to dinner the week after next. After the World Series. She told me she misses you."

"Aw, I miss her too. What about Japan?"

"Hong Kong?"

"Mumbai?"

Iggy laughed. "Hell, let's throw darts at a map."

Matt smiled. "Come on, there's got to be someplace you've always wanted to go."

Iggy tilted his head and seemed to consider it. "Maybe Latin America. Brazil or Argentina. Plus, if we go during the winter, it will be summer there."

"Good point. Okay, now we're talking. Maybe we'll go to Rio. Somewhere with nice beaches and decent nightlife."

"Okay. You're on. That sounds like fun."

Matt glanced around the restaurant, and when he didn't see anyone looking their way, he reached under the table and gave Iggy's hand a squeeze. He let it go quickly but was pleased when Iggy smiled at him from across the table.

"I'm sorry," Iggy said.

"What are you apologizing for?"

"Everything has been getting to me lately. It's not you, it's just.... Well, it's kind of everything."

"The season's about to end. Then you can take it easy for a while." Matt lowered his voice. "Think about us on a beach in Brazil, me rubbing sunscreen on your back."

"That does sound amazing."

"We're going to be okay, Iggy. It's like you said when I went to Dallas. We'll find a way to make it work."

Iggy nodded. "You're right—the sauce on this chicken is pretty fantastic. The pesto on the gnocchi is pretty good too, if you want to try it."

Matt took his fork back and used it to spear a couple of gnocchi. The pesto tasted light and fresh. "My mother's is better."

"You're obligated to say so," Iggy said with a smile.

"She actually doesn't make pesto very often. I grew up in a house where the red gravy was served with almost every meal."

"Red gravy?"

"You may know it as marinara. My mother's is the stuff of legend, by the way."

"I know. I've had it. Why do you think I never order Italian dishes with red sauces? Your mother's cooking has ruined me forever."

"Only fair. I haven't been able to eat Latin food since your mother made that meal we had last year. Do you think we can talk her into cooking when she's here next week?"

"I think you'd have a harder time talking her out of cooking. Ten bucks says the first thing she says when she sees me is that I'm too skinny."

"You are not too skinny. Has she seen your abs?"

"Everyone in the country has seen my abs."

Matt laughed. "Oh, true. I forgot. Man. That paella she made with the fresh fish. I still dream about it."

"I wish I had known earlier that the way to your heart was through your stomach."

"I *am* Italian." Matt grinned. "I wish I had known earlier that your mother was such a good cook. Maybe she'll make enough that we'll have leftovers."

Iggy smiled and ate a few more gnocchi. "I don't know that it's really fair to make a woman cook when she's here on vacation."

"I know, I know. Wishful thinking. I bet the food in Brazil will be just as good."

"Maybe not, but I'm sure we'll enjoy it."

Chapter Twenty-Two

IT FELT like a dream.

Iggy stood on the field, tired and dirty but also elated. Some players went their whole careers without a moment like this, and yet here he was, after a mere three seasons in the big leagues, soaking in his first World Series win.

It was a hard-fought victory, with the Eagles eking out a win in the very last inning of Game 6 to take the whole thing. Although Iggy had played pretty well all series, if he did say so himself—eight runs scored, including three home runs, a dozen runs batted in, and several crucial defensive plays—he'd been in the dugout when Manuel Cruz had run home, giving the Eagles the one run they needed to win the game.

And still the press had been talking about declaring Iggy the Series MVP, even though Alvarez, Cruz, and Caballo had played just as well, even though Roger had pitched a nearly flawless six innings in Game 4, even though the victory genuinely felt like a team effort.

Indeed, when Teddy Rothschild took to the stage that had been spontaneously erected over the pitcher's mound, he declared Alvarez the MVP. Iggy thought that was just fine; he didn't care for Alvarez much as a person, but he'd played brilliantly all season, and he had scored the tying run in two of the four games the Eagles won.

The only thing that would have made this better was if Matt had been there, but alas, the game had been held at the opposing team's stadium in St. Louis, and Matt hadn't been able to get tickets, though not for lack of trying.

A little while later, as the team celebrated in the locker room by spraying champagne everywhere, Roger walked up to Iggy and slapped him on the back. "So, rookie, how's it feel?"

"This is my third year in the majors. I'm not a rookie anymore."

"But it's your first World Series. How does it feel?"

"Pretty damn good. But this must be old hat to you. How many is this now? Three?"

"Four, actually." Roger puffed out his chest. Then he laughed. "You know what? It never fucking gets old."

Iggy laughed with him. "Glad to hear it." There was enough noise and commotion that he felt safe saying under his breath, "I wish Matt were here."

Roger nodded. "Me too. But I tell you what. When we're back home, we should all go out for a drink. I'll bring Lauren; we can invite Cruz. It'll be like old times. Yeah?"

"Sure, Roger."

"Speaking of Lauren, she's waiting for me outside the locker room, so I better finish up here."

Of course Roger had been able to score tickets for his wife. But Iggy didn't want to become bitter. Not on a night like tonight. Not when everything he'd been working for had happened. Not only was this the first World Series he'd ever played in, but the Eagles had won, and he still didn't quite believe that.

EMMA WINSTEAD was taller than Matt expected. Showbiz people were almost always short, but Emma—she'd insisted he call her Emma—was nearly six feet tall even when she wasn't walking around with those ice picks she called shoes.

She walked into the greenroom and smiled at him. "Hi, there. I like to greet all my guests before they come on the show. It tricks the audience into thinking we're not total strangers when you come onto the soundstage. How are you?"

"I'm all right."

"Nervous?"

Matt wondered if the hurricane-force winds moving through his stomach could still qualify as "nervous." "Uh, you could say that."

She smiled again. "You'll be fine. Try not to fidget on camera. Smile a lot."

"Okay."

"Seriously, I want to help you. I'm here for you. A.J. and I have been friends a long time, and he tells me you're a nice guy. I believe him. So be that guy." She took a deep breath. "A.J. gave me an approved list of questions, but is there anything totally off-limits?"

"I won't talk about my boyfriend," said Matt.

"Noted. Can I say you have one? The ladies in the audience like that sort of thing."

"I guess." He'd said as much in the book, hadn't he? "I won't say his name."

Emma nodded. "Basically what's going to happen is I'm going to introduce you, we'll chat about baseball, I'll introduce the book, you be charming and smile a lot. Then I'll tell the audience that you have something you want to tell everyone, and then you say it however you want. Got it?"

Why had Matt agreed to come out on national television? Why had he let A.J. talk him into doing a daytime talk show with a mostly female audience? Why had Iggy said, "Oooh, I love Emma Winstead. She's so dishy!" in a way that made Matt think this was a good idea?

This was a terrible idea.

It was one thing to know something in your gut, but it was another thing entirely to say it out loud.

By the time a PA came by to escort him to the soundstage, Matt was pretty sure he was going to throw up. He just hoped it wasn't on Emma Winstead.

The PA made him stop just short of the stage. Matt gazed out at the set that was made to look like someone's living room. It might have been convincing if there hadn't been a live studio audience. The audience itself was especially terrifying; Matt estimated that there were maybe a hundred people there, most of them women.

"Emma's gonna introduce you," the PA said, pinning a wireless mike to his lapel. "When she says your name, walk out slowly. Wave to the audience. Smile. Walk over to the green chair, but don't sit until Emma invites you to. Answer her questions. Don't get up until the director says cut. Got it?"

"Got it."

She slapped his back and said, "Good."

He heard the director shout, "And we're back in five, four, three...."

Then the cameras were rolling. Matt tried to swallow his nerves. God, he wished Iggy were here. Iggy would know how to calm him down. He'd tell a dumb joke or just give him a hug. But Matt knew he had to do this alone. His only consolation was that, now that the baseball season had ended, Iggy was guaranteed to be home when all this was over.

Iggy was guaranteed to be in *Matt's* home, he realized. Iggy didn't really live there.

That made him feel worse.

Emma said, "You guys may know my next guest as the former Brooklyn Eagles' first baseman. He's quite a looker if you know what I mean." Someone in the audience hooted. "Yeah, he is! He's a pretty swell guy all around. He's got a new book hitting shelves tomorrow, and he's here to talk about that, so please welcome to *The Emma Show* Matt Blanco!"

Matt did as he'd been told. He walked onto the stage slowly. He pasted a smile on his face. He waved at the audience. How many press conferences had he had to do after bad games? How many public appearances had he made when he hadn't wanted to see people? He could fake his way through this.

With that small comfort, he walked over to Emma, shook her hand, and sat in the green chair when she invited him to.

Once the audience had calmed down—they'd received him enthusiastically, though Matt was pretty convinced half of them had no idea who he was—Emma grinned at him and said, "Hey there, Matt. How's it going?"

"It's going pretty well, Emma," he said, sitting up a little, grinning at the audience, trying to play the part of a confident man even while his stomach seemed to be trying to eat itself.

"So you are legendary first baseman Matt Blanco." She glanced at the card in her hand. "Almost six hundred career home runs, fourteen seasons in the majors. Plenty of people say you're almost guaranteed a spot in the Hall of Fame. How does that feel?"

Matt plastered on that smile. "Well, I'd be lying if I said I didn't miss the game, but it's hard to have any regrets with stats like that."

Emma laughed. "Indeed. And you retired last year. A knee injury, right? How is that now?"

"The knee still bothers me sometimes, but it's almost completely healed now."

"That's good to hear. And the Eagles just won the World Series. Can you believe that?"

"Man, it's great. I still love my team, you know? A lot of those guys are still close friends of mine."

"Yeah, I read that you and pitcher Roger May are pretty close."

"We came up through the minors together. We played together almost twenty years. He's like my brother."

"I imagine you must build some pretty close friendships with your teammates."

"Yeah, you do."

"You talk about that some in your new book."

And here it went, thought Matt. Emma picked up a copy of the book—the cover was taken up mostly by a close-up shot of Matt holding a baseball bat so that it casually leaned on his shoulder—and showed it to the camera. The audience oohed and aahed appropriately.

"Now, I want to talk about the book," Emma said. "Because I've read it, and it's incredible. There's some really touching stuff in here. One of the things you said is that though you were close friends with a lot of your teammates, there was one secret you never told them. Can you tell us what that was?"

This was his moment. The whole fucking world was staring at Matt Blanco. He'd been telling himself all morning that all he had to do was say two little words and that forty-year-long chapter of his life would finally be over. And, if it was possible, his panic kicked up a notch.

He fumbled. When he realized he was taking a long time to answer, he said, "It's so hard to say out loud."

Emma reached over and touched his knee. "I know, honey. Can you tell us anyway?"

Matt took a deep breath. He needed to just say it. Everyone would know within the next twenty-four hours anyway. "Well, Emma. I'm gay."

He dug his fingers into the upholstery on the arms of the chair, as if that would help him brace for impact.

The audience murmured, but Matt couldn't tell if they were good or bad. Too terrified to look, he focused instead on Emma, who smiled at him sweetly.

"Your book is mostly about what it was like to be a closeted professional athlete. I imagine that must have been incredibly hard for you."

"Not all the time, but sometimes, yeah." If he just focused on Emma, it was like they were having a simple conversation. Matt worked hard to pretend the audience wasn't there.

"Like with your friends on the team. They didn't know the truth about you."

"A couple of my closest friends knew, but most of my teammates didn't. It's just, you know, there's so much teasing in the locker room, a lot of gay jokes, and it's not always clear who would be okay with it and who wouldn't be. You get guys who say these things, like they don't want a gay guy on the team because it would be uncomfortable or threatening or whatever. But, you know, I'm just like every other guy on that team. I'm not in the locker room to pick up men. I'm there to get ready to play baseball. But a lot of the straight players don't seem to get that. I lied. I lied for years." And apparently now that he'd started talking, it was hard to stop.

"You say in the book that your family knew. Did they accept you?"

"Yeah. My parents were great that way. I told them when I was twenty-five, and I've never doubted for a moment that they love me. I was lucky. I know a lot of kids didn't have it so well."

"Yeah. You also write about a guy in the book, someone you fell in love with. Are you still together?"

Matt couldn't keep himself from smiling as he thought of Iggy. "We are, yeah. Going on three years now."

The audience clapped, which made Matt smile wider. He chanced a look at them. Because of the lighting in the studio, he couldn't really make out most of their faces from where he was sitting, but people seemed to be cheering instead of booing.

"That's really wonderful," said Emma. "So what made you want to write this book?"

Matt sighed. The nausea was starting to lessen now. He'd said what he needed to, and the world hadn't ended. "It was my boyfriend's suggestion, actually. But as soon as he said it, I started thinking about how I felt as a boy. You know, you hear about these kids now, the ones really struggling, the ones who kill themselves. I know how that feels, because I was that kid once too. But I imagined what it would have been like if one of my idols had come out, if he'd said, 'I know what you're going through, and you can get through it and live a great life.' So that's what I decided to do."

"I think you're doing a great thing, Matt, both for those kids and for the game of baseball. You've written really honestly about your experiences in the book, and who knows, maybe it will inspire some change."

"I really hope so, Emma."

"Well, we have to take a break, but when we come back, I'll have more with Matt Blanco. Don't go anywhere!"

Matt breathed a sigh of relief when the camera cut.

"You're doing great, honey, really," Emma said.

"Thank you."

"I know it's hard."

"It's a very strange experience."

"Can you answer a few more questions? Nothing more probing than anything you've said in the book."

"Yeah. The hard part's over. I think I can answer your questions."

Emma smiled. "I do think you're doing a good thing. An athlete as high profile as you coming out of the closet? That's pretty amazing."

"Thanks."

"Okay, back in sixty seconds," said the director.

So Matt settled in for the rest of his interview.

Chapter Twenty-Three

THE PHONE rang off the hook for two weeks.

Matt didn't answer it unless he recognized the number on his caller ID. He didn't want to do more interviews, although he had agreed to the few that A.J. had set up. He didn't really want to talk to former players either, although plenty of them had called. The voice mails were mixed: together he and Iggy had determined that for every two or three calls from people who wanted to congratulate him and wish him well, there was one guy who felt the need to call him and tell him how gross he was, how he couldn't imagine how they'd ever shared a locker room. One former player—not anyone Matt was close to but a guy who'd played with the Eagles for one season ten years before—had gone so far as to call Matt a sick fuck right there on his private voice mail. Matt wanted to change his number.

But the majority of the responses were positive. Even Jake Caballo called to apologize for every gay joke he'd made in the locker room. "I had no idea, man," he'd said when he got Matt on the phone. "I swear if I did, I never would have—"

"Water under the bridge," Matt had replied.

And it was true that Matt didn't bear his former teammates much ill will. In fact he generally felt lighter, like a weight had been lifted. Because even while some conservative news sources condemned him—among other things, a parents' group was ceremonially burning a pile of Blanco merchandise—he felt like he'd found freedom. He wasn't lying to anyone anymore. He was just… himself.

The funny thing was that people kept telling him how brave he was. But Matt didn't feel especially brave. He felt cowardly for keeping it a secret for so long.

But it sure as hell was nice, three weeks after his appearance on Emma Winstead's show, to be flying into Buenos Aires with Iggy. They'd had to hire a private jet, which had made Iggy laugh when they'd made arrangements—"Talk about your first-world problems," he'd said—but Matt kept getting mobbed when he went out in public, and he didn't want to draw extra attention to Iggy.

And so it was that one night, as they had dinner at an outdoor cafe—which gave Matt an excellent opportunity to admire the architecture in Buenos Aires—Iggy said, "You know, I'm really proud of you."

"Really?"

"Yeah. I know how much you were sweating going on *The Emma Show*, and I know how worried you were about how the book would be received, and yet here you are. No worse for wear. Right?"

Matt glanced around the restaurant. He spotted another gay couple cuddling together in a corner. "Can I try something?" he asked.

Iggy raised an eyebrow. "Okay."

"Give me your hand."

Iggy held his hand out, palm down. Matt pressed it onto the table, and then he threaded their fingers together. Iggy looked at their tangled hands for a long time and then said with no small amount of awe in his voice, "We're holding hands in public."

"We sure are."

"That's…. Wow."

"I know."

"And you thought you'd never be able to do this." Iggy looked up and smiled.

"Well, we did have to hire a private jet and fly five thousand miles to be able to do this."

Iggy laughed. "I guess we did."

When a waitress came to take their orders, Iggy tried to take his hand away, but Matt held firm. The waitress smiled at them. Iggy rolled his eyes and ordered for them in halting Spanish.

When the waitress left, Matt said, "I've heard you speak Spanish beautifully. What was that about? Am I really so distracting?"

"No." Iggy shook his head. "I was trying to hide my accent. It took me a moment to remember my school Spanish. A lot of other Latinos find the Dominican accent to be ugly."

"Really?"

"Yeah, I heard that all the time when I was a kid. The Mexican kids I went to school with made fun of me for it."

"Well, for what it's worth, *I* think you are really sexy when you speak Spanish."

"That's because you can't understand half of what I'm saying."

"Still." Matt smiled.

Iggy smiled back and squeezed his hand.

IT WAS fun to watch Matt act like a kid in a candy shop, his eyes wide as they walked around Buenos Aires. He was constantly reaching for his camera to take photos of the buildings he liked, and he'd tell Iggy he thought the city looked like some he'd visited in Europe. That Matt knew so much about art and architecture was a surprise to Iggy.

"Well, babe, while you were winning a World Series ring, I was studying," he said when Iggy pointed it out.

Matt was in rare form the whole trip. Gone was the melancholy of the previous year; gone even was the fidgety nervousness of the weeks leading up to the book's release. Instead Matt seemed happy. He made jokes, he got excited about places they visited, he was effusive in his praise of the meals they ate. Iggy found it impossible not to get caught up in his enthusiasm.

He let Matt talk him into tango lessons, followed by a lively performance one night where they sat in the audience and watched lithe dancers move sensually across the floor. One afternoon they took a tour through the city on a colorful tour bus. They went shopping, and Matt picked out outfits for Iggy. When they walked through the Plaza de Mayo one afternoon, Iggy looked for signs that Matt's knee was bothering him, but it didn't seem to be. In fact, Matt pointed out the Casa Rosada and sang a couple of lines from "Don't Cry for Me Argentina."

They lay in bed together on their last night in town. A warm breeze wafted in through the open window, and Iggy enjoyed the way the night air felt on his skin, the way Matt's arms felt around him.

"I'm sad to be going back home tomorrow," Iggy said.

"Yeah. This has been a fantastic trip." He kissed the side of Iggy's face.

"It's been so easy to be with you here."

Matt squeezed Iggy tight. "Yeah."

Iggy pressed his ass back a little in an effort to get closer to Matt and was greeted with Matt's cock growing hard against his thigh. "Well," Iggy said. "Are you just happy to see me?"

"I'm always happy to see you." Matt kissed the shell of Iggy's ear before he gently sucked on his earlobe.

That was enough to wake Iggy's body up. Warmth spread through his chest, through his limbs. His skin started to tingle. "How is it possible for me to want you again?"

Matt wrapped his hand around Iggy's cock. "I'm irresistible."

"You are; it's true."

"Mmm. I love you, Ig." Matt nibbled at Iggy's neck. "I worried that maybe we'd lost that for a while, that things between us were strained, but this trip... I can't really explain it, but I feel like I'm alive again."

"Yeah, I know what you mean."

Matt thrust his hips against Iggy's, and his hard cock slid between Iggy's asscheeks while Matt continued to lazily stroke Iggy's cock. The sensation was thrilling and arousing, and Iggy got hot and bothered for what felt like the millionth time during that trip.

"We're about to make love again, aren't we?" he asked.

"Something about the air in Argentina. Man, those tango dancers yesterday? The way they moved. The whole thing was so hot. I wish we could take tango lessons when we get back home."

"Really?"

"Yeah. I'd love to be able to dance like that with you. The way your body moves sometimes is so sexy. I watched the way you danced during the lesson." Matt thrust forward against Iggy's butt again, his cock sliding now against Iggy's asscrack. Matt's skin was soft and warm where it touched Iggy's. Iggy loved that Matt was using his body to get off, and he was turned on by the fact that Matt wanted him so much.

Matt groped at Iggy's skin with the hand that wasn't on his cock. He thrust against Iggy's ass at a steady pace, and his breath came faster. Iggy reached a hand back and placed it on Matt's hip, encouraging him to keep moving, to keep stroking Iggy's cock, to continue to make Iggy feel like he was the hottest thing in Argentina. He wanted them to get off together. He considered turning around and asking Matt to make love to him on their last night in this place, but what Matt was doing felt *good*. Matt knew exactly how much pressure Iggy liked, knew all the secret places to touch. Theirs was not the frenzied love of a new relationship but instead something learned and practiced, though no less exciting.

The heat and friction mounted as Iggy and Matt moved together, pushing and pulling each other toward ecstasy, pressing their flesh together. Iggy's body arched, and he thrust into Matt's hand, needing just a little more to get off, just a little more, just a little....

Matt sank his teeth into Iggy's shoulder as he came, wet heat hitting Iggy's back, and the mere knowledge that Matt was coming against him got Iggy off. He grasped Matt's hand on his cock and squeezed just enough to make the pleasure that had been pooling in his stomach unleash itself, and then Iggy was coming. He threw his head back and groaned, and everything went white.

They lay together silently for a long time afterward. Iggy started to drift off to sleep, but before he did, Matt said, "This trip. So incredible. You're incredible."

"I love you, Matt. But man, go to sleep. We have a flight tomorrow."

Matt chuckled, his chest vibrating against Iggy's.

Iggy went to sleep, content to be enveloped in the warm night air and Matt's arms. Because whatever might be awaiting them back in New York could wait.

Home

WELCOME TO THE NEW SEASON OF EAGLES BASEBALL

by Cary Galvin, Sports Net

Coming off last season's World Series win, it looks like this organization has got a heck of a season ahead of them this year as well. These guys looked excellent in spring training. But before I get into that, let's talk about the elephant in the room. Matt Blanco's memoir sure made a splash in the off-season.

The big confession aside, the book itself is a pretty interesting look at the inner workings of a professional baseball team. And Blanco being Blanco, he was never mean to anyone in the book, never named names, just said he'd had a hard time with some aspects of the way the game was played.

It's those aspects of the game that are my primary concern. As a gay man myself, I've often wondered when it would be possible for an active professional baseball player to come out publicly. It has long been my theory that major-league locker rooms aren't nearly the bastions of intolerance they're often thought to be, although of course there are still plenty of people in these organizations who don't want to see a gay player. But it makes you wonder, doesn't it? Blanco's memoir was widely praised. Could this mean attitudes have changed enough for a gay active player to live life openly?

But back to the Eagles. This new class of rookies has been doing some interesting things....

Chapter Twenty-Four

TEDDY ROTHSCHILD sat with his fingers steepled at his chin. Iggy felt a little intimidated looking at him. Teddy was generally not known as a man who put up with any nonsense, and he looked especially stern staring across his desk at Iggy, his lips pressed into a thin line.

"Maybe we should get started," said Chris McGrath, Iggy's agent.

Haverman crossed and uncrossed his legs. "Is there a problem, Iggy?"

Iggy glanced at Chris, who nodded for him to go on. "Not a problem per se," said Iggy, "but I think there's something you should know. It may become an issue, and I want to know what I should do about it if that happens. I would appreciate everyone's input on the matter."

"You're injured," said Haverman. "I fucking knew it. It was that slide into third the other night, wasn't it? I saw you twist your ankle, and I thought—"

"No, Bill, I'm fine. Nothing's wrong with me."

"Shit, steroids." Haverman shook his head. "Goddammit, I should have known. I thought you were smarter than that, Ig."

Iggy sighed, frustrated. "No, I'm not taking steroids, or any PEDs. Come on, Bill, I thought you knew me better than that."

"What is it, then?" asked Teddy.

Iggy glanced at Chris again. "Well, sir, I'm moving in a couple of weeks, for one thing. I bought a house in Brooklyn."

Teddy put his hands on the desk. "That's good." There was a fair amount of caution in his voice. "We like when our players live locally."

Iggy looked at the ceiling. He knew he just had to come out with it and take the consequences. He was getting so tired of keeping it a secret. He tried to make his mouth form the words a couple of times, but nothing came out.

"God, Iggy, what is it?" asked Haverman.

Iggy thought about the expression on Matt's face when they'd toured the house, the longing in his eyes as they'd walked through the empty rooms of the recently renovated brownstone. Iggy had finally talked him into living together, and as with everything Matt did these days, he'd dived into the project headfirst. The house was perfect: well maintained, spacious, and close to the stadium. It was the sort of house, the realtor insisted, that was great for a couple. Iggy thought about how happy Matt had seemed when they closed, how sweetly Matt had kissed him afterward. Despite the risk, Iggy knew buying the place had been the right decision.

When Iggy lowered his head, everyone in the room was looking at him.

He took a deep breath. Matt had told him that morning that it was just two little words. Iggy tried to think of it that way as he said, "I'm gay."

Everything in the room stilled.

Iggy let out a breath. "There. It's out there. I'm gay. I bought a house with my boyfriend. He's having all my stuff moved when the team is on the road next week, because he thought it would be more discreet if we weren't seen moving together. Except now we own this house, so there's a certain inevitability that we'll be seen together. And I thought you should know so you can tell me what I should do with the press should they catch wind of this, or if you're just going to fire me, or whatever the fallout will be."

Haverman and Teddy sat there for a long moment. Iggy resisted the urge to chatter to fill the silence.

"Wait," said Haverman. "This is the issue? This is what this is about? You're gay?"

"Yeah, that's all this is," said Chris. "See? Small issue."

Teddy cleared his throat. "What are you going to do?"

"Me?" Iggy said. "Nothing. I mean, I've thought about coming out publicly, but I know what the fans are like, and I was worried about how the team would react, and Matt keeps saying…. Well, I'm just not sure it's a good idea. I know there have been a few professional athletes who have come out, but—"

Haverman held up his hand. "Matt? Matt Blanco? Have you been talking to him about this?"

"He'd know, wouldn't he?" said Teddy.

"You should tell them the whole story," said Chris.

Iggy bit his lip. "Uh, well. Matt Blanco is my boyfriend."

"Jesus Christ," said Teddy.

"Blanco? Really? Did you hook up with him after his book came out?" Haverman seemed genuinely curious.

"Uh, no. Matt and I have been together for four years. Since, uh, his last season with the Eagles. His last real season, I mean."

Everyone went silent again.

Chris was the first one to speak. "As you can see, Iggy and Matt have been the picture of discretion since they got together. They can keep it up, but Iggy thought you should know the whole truth just in case the media finds out, so that we can devise a strategy."

"So you're the player Matt wrote about in his book?" said Teddy.

Iggy nodded. "You guys didn't seem to have any problem with anything he wrote about in the book, though. There was no reaction from the Eagles' front office, besides that you supported him. But he's sort of treading water now. He auditioned for a sportscaster job and was turned down, we think because he's gay. He was told the fans don't like him anymore. So I thought I could come to you with this, and maybe you'd fire me, but maybe you'd get behind me, and I really hope it's the latter, because I love playing here. Like, in my soul, I love this team. But I love Matt too, and I'm very tired of sitting around waiting for the other shoe to drop. I don't know how much longer I can keep this up. And I thought you should know that." He sat back in his chair and grunted. "This is coming out all jumbled. I'm sorry."

Teddy pursed his lips. "Look, Iggy. I don't have a problem with gay people. I'm surprised, but it's not a problem for us. Is it, Bill?"

Bill shook his head.

"But I do think it's important to stay discreet. If at all possible."

"But what if it hits the press?" Chris asked.

"Do we deny it?" asked Bill.

"No," said Teddy. "I want to do a little research, find out something about fan reaction. But we don't deny it. It comes out, we deal with it."

TWO WEEKS after his meeting with Teddy and Haverman, after eight days out of town, Iggy got a cab from the airport to the new house. Though he'd been to the house a half dozen times and had his key firmly in hand, it still felt like he was breaking into a stranger's house when he pushed through the front door.

"Matt?" he called as he came in. He dropped his luggage near the door.

"Kitchen," shouted Matt from the back of the house.

Iggy waded through the sea of boxes and found Matt in the kitchen, unpacking dishes. He leaned forward a little and puckered his lips, so Iggy kissed him.

"Hi," said Iggy.

"Hi. Welcome home."

Something about that warmed Iggy down to his bones and helped the past few days—a tough road trip during which the Eagles had lost more than they'd won—fall away. He smiled and walked around the boxes. He pulled Matt into his arms for a tight hug.

Matt laughed. "How was your flight?"

"Fine. Uneventful." Iggy pulled away. "Oh, Bill wanted me to give you this." He pulled an envelope out of his pocket.

Matt raised an eyebrow and took the envelope. Before he opened it, he asked, "Do you know what it is?"

"A pass to your permanent seat in Section Fourteen at FSB Stadium."

Matt furrowed his brow. "Section Fourteen? But that's where the wives sit." He blinked a few times and looked Iggy in the eye. "I'm a baseball wife now, aren't I?"

Iggy rubbed Matt's shoulder. "Well, to be fair, all friends of the team sit in Section Fourteen. Former players end up there all the time. Hell, the President of the United States sits there when he comes to games. If you're worried about drawing attention to yourself, I don't think it's a big deal. But somehow Bill found out you've been buying tickets to home games online, and he didn't want you to have to do that anymore."

"It's not like I can't afford it," Matt said, stuffing the envelope in his pocket.

"You can sit with Lauren. Also, this way, I'll always know where to find you in the stands."

Matt smiled and nodded.

Feeling embarrassed by that little display of emotion, Iggy said, "So how's unpacking going?"

"Fine." Matt pointed to one of the boxes. "You have some really ugly dishes, you know that?"

"The ones with the stripes were a housewarming gift from my mother. We have to keep them. She's going to ask about them when she visits."

Matt grimaced. "All right."

Iggy laughed. "Man, I'm tired. I need some dinner, some sweet loving, and a whole lot of sleep, not necessarily in that order."

"I think I can help with those things." Matt smirked. "Although the new oven's not gonna be here until Tuesday, so dinner will have to be delivery. Unless you want to go out. There's a cute little taco place down the street."

Iggy found himself grinning. "I missed you," he said.

"Me too. Come here, I want to show you something."

Matt took Iggy's hand and led him back through the house and out the front door. When they got to the sidewalk, Matt turned them around so they were facing the house.

Iggy studied the front of the house but didn't notice anything out of the ordinary. "What are we looking at?"

Matt threw an arm around Iggy. "This is our home."

Matt didn't need to explain further; Iggy got it. Looking up at the house suddenly felt like the culmination of everything they'd gone through for the past four years: from the first moment they met, to the first time they kissed, to Matt getting traded and hurting his knee, to the book, to everything Iggy wanted. He leaned into Matt, who kissed his temple. Iggy felt a little surprised that Matt was being so affectionate outside in public, but then, the sidewalk was deserted.

Iggy's stomach rumbled. He sighed. "So about that dinner?"

"Let's just get something delivered. Then we can get to the sweet loving faster."

Chapter Twenty-Five

AFTER A homestay, the Eagles were off to Cleveland and then Pittsburgh, and Iggy found himself getting increasingly tired and restless as the week wore on. It was hard to put a finger on exactly what the problem was, but he knew something was off. It didn't affect his playing until the first game of the series against Pittsburgh, when he flubbed a catch that allowed the Pittsburgh runner to get to second and, eventually, to score.

He lay awake in bed in the hotel that night, thinking about calling Matt, when his phone rang. It was Cary.

"Did you see the game today?" Iggy asked.

"Yeah, that was a rough catch. They replayed it on *Baseball Tonight* about six times."

"Oh God. I don't need to know about things like that."

"Eh, you'll be better tomorrow. I have another reason for calling. And it's kind of urgent."

"What is it?"

"You're, um, well. There's a story that's going to hit the Internet, probably tomorrow."

"About me? Spit it out, Cary."

"Someone's onto you. You were spotted having dinner with Matt the last time you were in New York, which isn't exactly damning, but my understanding is that there's a small-potatoes New York gossip blog that has a story outing you as the mystery player in Matt's book."

Iggy felt sick suddenly.

"It's a pretty under-the-radar thing, not anything that any of the sports blogs would have picked up on normally, except a big-time gossip blog caught hold of the story. And even then, usually stories about the personal lives of players are the least viewed on our site because the fans don't really care what you do off the field. But this is kind of big. My boss wants me to investigate and report on it."

"Holy shit."

"I told him I couldn't do it because of my personal relationship with you."

"Okay." Iggy's ears started ringing. "Shit. Shit."

"Unless."

"Unless what?"

"Well, you're always saying how much of a toll keeping the secret takes on you. Maybe this is the end of the road. If I break the story, at least someone you trust is behind it."

"I guess. I have to talk to my agent. Christ, what am I going to do?"

"It's not like it used to be. There are a handful of out athletes playing for professional teams today. And you're on top right now. You've been putting up good numbers all season—for the last three seasons—and the fans really like you. Most of the team already knows, anyway, right? This won't affect your career."

"Rothschild wanted to keep it quiet."

"Well, he may not have a choice in the matter."

EAGLES MANAGEMENT opted not to comment on the story and instructed Iggy to do the same, which worked fine for the second game against Pittsburgh—during which Iggy hit a home run and played an error-free defense—but it was clear going into the third game that the story had spread.

Iggy went up to the plate in the first inning and was greeted with what sounded like boos. He'd gotten pretty used to zoning out commentary from the stands, so he moved into his batting stance and prepared to hit. First pitch was a fastball, and he swung and missed it. Out of the corner of his eye, he saw a fan in the box behind home plate get up and shake his ass at the field. Iggy closed his eyes and tried to concentrate. He picked up his old routine for getting through the game: mental recitation.

Felicitas on the mound. He's got a mean curveball. It'll be slow and to the left. Or he might throw another fast one, right through the middle of the strike zone. Bat up, foot down, hips back, lean forward. Wind up. Pitch. It's low. Swing.

Iggy felt his bat connect with the ball, and he took off for first base. It was a grounder that rolled between the second baseman and the shortstop, creating enough of a stall getting it into play that Iggy reached first base successfully.

As he waited for the next batter in the lineup to hit, he looked up at the stands and noticed three guys standing a little above home plate. They lifted their shirts to reveal letters painted on their stomachs. Read across, they spelled, *FAG*. One of them pointed at Iggy.

Iggy broke out in a cold sweat waiting for Caballo to hit the ball. He crouched a little, thinking the delay might give him enough time to steal second. Then Caballo hit a pop-up, so Iggy took off for second anyway. The left fielder caught the ball, getting Caballo out.

Standing at second, Iggy heard a droning chant from the stands. It sounded like, "Ig-gy, Ig-gy," but he wasn't quite sure.

The next batter struck out, leaving Iggy nervously stranded at second while he waited for Cruz to bat. Cruz walked, and the Pirates' pitcher wiped his forehead. Iggy went back to concentrating on the game, wondering if he'd be able to steal third, wondering how fast Felicitas's reflexes really were. But then it didn't matter, because Greg Letum hit a pop-up that looked like it might go foul until the Pittsburgh catcher caught it. End of inning.

Iggy ran back to the dugout to get his glove and made eye contact with Haverman, hoping that he'd imagined what was going on in the stands. Haverman bit his lip, which seemed like a bad sign.

The next inning progressed without further incident, but Iggy was up again in the third. The crowd was a little drunker and a little more candid. The taunts were juvenile nonsense on the surface. "You hit like a girl, Rodriguez!" someone shouted. Then, after Iggy got his second strike, he heard quite clearly from someone sitting behind him, "After you strike out, why don't you come on over here and suck my cock, Rodriguez." Iggy was so flustered he missed the fifth pitch by a wide margin.

"Don't let this shit get to you," Haverman said when Iggy retreated to the dugout. "You have to block it out."

Iggy tried to keep that in mind when he trotted out to the field to start the fifth inning, but now people held up signs in the stands. Iggy couldn't read most of them because of the distance, but one he could read had giant black letters that spelled *No gay in baseball!*

His panic mounted as the inning progressed. The ball only came his way twice: once when the second baseman got hold of a grounder that he tossed at Iggy, after which Iggy easily made the out at third; then again when a batter hit a pop fly that Iggy caught. Neither play was hard to make, or at least not so hard that Iggy's well-honed instincts couldn't take over and do the work for him. Which was good, because the gay slurs were increasing.

The inning ended, and Iggy went straight for Haverman. "Take me out of the game," he said.

"No," said Haverman. "You leave and these assholes win."

"I don't think I can play anymore."

Cruz walked over. "You're not thinking of leaving the game, are you, Ig?"

"I'm starting to panic," said Iggy. He didn't know how else to explain the tightness in his chest or the trouble he was having breathing.

"If I take you out, then everything those fans are saying will be justified. It'll be better for you in the long run if you stick it out. So I'm keeping you in the game unless I think it's dangerous. Okay?"

Iggy glanced at Cruz, who nodded. He took a deep breath. "Okay. I'll do my best."

Things only got worse after that.

AT HOME, Matt flipped on the game about an hour after it started. He cracked open a beer and ate a handful of popcorn out of the bowl he'd put on the coffee table. As the din of the crowd crescendoed over the speakers, Matt realized the general tone of it sounded a little angry. The announcers were spouting some trivia—which included "the single-game home run record for this stadium is three, achieved by the Eagles' own Matt Blanco back in 2001"—and then they were back on the game.

"Well, top of the sixth," said one of the announcers. "Gotta say, it was looking for a minute there like Haverman was going to take out Iggy Rodriguez, but there he is, still in the game."

That had Matt's full attention. He worried Iggy had been hurt, but it must not have been bad if Haverman had kept him in the game.

"If you're just joining us," said the other announcer, whose voice Matt recognized as belonging to Bill McClintock, "we're at PNC Park, watching the Pirates take on the Eagles in a real nail-biter of a game. These Eagles batters haven't been able to get much past Felicitas, and Roger May has given us five scoreless innings so far."

"But the real story this afternoon might be the reception the Eagles are getting from the fans at this ballpark." The other announcer sounded like Ray Swenson, who had once been a mediocre outfielder for Dallas but who had made good as a sportscaster. Or, sorry, "baseball analyst," Matt thought with a little bit of bitterness. "You ever see anything like this, Bill?"

"Only in that old footage of Jackie Robinson, you know? He got a lot of terrible mud hurled at him his first few games."

"Rodriguez seems to be holding up remarkably well. These fans are not treating him nicely."

It finally clicked for Matt what was going on, and he sat back on the couch, utterly horrified.

"You hate to see stuff like this," McClintock said. "Rodriguez has been putting up solid numbers all season. He's currently batting .371 with an on-base percentage of just over .500, and that's nothing to sneeze at. That's what really matters. He's been a great asset to the Eagles since they signed him."

"And Haverman must have faith in him if he's keeping him out there," said Swenson.

"But the crowd here is affecting his game. That strikeout in the third sure was ugly."

"You think the rumors are true?"

"Does it matter?"

Matt sat forward as the camera panned in on Iggy, who stood staring toward home plate. Matt didn't think it would be obvious to the casual viewer, but he could tell something was definitely not right. Iggy kept wiping his forehead, and his skin looked a little greenish. He also kept shifting back and forth on his feet.

Matt would have given anything to be able to talk to Iggy right then, to comfort him and try to help calm him down. The camera panned to some of the signs in the stands—someone in a Pittsburgh jersey held up a sign that said *NO HOMO!*—and there was a lot of angry shouting. Matt could only sit back and watch.

It got really bad in the eighth, when fans who said particularly heinous things or who held up signs with obscenities started getting ejected from the stadium. A fight broke out in the bleachers. Iggy managed a base hit, but his batting stance was off while he did it. Caballo hit a home run after that, batting in Iggy and finally putting some runs on the board, meaning when the game was mercifully over twenty minutes later, the Eagles had squeaked out a 2–1 victory.

Matt gave it ten minutes before he couldn't take it any longer. He pulled out his phone and called Iggy.

"Hi," Iggy greeted him. There was a lot of commotion in the background. "I am very glad you called, but I can't really talk right now."

"I know, just… I had to talk to you. I wanted you to know that whatever happens, I'm here for you when you get back."

"I wish I was there with you."

"Me too."

"Haverman is pulling me into the postgame press conference. He, Chris, and Rothschild are all arguing over how to react, but I think that… I think I have to come clean."

Matt's heart ached for Iggy. It was incredibly frustrating to be so far away and unable to do anything. "I think you should do what feels right."

"What feels right is for me not to lie anymore. I don't want to hide or make excuses. This was…. This game was one of the worst things I've ever gone through, but Haverman thinks it'll blow over in a few weeks when the next scandal erupts, so I just have to get through this. And if games are going to be like this from now on, I don't see the point in lying." There was some static on the line, and then Iggy said, "Yeah, I'll be right there."

"Listen, Ig, I love you. Call me when you can."

"I will. Love you too."

Then he was gone.

The postgame analysts chattered for another minute about the other players in the game, and then they went live to the press conference, at which a beleaguered-looking Bill Haverman held court.

He said, "I hate to put Iggy on the spot, but in light of what happened today, he has a statement. Ig?"

The camera panned to Iggy, whose brow was furrowed in misery. He was clearly sweating and still looked a little green.

He glanced at Haverman and then said, "I didn't have time to prepare anything, so forgive me for speaking off the cuff, but here goes." He took a deep breath. "Yes, I'm gay. I'm not ashamed of that fact. But it has nothing to do with how I play the game, and I'd say that what happened today was a big reason I stayed in the closet, although, yes, the Eagles organization knows, as do most of my close friends and family. And my partner, obviously." He took another deep breath. "Look, all I ever wanted was to play baseball. I've dreamed of playing for the Eagles since I was a little boy, and four years ago, I got my wish. I'm grateful for the opportunity, and I work hard for the team. I've had an off week, but my stats this season speak for themselves. And it's my hope that the major leagues are ready for an openly gay player, because I would very much like to keep playing baseball. That's all."

The camera panned back to Haverman. "I'll take questions about tonight's game and tonight's game only. Iggy's said his piece, and we're gonna leave it there."

The pressroom went nuts. Haverman answered a few questions about other players, but once it became clear that everyone in the room had questions about Iggy, he abruptly ended the press conference. The TV station cut back to the studio.

Matt wondered what would have happened if all of this had unfolded ten years before, when he'd been only a little older than Iggy was now. He reflected on every time he'd fretted about something he'd done for fear of someone finding out; he thought about every time he'd wanted to get caught because at least that would relieve him of the pressure of keeping his private life so private. He thought about Roger and Cruz and how accepting they'd been when they'd found out. He thought about every athlete who had come out in the past five years, paving the way for Iggy.

Although the bottom line was that Iggy had changed his whole life. And if not for Iggy, Matt might still be in the closet. He'd also be horribly alone.

Chapter Twenty-Six

MATT AND Lauren settled into their seats in Section Fourteen. Matt was still trying to get used to this baseball wife idea, but after everything that had happened, he felt it was pretty important to be at the game. Iggy had been so out of sorts that morning, nervous and fidgety and saying he didn't want to play. Matt had talked him into it, had in fact driven him to the stadium and then kissed him stupid before he got out of the car.

In Section Fourteen, a bunch of the WAGs—wives and girlfriends—greeted him. He couldn't remember most of their names, even though he had attended some of their weddings. They all seemed happy enough to see him. Each woman was wearing her husband's jersey. Matt had almost pulled on a Rodriguez T-shirt that morning but thought better of it. He'd settled on a red-and-blue striped polo shirt—Eagles colors, but not an endorsement of any particular player.

The space was nice. Matt had never sat in this part of the stadium before. The section was on field level, a little to the left of home plate. A waitress came by and asked if he wanted something, so he ordered a beer, which she promptly returned with. It was served in a plastic cup that said *Brooklyn Eagles: World Champions!*

"Pretty swanky," Matt said to Lauren. "Why didn't I start watching games from this section earlier?"

"Because you were sneaking into games instead."

Then, somewhere off to his right, a kid shouted, "Oh my God, Matt Blanco!"

Matt turned and looked. A skinny boy, maybe twelve years old, was hanging over the railing on the other side of the aisle. "It is you, right? Man, you're the greatest."

Matt laughed. "Thanks, kid." He waved.

"And you thought you didn't still have fans," said Lauren.

"We've got a cock in the henhouse, I see," said one of the wives.

Matt shrugged. "You ladies don't mind, do you? Also, I'm gay, remember? I won't try to steal any of you from your husbands."

There was some giggling, and then a blonde woman—Caballo's wife, if Matt was not mistaken—stood up and posed for him. She was wearing a jersey cut to fit her female body, and someone had taken the time to cover it with rhinestones. "So, Mr. Gay Baseball Player, what do you think of my jersey?"

It was tacky, was what Matt thought. "I'm not that kind of gay. I don't know anything about fashion. I spent most of my life wearing baseball jerseys and workout clothes."

"Oh, speaking of fashion," said Lauren. She dug into her bag and came back with a purple baseball cap. "This is for you."

"Purple? Really?" He took the hat. It had the Eagles' logo emblazoned on the front.

Lauren gestured around the stadium. "Matt, everyone is wearing these. The players will be wearing them today. To show solidarity with Iggy."

"They… what?" Matt looked around. How could he not have noticed? The first pitch was still a good ten minutes away, but the stands were crowded, and sure enough, there were a lot of purple hats.

Tears stung Matt's eyes, but he blinked them away. "Holy shit," he said. "How did they make this happen?"

"Roger told me the team decided when they got back from Pittsburgh. They didn't tell Iggy because they wanted it to be a surprise. They're selling these purple hats in all the parking lots, on the carts outside, even in the stadium. It took some magic to get a few thousand purple hats made that fast, and they're not the best quality, but…."

Matt saw on closer inspection that the logo on his hat was glued instead of sewn on. But it didn't matter. He swapped hats, putting his own cap in his lap and pulling the purple one on.

Lauren shook her head.

"What?"

"How is it you can pull on a baseball cap and it fits just right?" She put a purple cap on over her head, pulling her long brown hair through the loop in the back. "They never sit right on my head."

Matt grinned. "I think my head just naturally changed shape over the years to best accommodate a cap."

He looked at the cap in his lap. It was fairly new, bought at the beginning of the season, made in Matt's hat size. It had a tiny number three embroidered on the back. He had a dozen more like them at home. "You got a pen or a marker?" he asked Lauren.

Lauren pulled a black marker out of her purse.

"Excellent." He called across the aisle, "Hey, kid. Come here."

The kid climbed over the railing. An older man, presumably the kid's father, made a halfhearted attempt to get him to stop. The kid stood against the railing on Matt's side of the aisle with an eager expression on his face.

"What's your name?" Matt asked.

"Tim."

Matt nodded and wrote *For Tim from Matt Blanco* on the bill of his hat.

The kid's eyes went wide. "Oh my God. Are you giving this to me?"

"Sure. Least I could do for my biggest fan."

When Matt handed the cap over, the kid held it reverently in his hands. Then he leaned close and said, "Can I tell you something?"

"Sure, anything."

Tim bit his lip. After a long pause, he whispered, "I think I might be gay. I haven't told anyone yet."

Matt's heart broke for this kid. "It's gonna be okay" was the best thing he could come up with to say. "Is that guy with the mustache your dad?"

Tim glanced back at the older man. "Yeah."

"He a good guy?"

Tim shrugged, which seemed more of a standard adolescent response than anything else. "I guess so."

"I think you'll be just fine, kid."

"Your life turned out pretty good, didn't it?"

Matt nodded. "It was tough, don't get me wrong, but things are pretty good now. I got to play for the best baseball team in the world, and now I have a guy at home that I love. So yeah, I'd say my life turned out pretty well."

"I play Little League ball," Tim said. "First base, just like you."

"Do you love it?"

"Baseball is the best."

Matt reached over and ruffled Tim's hair. "Stick with it. And cheer extra loud today for my friend Iggy Rodriguez, all right? He had a rough time in Pittsburgh."

"I will. I saw that on the news."

"I think you'll be all right, Tim. Good luck."

"Thanks, Matt!"

Tim ran back across the aisle and sat with his father. Matt watched him show off the cap.

"That was a good thing you just did," Lauren said.

"I'm just glad I could do it."

The Eagles trotted out to the field then. Sure enough, they were all wearing purple caps. The stadium went bonkers, cheering and clapping. The players on the field waved, except for Iggy, who stood at third base looking completely bewildered.

Lauren elbowed Matt and pointed to the Jumbotron. There, with white text against a purple screen, it said: *The Eagles stand with Iggy Rodriguez!*

Matt worried he would cry again.

The announcer said, "Will everyone please stand for the national anthem." Then the game began.

DESPITE EVERYTHING, Iggy's stomach still churned as he went up to bat in the ninth inning. The game was tied at two apiece, but that wasn't really the issue. He'd been feeling agitated all day.

The purple hats were a nice gesture. A lot of the guys were also wearing rainbow pins on their jerseys, the sorts of things that people in the stands wouldn't have seen but that would show up on TV. Iggy wasn't sure what he'd expected, but purple caps and rainbow pins certainly weren't it. Roger had told him before the game that the team had wanted to do something to show they completely supported him. "We're on your side, Ig," he'd said.

"Yeah," Caballo had said. "I know I make a lot of tasteless jokes, but it's like I told Blanco when his book came out. I didn't mean them. I don't care about having a gay teammate."

Iggy had been so touched and humbled by the gesture that he came close to breaking down in tears right there in the locker room, but he'd managed to hold it together and instead exchanged backslaps and a few hugs with his teammates.

"Plus we kinda suspected for a while," Jones had said. "You and Blanco, right?"

"Does everyone know?" Iggy asked.

A few of the players shrugged. "You're not as subtle as you think you are," Caballo said.

Back in the game, Iggy stared down the opposing relief pitcher, a guy in his second year in the majors who looked barely out of high school. Nervous too. Iggy supposed that, a few weeks shy of his twenty-ninth birthday, he wasn't exactly an old-timer, but that kid on the diamond looked so young. That was how the passage of time worked in baseball. That was what had happened to Matt, what would happen to Iggy. Iggy was hot shit right then, and he knew it, but in a few years, the next hot player would come along.

But now Iggy could live his life out in the open. And his team stood by him. That was an amazing thing.

A new conviction came over him, a knowledge that anything was possible now. He and Matt could be a couple in public, could stop lying. He probably had more nights like that one in Pittsburgh in his future, but it didn't matter, because the team—and the fans, based on all the purple in the stands—stood by him. Matt loved him. He was playing baseball for the World Champion Brooklyn Eagles. He could do anything.

That included hitting this ball out of the park. The first ball got past him, but he attributed that to overthinking. He scraped his cleats against the dirt and then readjusted his batting stance. He closed his eyes for a second, just wanting to get back in the right headspace. He knew Matt was in the stands somewhere, and that was a comfort too. A glance at the scoreboard told him what he already knew: last inning, tied at two, two outs. If Iggy got a run off this pitch, the Eagles would win the game. And he could totally get a run off this pitch.

He glared at the pitcher, who took off his cap and wiped sweat off his brow and then picked up a chalk bag and tossed it a few times. When his hands were good and chalky, he bent at his waist. He went into the windup, and then the ball came at Iggy dead-on. Iggy swung. His bat made a satisfying *klok* as it collided with the ball, so he took off running for first. The cheering in the stands told him it was probably a fair ball, though he was afraid to look. But then the home-run horn sounded in the stadium. And that was it. Iggy had hit the winning run out of the park. He jogged around the rest of the bases, and by the time he got home, his whole team had rushed the field. They hugged him and slapped him, and then they hoisted him up on their shoulders. The whole stadium got to its feet. Chants of "Iggy, Ig-gy!" sounded all around him, though this time they were happy and enthusiastic instead of mean-spirited.

It was the most amazing thing Iggy had ever experienced. It felt even better than winning the World Series.

As the stadium started to empty, Iggy signed a few autographs, but then his teammates pulled him back inside. When he and Cruz were in the hallway back to the locker room, he heard a familiar voice say, "Where's Iggy? I need to see Iggy."

"Matt!" Iggy called.

It was hard for them to find each other in the cheering crowd that had assembled in front of the locker room—a crowd that included not just all forty men on the Eagles roster but also reporters, wives, girlfriends, and most of the front office staff. Then there was Matt, standing in the middle of everything, the purple cap on his head slightly askew.

Iggy pushed through everyone until he got to Matt.

"That was incredible," Matt said.

"Yeah, jeez, I still can't believe—"

But before Iggy could finish the thought, Matt had pulled him into a tight hug. And that was maybe the most amazing thing of all. Iggy put his arms around Matt in return, pressed his cheek into Matt's shoulder, and they just stood there in the middle of this crazy celebration, holding each other as if the world were ending, because maybe it was.

"I love you so much," Matt whispered in Iggy's ear.

Iggy pulled away and looked around. A few people were staring at them, but the celebration didn't seem to have lost its fervor. Iggy waved, trying to get everyone's attention. "I just want to say something real quick!" he shouted. That got everyone to look at him, at least. Everything quieted down. "I just wanted to say that your support means so much to me. This has been maybe the most incredible game of my life. I thank you all from the bottom of my heart."

"Yeah, Iggy!" someone shouted.

The crowd seemed to collapse on itself again, everyone shouting and cheering, players starting to make their way into the locker room.

"You did it," Matt said. "First active-duty baseball player to come out. Not so bad, huh?"

"It's not always going to be this easy. I mean, don't get me wrong, this was incredible. I feel so humbled. But what about next week when we go to Atlanta, or the week after when we go to Texas? Not every stadium is going to be so nice to me."

"No, probably not."

"But we all love and support you, Iggy," Lauren said. Iggy hadn't even seen her there.

"Thanks," said Iggy. "I love you all too." He touched Matt's shoulder. "You most of all."

Matt grinned. "Go change out of your sweaty uniform. I want to take you home."

KATE MCMURRAY is an award-winning romance author and fan. When she's not writing, she works as a nonfiction editor, dabbles in various crafts, and is maybe a tiny bit obsessed with baseball. She is active in RWA and has served as president of Rainbow Romance Writers and on the board of RWANYC. She lives in Brooklyn, NY.

Website: www.katemcmurray.com
Twitter: www.twitter.com/katemcmwriter
Facebook: www.facebook.com/katemcmurraywriter

THE
Long Slide
HOME

KATE McMURRAY

THE RAINBOW LEAGUE

The Rainbow League: Book Three

Nate and Carlos have been the best of friends since their childhood playing baseball together in the Bronx. For the past few years, Nate's been in love with Carlos, though he's never acted on it and Carlos has never given any indication that he returns Nate's feelings. Nate has finally given up, determined to move on and find someone else, especially now that Carlos has shacked up with his boyfriend, Aiden.

Carlos doesn't understand why Nate has suddenly gotten weird, acting cold and distant at team practice for the Rainbow League. But if that's how things are going to be, Carlos is done trying to figure Nate out. But then Aiden reveals he has a violent side, and Carlos needs his best friend's support. On top of that, he starts to realize his feelings for Nate might not be limited to friendship. But in the aftermath of his relationship with Aiden, and with Nate having problems of his own, the timing is all wrong to make a real relationship work. As emotions run high, both have a hard time figuring out what is real and what is just convenient.

www.dreamspinnerpress.com

KATE McMURRAY

DEVIN
DECEMBER

A freak blizzard strands flight attendant Andy Weston at LaGuardia Airport on Thanksgiving. Tabloid reports about Hollywood It couple Devin Delaney and Cristina Marino breaking up in spectacular fashion keep Andy sane. And then Devin Delaney himself turns up at the gate Andy is working. Against all odds—and because there's nothing else to do—Andy and Devin begin to talk, immediately connect, and, after Devin confesses the real reason he broke up with Cristina, have a magical night together snowed in at the airport. But the magic ends when Devin boards his flight home the next morning, and Andy assumes it's over.

Then Devin turns up on his doorstep. Andy is game for a clandestine affair at first—who could turn down one of the hottest men on the planet? But he soon grows tired of being shoved in Devin's closet. As Christmas approaches, it's clear that this will never work unless Devin is willing to make some big changes. Devin has a holiday surprise in store—but will it be enough?

www.dreamspinnerpress.com

CPSIA information can be obtained
at www.ICGtesting.com
Printed in the USA
FFOW04n0513090617
36440FF

9 781634 771757